THE
LION AT THE DOOR

ALSO BY NEWTON THORNBURG

DREAMLAND
BEAUTIFUL KATE
VALHALLA
BLACK ANGUS
CUTTER AND BONE
TO DIE IN CALIFORNIA
KNOCKOVER
GENTLEMAN BORN

THE
LION AT THE DOOR

NEWTON THORNBURG

WILLIAM MORROW AND COMPANY, INC. NEW YORK

Recognizing the importance of preserving what has been written, it is the policy
of William Morrow and Company, Inc., and its imprints and affiliates to have
the books it publishes printed on acid-free paper, and we exert our best efforts
to that end.

Library of Congress Cataloging-in-Publication Data

Thornburg, Newton.
The lion at the door / Newton Thornburg.
p. cm.
ISBN 0-688-08820-1
I. Title.
PS3570.H649L5   1990
813'.54—dc20   89-13320
                                                                     CIP

Printed in the United States of America

First Edition

1 2 3 4 5 6 7 8 9 10

BOOK DESIGN BY JAYE ZIMET

To Chelsea and Caitlin,
my little girl's
little girls

It's like a lion at the door;
And when the door begins to crack,
It's like a stick across your back;
And when your back begins to smart,
It's like a penknife in your heart . . .

(A NURSERY RHYME)

THE
LION AT
THE
DOOR

1 Despite the number of beers he'd had, Tom Kohl felt uncomfortable sitting at the bar of the chic little cocktail lounge in his filthy overalls and T-shirt and muddy boots, with his broad back and thick legs dwarfing the barstool. But his truck was down again, which meant that cousin Ken had picked him up after work, and naturally a beer wouldn't do for Ken, just didn't quite slake his upscale thirst as effectively as Chivas on the rocks. And since hard liquor in Washington state was not available in beer taverns, only in restaurant bars, Kohl reluctantly had gone along with him, stopping off at yet another of the area's fashionable watering holes for a few quick ones, enough anyway to dampen the dust in his throat. But as it sometimes happened, the dampening had gone on and on, to the point where Kohl had just seen the lights come on outside, in the plaza, as the locals called it.

Ken as usual was white-glove clean, casual in a safari shirt and twills, his shaggy, handsome head giving off the faintest scent of a cologne for which he and Diane undoubtedly had shopped long and hard. For the others in the bar, though, Kohl suspected that the only scent getting through was the one produced by his own sweat glands after ten hours of construction labor under the hot summer sun, or at least what passed for the sun in Seattle. And that didn't seem to be his only crime either, judging by what he could hear of the conversation at a table a dozen feet behind him.

In the bar mirror he glanced now and then at the table's occupants: the very nervous man in the off-white suit and the three very carefree women with him, high-mileage types in their late thirties, expensively coiffed and dressed, and well past a third round of daiquiris judging by the decibels they were generating. As the man tried to quiet them down, he kept glancing uneasily over at the bar, probably worried that he would be the one Kohl would choose to remonstrate with in the end. But the women ignored him.

"What do you think *it* eats?" Kohl heard. "And where?"

Then two of them in unison: *"Anywhere it wants!"*

"Or anyone!" said the other, to squeals of laughter.

Whispering much too loudly, one wondered if the others thought its age could be estimated by the sweat rings under the armpits, and the man threatened to leave if they didn't shut up. Oddly, they seemed to be getting to Ken even more than they were to Kohl. Every now and then he would turn on his stool and give them a withering look.

"I tell you, Tommy," he said now, "they keep on, I'm gonna unload on 'em."

"Forget it," Kohl told him. "They're a little high, that's all."

"I don't forget lousy manners."

"Well, you were the one who wanted to come here," Kohl reminded him. "It isn't exactly a working stiff's bar, you know."

"So what? They're the only ones making a fuss."

Kohl shrugged agreement. And the odd thing was, he really couldn't figure what all the fuss was about. Oh, he was aware that he looked out of place, but they were carrying on as if he were a three-hundred-pound garbage engineer or something, not just a husky six-footer with a day's dirt still clinging to him. For all he knew, though, it could have been his hair and beard that got them, the two months' growth ringleted from all the sweat it had soaked up that day. One of the carpenters at work called him Zeus because of the curls, and it made him wonder now—not very seriously—if that was the ladies' problem, that Greek gods weren't supposed to wear overalls and smell of labor. Whatever, he'd had enough of it by then, enough of the women, enough beer.

"Time we cut out," he said to Ken, who for the moment seemed to have forgotten about the women and was getting that soft, damp look around the eyes, which meant that he would soon be picking up his scotch and towing Kohl back to a table in Siberia for some man-to-man blubbering about the good old days, growing up together on adjoining farms in Illinois. In reality it was a life Ken had fled like the plague right after college ten years before, while Kohl had left it only recently, and not by choice. Yet to hear Ken tell it, you would have thought it was *his* heart buried back there in the black loam. Kohl understood, though, because his cousin wasn't enjoying the best of times either, the way things kept going sour on him while his Diane prospered so spectacularly. And that naturally wasn't easy to talk about, your real pain. So Ken fudged a little, mourning the good old days instead of all these bad new ones.

Unfortunately Kohl wasn't in the mood for nostalgia any more than he was for the ladies' commentary. He downed the last of his beer and got to his feet, waiting while Ken drained his glass. And just then one of the women chose to jump in again, wondering aloud if her friends thought "Mr. Clean is that thick *everywhere*." Now maybe if he'd had only a few beers or if the women hadn't been quite so obnoxious, Kohl would have let it pass. But they really seemed to be asking for it—for something, anyway—so on the way out he took a slight detour in the direction of their table, figuring that a moment of terror might do them all a world of good. The man immediately pushed back his chair and held up his hands, showing Kohl that he was unarmed, innocent, maybe even a heart case. The women were made of sterner stuff, however, and only one of them was unable to keep her eyes from skittering. But all Kohl did finally was smile and tell them to have a nice day. Not Ken, though. At the front door Kohl looked back and saw that his cousin had stopped at the women's table, in fact was leaning down over it and grinning lasciviously.

"So you want to know how thick it is, do you?" he said. "Well, all I can tell you is this—in high school gym we used to call him Tuna Can. That answer your question?"

While the ladies grimaced and groaned, Ken came on toward Kohl, smiling happily. The two men went on outside then, into the cool dark of the lakefront.

"Tuna can!" Kohl laughed. "Where the devil did you get that?"

Ken was still smiling. "Oh, just a joke I heard. It does present a vivid image, doesn't it? Something for those ballbreakers to think about later, in bed."

Kohl still felt little but indifference toward the women and their remarks, probably because he was too tired to feel much of anything. "They were just blowing steam. A rough day at the office maybe."

"My heart bleeds," Ken said. "I kept wondering if Diane would carry on like that with some of her Amazon colleagues. Christ, can you imagine the farm wives back home doing that to a stranger? Say a visiting salesman in a three-piece suit?"

Kohl looked at his cousin to see if he was serious. "Only louder and drunker," he told him. "And with their men jumping in too."

Ken shook his head. "Didn't used to be like that."

"Well, now it is. From sea to shining sea, old buddy. We've become a nation of slobs."

Frowning at the idea, Ken tripped and almost fell over one of the parking-lot curbs.

"Maybe I should drive," Kohl said.

Ken laughed at him. "Four, five drinks—what're you talking about? I'm sober as a judge."

"That's what I was afraid of."

Ken had parked on the far side of the lot, which was lined with narrow avenues of trees and other greenery, in keeping with the prosperous look of the plaza, all the fancy shops and restaurants that faced the parking lot and the lake beyond. Just over the trees was Kirkland's main lakefront park, where Ken and Kohl once had gone skinny-dipping at three in the morning, sharing the paralyzing fifty-degree water with an aviary of startled ducks, geese, and gulls. It had been a freezing March night during Kohl's first week in town, and when they finally got home, soaked and shivering and frisky as a pair of college drunks, Kohl got his first glimpse of frost in Diane's eyes.

"How cute," she'd said. "A couple of good old boys out on the town."

Since it was her house, Kohl had started to apologize when Ken cut him off, sticking his face right into hers.

"And we good old boys are old enough to do what we fucking want, *when* we fucking want to do it. *Capische?*"

She had stepped back then, waving his breath away. "Assholes," she said. "Good old boy assholes."

At 115 pounds, she was about half Kohl's size, yet managed far too often to make him feel like a little kid, a *dumb* little kid. If it hadn't been for his financial straits—and Ken's insistence that he stay on—he would have left that first week. Or at least that was what he kept telling himself.

Kirkland once had been a sleepy village separated from Seattle by the twenty-mile-long Lake Washington. But during the Second World War the building of a pair of bridges changed all that, transforming town and country alike into what came to be known simply as the Eastside, a vast bedroom community of large new houses and sprawling apartment buildings, the American Dream in natural wood and floor-to-ceiling glass. Neighborhoods ranged from comfortable to posh to obscene, with the old towns, like Kirkland, now centers of yuppie commerce, street after street of boutiques and eateries with names so cute and clever the latest restaurant had resorted to a simple neon sign saying EATS, just like the one in the window of the Blanton, Illinois, café where Kohl over the years had drunk enough coffee to float a Charolais bull. The only difference was no one in Blanton had realized the sign was chic.

The street running south along the lake from downtown Kirkland was lined with pricey condos, a couple of parks, and a scattering of small old lakeside houses whose owners were undoubtedly holding out for the moon and change. The condos, like all buildings in Kirkland, were no more than three stories high, yet the population was dense enough so that the street was solidly edged with parked cars. Given such conditions, the speed limit was only thirty, which Ken for the most part did not exceed, even though it was never easy for him to hold down the throaty eight that powered his Bronco four-by-four.

"Diane's working late tonight, uh?" Kohl said.

Ken shrugged. "That lakeside house she sold last week—she's treating the buyers tonight. Vittles at Benjamin's."

"Can't see how the lady keeps her figure."

"Of course she doesn't *eat!*" Ken laughed. "She talks and smiles and maybe even plays kneesies, for all I know. And when it comes time for the new buyer to move on, guess who he'll call and list it with."

Kohl was figuring commissions. "I guess with that one sale she made more than I will busting my ass all year."

"Four percent of seven hundred thou—yeah, I'd say so."

Kohl turned down the visor mirror and stroked his beard. "Maybe if I slimmed down a bit and got a new hairdo and learned how to smile more winningly—" Batting his eyes, he flashed his teeth at Ken, who laughed out loud, throwing his head back for a second or two, no longer. Yet in the space of that time a figure appeared out of nowhere just ahead, a man moving between parked cars into the roadway and looking in the opposite direction at a huge semitrailer truck coming slowly north on the street, lit like a Christmas tree, the thunder of its engine and tires obviously drowning out the sound of the Bronco as it rounded the slight curve and bore down upon the man. Kohl yelled *"Watch it!"* and reached for the dashboard as Ken hit the brakes and the man finally wheeled, raising his briefcase to ward them off, almost as if he were holding a cross up against evil. And Kohl watched and watched as the face brightened in terror and the screaming of their tires ended in a rending *whump!* that sent the man cartwheeling over the parked cars just as his released briefcase smashed into the windshield, transforming it into a floppy silver net that in turn snared the case like a bird in flight. And though the four-wheeler was fishtailing, Ken somehow managed to keep from hitting either the semi pounding toward them on the left or the parked cars on the right, beyond which a pair of late joggers had turned to look and now were reacting in terror, ducking and jumping backward to escape whatever it was that had just landed on the sidewalk in front of them. Only gradually, another second or two later, did it dawn on Kohl that Ken was not stopping, that instead he had floored the accelerator and was roaring away from the accident, one hand pulling at the sagging, crack-frosted windshield in order to see out.

"For Christ sake, man!" Kohl yelled. *"You gotta stop!"*

Ken was shaking his head. *"I can't, Tommy!"*

By then they were a quarter mile down the road and Ken suddenly turned off, slamming through the Bronco's gears as they raced up a steep blacktop lane into an area of expensive lakeview homes. Kohl's heart was thumping in his neck and his hands shook as he too worked at the sagging windshield, trying to pull it down out of the line of sight. When it finally came, the briefcase dropped onto the floor amid a shower of powdery glass. Out of patience, Kohl took hold of the wheel and turned them onto the blacktop's gravel shoulder, forcing Ken to brake.

"Man, get hold of yourself!" Kohl shouted. "We might've killed that guy, don't you realize that? We've got to go back! We've got no choice!"

Again Ken shook his head. "I can't, Tommy! *I just can't do it!*"

"There were people on the sidewalk, Ken." Kohl was trying hard to sound calm and reasonable. "They saw us! Christ, they probably even got our license."

"So *they* can help the guy. We can't do anything for him they can't do!"

"But it's hit-and-run, man! You *want* to go to prison?"

Ken yanked at the wheel and gunned the engine, skidding out of the gravel back onto the road.

"This way I got a chance, Tommy!" he said. "At least a chance! But I go back there—and if the guy dies—then it's vehicular homicide! Prison for fucking certain!"

Kohl did not understand. "Ken, *he* stepped out in front of *us*! The trucker *had* to see it. And probably the joggers too."

Ken was breathing so hard it took him a while to get it all out. "Last year I lost my license for three months on a DWI. I was taking Valium for a back strain and only had a few drinks— four maybe, honest to God—and I just passed out at the wheel. Rolled the goddam car." He looked over at Kohl now, his eyes brimming with tears and desperation. "I got no choice, Tommy. They test me for alcohol and that's that. Go to jail. Do not pass go."

Kohl felt an immense helplessness. He knew it was a terrible decision, one that Ken would almost certainly live to regret. But the car was his, he had been driving, it was his accident. It was his call. The fact that it made Kohl an unwilling accessory didn't even enter in. Despite a decade of separation, the two of them were like brothers, had always been like brothers.

Within minutes Ken pulled in at home and followed the driveway around to the garage. The moment he turned off the ignition, he slumped over the steering wheel as if he'd been shot.

"I'm gonna be sick," he said.

Kohl wasn't sure if he was more disappointed or relieved that Diane wasn't home yet. If she'd been there, then that would have been that. There would have been no question of carrying out the cover-up he'd hurriedly devised at Ken's urging— no question of it for the simple reason that she would never have gone along with it, not in a million years. Even if Ken begged her or raged at her, it wouldn't have done him any good, because Diane simply wasn't the type to let herself become an accessory to a hit-and-run. Now, a big dumb farmer from Illinois might do it, Kohl reflected, but certainly not the Eastside's youngest real estate superstar, not in this life anyway.

So he had been disappointed at not seeing her Cadillac in the drive, where it forked past the front door. On the other hand, its absence meant he could move ahead without interference, do what had to be done if Ken was to have any chance at all of escaping the mess. The Bronco's bumper, grille, and hood were caved in, but the headlights still worked, and amazingly there was no blood anywhere on the vehicle as far as Kohl could see, in the light from the garage. He pulled the rest of the windshield free and dropped it onto the car floor. Almost as an afterthought, he picked up the briefcase and tossed it to Ken, who was doing a pretty fair impression of a sleepwalker.

"Take it inside and hide it for now," Kohl told him. "Someplace where she won't find it."

But Ken just stood there staring down at the case as if it were a bomb.

"Ken!" Kohl said. "This is your show! You'd better get with it!"

"Right. Sure, Tommy." He hurried inside then, still handling the case as if it might go off at any second.

While he was gone, Kohl loaded one of Ken's dirt bikes into the back of the Bronco. Then he got into the driver's seat and lit a cigarette, hoping that the appearance of calm might somehow become the reality. When Ken returned, he went around to the passenger side to get in, but Kohl stopped him.

"No, you stay here, remember? I'll dump it alone and come back on the bike. And remember what you tell Diane—I dropped you off and went back to the bars. In the morning the Bronco is missing and we report it stolen. Okay?"

"You think it'll work?"

Kohl didn't answer. He had already started the engine, and now he backed around and slowly drove off, giving Ken a thumbs-up on his way out to the street. No, he didn't think it would work, not with three witnesses on the scene. If even one of them could give the make of the vehicle, let alone its license number, he figured the police would be able to put it all together. But it was nighttime, and witnesses were witnesses. With an abundance of luck, just maybe he could pull it off.

As he drove away, he wondered again where the devil Diane was. It was well past ten o'clock, and that was late for one of her post-sale client dinners. Her house was situated at the top of a long dead end, a blacktop street so narrow that if they passed each other on it she would clearly see the four-by-four's missing windshield and battered front end. And that was his one last hope of getting out from under the mess, letting his muddled sense of blood loyalty give way to her unflagging common sense.

Unfortunately, he negotiated the street without meeting her or anyone else and was soon out on the freeway, heading south toward Interstate 90, which he would then follow east up into the foothills of the Cascades. As he drove, it occurred to him that his behavior—calmly carrying out a felony—was probably something like the battle fatigue of soldiers. Because as far as he was concerned, this was not even a minor skirmish compared to the wars he'd fought and lost over the last five years, beginning with the farm depression, the first scary realization that if things didn't change he and his parents would lose their farm. After that there was his mother's cancer, the lymphoma that over a three-year period took all their savings before it finally took her life and in the process drove Kohl's young wife Julie back home to Mommy and Daddy in town. Then came his father's fatal hunting "accident," in which that expert old wingshot crawled through a barbed-wire fence with his twelve-gauge not on safety just weeks before the coup de grâce—the auction—that cold and sunless day when what little Kohl had left disappeared like so much wastepaper in the biting November wind.

As a result, none of this particularly scared him, not even the prospect of being picked up by the police and charged with something like aiding and abetting. Professional criminals were always copping pleas, he reasoned, so why couldn't he do the same? And anyway, he had no real choice in the matter. Ken wasn't only a blood relative, he was the one person in the world to throw Kohl a lifeline after the auction was over and all he had left was his pickup truck and his clothes, such as they were. *Come out and stay with us,* Ken had said. *And take your time. Get on your feet.* So Kohl's only qualm about what he was doing was that if it didn't work out, things would go worse for Ken, much worse than if the two of them had stopped and faced the music right after the accident.

But none of that mattered now. Within a half hour Kohl was back in the mountainous area east of the town of Issaquah. Although he didn't know for sure, he suspected that the area was a state park or nature preserve, since it was so free of development. Even in the lower, more level areas there was no sign of the urban sprawl that elsewhere was moving up into the foothills like a reverse flow of lava. He had been here only once before, two months earlier, on the day Ken had traded his three-year-old Datsun sports car for the Bronco and immediately wanted to give it a rigorous off-road test. For what seemed like hours they went roaring up and down the narrow mountain trails, sliding along the edge of precipices that offered unrestricted views straight down of bright green rivers of bracken and ferns and conifers that could have swallowed them and the four-by-four as easily as the sea.

So Kohl knew where he was going, even in the dark and in the cold mountain air, with an occasional bug splatting against his unprotected face. And in time he came to a curve that he remembered better than any other, sitting next to Ken in the passenger seat and gazing down a seventy-degree incline at the greenest grave a man could want.

"You trying to scare me, cousin?" he'd asked.

And Ken had laughed. "Yeah. Am I doing it?"

"You bet your ass you are."

Now Kohl stopped at the edge of the road and got out. His mouth was dry and he imagined his heart was going a little faster than it normally did, but otherwise he felt calm, even cool. The Great Criminal at work, he thought, smiling ruefully. He lifted the dirt bike out of the back and got a rag and wiped down the Bronco's door handle and steering wheel, just in case the police found the vehicle and went so far as to dust it for prints, a not very likely eventuality, he had to admit. Still holding the rag, he turned the steering wheel toward the drop-off and then pushed the Bronco over the edge.

Standing there in the moonlight, he was struck by the peacefulness of the operation, how quietly the heavy vehicle skidded and rolled and bounced its way down the slope, until it finally disappeared into the blackness at the bottom. Pleased, he lit a cigarette and continued to stand there for a few minutes, taking in the awesome view spread out before him: the million lights of the Eastside and Seattle divided by the long black band of the lake and backdropped by the Olympics beyond the Sound, their snowy peaks limned by a faint, unearthly light, some dim memory of sunset. And he decided that if a man had to commit a felony, he might as well do it in a scenic spot.

Just as he was getting ready to mount the dreaded little dirt bike and head for home, it hit him like yet another bug in the face that the bike's key was on the same keychain as the Bronco's and they were both a couple of hundred feet below, hanging from the mangled vehicle's ignition. If he could have kicked himself he would have. Instead he picked up the dirt bike in a surge of anger and, spinning with it like a discus thrower, launched the thing out into the chasm, where it seemed to hang for minutes in the light of the moon before it dropped out of sight and began its hectic journey down the mountainside, to join Ken's other toy at the bottom.

As he turned away, about to start the long walk home, a pair of headlights suddenly flashed on in the darkness up the trail about a hundred yards. For a moment he thought the vehicle might have rounded a curve or come over a rise, but then he saw by its taillights that the road behind it was flat and straight, which meant that the person or persons inside had been parked there in the darkness, *watching*. And that scared him. That really dried out the old mouth.

The lights started to come toward him, and he saw that the vehicle was an old midsize Buick, a tinny, rattling ghost of the gorgeous vinyl-topped Regal his uncle—Ken's father—had bought in the early seventies, when both boys were still in high school. Not wanting to join the Bronco down below, Kohl moved to the inside of the trail as the car started past him. But it braked suddenly and its passenger window whined down, revealing the bruised face of a young woman leaning over from the driver's side.

"You want a lift?"

Kohl could hardly believe he'd heard her correctly. "You always pick up strange men at night on lonely roads?"

She laughed. "When they look as big and mean as you, sure. Why the hell not?"

As he opened the door and started to get in she raised her

finger to her lips. "Be a little quiet, okay? My babies are asleep."

And they were indeed, like a pair of dolls that had toppled sideways on the back seat.

"They're twins," she said, driving on. "Tad and Kimberly. I'm Bobbi with an i."

The woman was a type Kohl had seen before in almost every country bar he'd ever set foot in: former high school pom-pom girls putting the finishing touches on a second or third divorce and usually having the scars to show for it as well as a brood of kids out in the pickup asleep. Like most such women, this one was cute and sexy, yet somehow still managed to look tough as a crowbar. Kohl figured she was in her mid-twenties, though in the soft dashboard light she could have passed for eighteen.

"I'm Tom," he said. "And I still can't believe you're doing this?"

"What? Picking you up?" She gave a laugh, throaty and careless. "Well, I'll let you in on a little secret. I'm running out on my boyfriend—one left hook too many." She crooked a finger toward her bruised cheekbone. "Drunk as usual, and mean as a pit bull. So I tossed his keys out in the bushes and picked up the babies and vamoosed. And I figured if he gets his truck started anyway and comes after me—well, you could handle him easy."

Kohl would have laughed except for the big question, the one still eating at him. "You were parked," he said. "Lights off. How come?"

She shrugged. "Well, when I left, I saw your lights up ahead. And you gotta wonder who the hell'd be up here this time of night cep that asshole I been livin' with—he's got a house trailer about a mile back. So I just turned off the lights and stopped. And boy, what I didn't see!"

Kohl tried to smile. "And just what is it you think you saw?"

"Well, it ain't none of my business, of course. Man wants to get rid of his wheels, that's his affair. I ain't the nosy type."

Kohl figured that a plausible lie would be better than nothing. "A little matter of insurance," he said. "Making the Rock pay for a change."

"Hey, I'm all for that." She gave him a quizzical look. "But how come the bike? You coulda just left it in the four-by-four to begin with."

Kohl did smile now. "My, what big eyes you have, Bobbi-with-an-i."

"That I do." She laughed. "But tell me. How come?"

"Simple—no key. I left it in the Bronco by mistake."

"Well, I'll say this—not too many guys could throw a bike like that. You must be awful strong."

"Well, that's why you picked me up, right?"

"Also because I'm a Good Samaritan."

"Whatever—I really appreciate it. And incidentally, you were right to do it—you've got nothing to fear from me."

She gave him a mocking look. "I know that, for heaven's sakes. Big guys like you a girl don't have to worry about. It's them scrawny little mothers you gotta watch out for."

Kohl laughed, for it was an opinion he readily agreed with, as he believed most large men did. But rather than just go along with her, he sensed that she would be more comfortable with kidding and raillery, and especially flirtation. "Even worse, though, are the women," he said. "Especially them cute, sexy little ones."

She smiled with obvious pleasure. "And don't you forget it, buster."

Bobbi explained to Kohl that she would have to drop the twins off at her mother's in Seattle before driving him to Kirkland. Her mother's was the first place her boyfriend, Rusty, would come looking for her, she said, so she had to get in and out of there as quickly as she could. Kohl told her not to bother about him, that if she would just let him out at the 405 interchange, he would hitch his way home or phone his cousin to come and get him. But Bobbi wouldn't hear of it.

"I like the company," she said, smiling wickedly. "And anyway, there's still good old Rusty, right? If he ketches up with us, and finds you—hell, I don't wanna miss that."

Kohl couldn't help admiring the girl. Her Rusty might have knocked her around now and then, but it was obvious that she was not intimidated by the man, and probably not by very much else either. In fact, Kohl had the uneasy feeling that if a mushroom cloud suddenly lit up the night sky over Seattle she would have kept right on jabbering, most of the time pumping him for information. Just how long had he lived in the area? What kind of work did he do? Why did he live with his cousin? And was his cousin rich? Did he live in a big house, since most houses on the Eastside were so "godawful huge," at least compared to her mother's neighborhood in Seattle and especially compared to Pottsville, the Oklahoma town where she had grown up?

Kohl had no problem understanding her interest in him, considering that she had watched him toss about eighteen thousand dollars' worth of wheels down a mountainside. And while he was grateful she had picked him up—grateful she was that reckless—he knew that didn't in any way make her an accomplice, someone he could trust with the truth. So for the most part, he answered her questions with lies. His name was Cobb, he said, Tom Cobb. And his cousin wasn't Ken Ryder but Ken *Anderson,* same as the former Bengal quarterback, a reference that apparently eluded her. And for some reason he volunteered the information that Ken and Diane were married, when in fact they were only living together, as they had been for the last four years. Not unexpectedly, Bobbi was keenly interested in this, their *ménage à trois,* but he assured her that it was all very innocent and boring.

"Oh, I'll bet," she said, laughing. "And how old are these two, anyway. *Too* old, uh?"

Kohl saw no reason to lie about their ages. "He's thirty-three, same as me. And she's twenty-eight, I think. But why should you care? You don't even know them."

The girl turned on her wicked smile again, as if by rheostat. "Whenever I hear about a hanky-panky situation, I try to picture it, you know? Picture the people."

"That's easy," Kohl said. "He looks like Pee Wee Herman and she looks like me."

Bobbi laughed loud enough to wake her babies, but they didn't stir.

"Looks like you!" she sputtered. "Oh, that poor girl! Tell me, has she got a beard too?"

"A light one."

She bit down on her fist in an effort to quell her laughter. "They sound like a real cute couple!" she got out.

"Oh, they are," Kohl said, almost laughing himself, because he knew how Ken and Diane would have bridled at the description, since the word "cute" hardly did them justice. The truth was, neither of them would have had any trouble earning a living as a model, they were that good-looking. Though Diane White probably wasn't a classic beauty, she was a lot more than just pretty, with her smartly cut honey-blond hair and perfect smile and brightly intelligent green eyes that could frost over so easily. Long-legged and slim, she wore a minimum of makeup and dressed expensively, mostly in business suits. But far from being vain about her attractiveness, she seemed at times to think of it as nothing more than a sales tool, a lucky leg up she had over her competitors in the selling of real estate.

Ken on the other hand could be downright fussy about his looks. Twice a month he'd come home from his hair salon in a snit: *"Goddam bitch never knows when to quit!"* And clothing was probably the closest thing he had to a religion: the Burberry rainwear and English tweeds, all the designer slacks and suede and leather jackets and Irish wool sweaters. To his credit, he was able to laugh at himself and all too often at Diane as well. Just the previous evening, dressed up for a dinner dance, he'd said to Kohl: "Well, here we are—Ken and Barbie stepping out!"

Even for a couple of dolls, though, things didn't always

run smoothly. Of late there had been a lot of anger in the house and talk of breaking up. And Ken, as he'd demonstrated in the bar earlier, seemed to live each day with a shorter fuse. On two separate occasions in the past few weeks Kohl had had to physically restrain his cousin when Diane had gone a little too far verbally, not just grilling him about some of his expenditures but calling into question his general character as well. For her, the "good old days" were the first two years of their relationship, when Ken had been a well-paid account executive with the largest ad agency in Seattle. With their combined incomes, they evidently had been not only one of the best-looking young couples in town but also one of the more prosperous. But then, as Ken told Kohl, there came that one unhappy day when he just couldn't put up with the "ratshit" job any longer—all the pressure and frustration and sense of utter uselessness—so he'd cleaned out his desk and walked. And for the next half year he did absolutely nothing, living on money he'd saved. And even when that was gone, he didn't exactly go back to work, but instead tried a little of this and a little of that, usually with Diane's help, since she was earning over one hundred thousand a year even then.

Finally there was *the boat,* the classic forty-foot Williwaw, which Ken bought for a song, as he often put it, when in truth it was Diane who had bought it, and not for a song either but for twenty thousand dollars. Ken was determined to restore the craft to its former elegance as a charter yacht that he would captain, this despite the fact that he knew virtually nothing about engines or woodworking or, for that matter, sailing. As a result, for the last year he had proved in spades the accuracy of the old saw about a yacht being a hole in the water into which one (in this case, Diane) throws money—over thirty thousand dollars so far. And that simply had to stop, she said. She had checked out a number of established charter outfits, and most of them were *losing* money. So what on earth did Ken expect her to do—keep throwing good money in after bad? It was a question he didn't bother to answer, except by going back to work on the Williwaw.

30

Kohl didn't doubt that Bobbi would have found all this fairly interesting, especially the parts about Diane's income and Ken's drop-dead good looks. At the same time, he would have given odds that the girl's own life was, if not more interesting than theirs, certainly more eventful. But at the moment he was much more concerned with other matters, such as the fact that he practically had to sit on his hands to keep from turning on the radio. A good ninety minutes had passed since the accident and he still didn't know if the man was alive or dead. And he desperately wanted to know if the police had a description of the hit-and-run vehicle. Did they have a license number? More to the point, was Ken already under arrest? Because if he was, then the dance was over for Kohl too. Much as he liked his cousin, he knew from experience that Ken was not one to shoulder a burden alone, not when there were others to share it with.

Yet Kohl didn't dare turn on the radio, not with Bobbi sitting next to him. After a description of the accident and the vehicle, he could almost see the look she'd toss him, the bright eyes and knowing smile, that old familiar face of country cunning.

When Bobbi pulled into the driveway of the tiny bungalow, her mother came out to help carry in the babies. The moment she saw Kohl getting out of the car, she stopped dead and put her hand over her heart, as though she wondered if it had stopped beating. Bobbi laughed at her.

"Hey, he's okay! He's just a guy I picked up on the road. Tom, say hello to my ma."

"*Picked up!*" the mother cried, shaking her head at Kohl. "The girl is such a caution."

Kohl couldn't help grinning. "That she is, ma'am."

The two women got the babies out of the backseat and took them inside, while Kohl waited at the car. When Bobbi came back out, she was waving her hand back and forth above her head, as though her mother's words were a swarm of insects. The older woman followed her only as far as the porch.

"But the man scares me, Bobbi," she complained. "He really does. He's *so* weird. He just scares the living daylights out of me."

"Oh, you'll be okay. He's all bluster. Just don't let him git to ya."

"What do I tell him when he gits here?"

"The truth!" Bobbi yelled from the car. "Like before. You don't know where the hell I am. He'll believe you."

"Dear God, I hope so."

"I know so. You'll be fine, don't worry. And listen, kiss the babies for me again, okay?"

With that, Bobbi slipped in behind the wheel and they drove off, heading back toward the lake. Almost immediately she got some country music on the radio, Waylon Jennings turned up so loud she practically had to shout as she told Kohl a little more about herself and especially her love life, more in fact than he wanted to hear, since he figured he probably knew it all already, from the moment she first looked over at him with that pom-pom-girl smile. And she made it very clear that her boyfriend Rusty was only a stopgap affair, someone she was putting up with until she got on her feet again.

"He's basically just a bum," she explained. "A boozer and a pothead. A chicken-thief kinda guy."

"Sounds like a real winner," Kohl said.

"Don't he, though?"

When they turned up Diane's street, Bobbi was impressed.

"I knew it!" she said. "Anybody can afford to throw away a new four-by-four, I just knew you'd live on a street like this. Your cousin must be loaded, Tom Cobb."

"Loaded with debt," Kohl said.

When he told her where to stop, she whistled softly. "And natcherly a Caddie in the driveway, right? They wouldn't happen to need a overnight maid or something like that, would they?"

Kohl wondered what the girl's reaction would have been if he'd explained that to Diane the house was merely a temporary investment she'd made, mostly for tax purposes but also to find a home for Ken's toys: all the snowmobiles and racing shells and dirt bikes, not to mention an unrestored old Jaguar XKE and, of course, the Bronco. As for the Cadillac, it was at best a necessary evil, an accommodation to the prejudices of Diane's many older clients from the Midwest and East, who often hated foreign products and especially foreign cars, including the BMW or Mercedes-Benz she would have much preferred to drive.

Kohl looked at the girl. "You really got a place to stay tonight?"

"My old girlfriend's, sure. Unless her old man came back home."

"What then?"

"Then I look someplace else. Hey, don't worry about me. I'll get by. I always do."

"If this was my place, you could stay," Kohl said. "You know that."

"Well, sure I do." She gave him a plucky smile. "Look, I'll be all right. Honest. You go ahead."

It embarrassed Kohl not to invite her in. But under the circumstances he knew he had no choice in the matter. As he opened the door to get out, he thanked her and clumsily reached over to shake her hand.

"Aw, come on now!" she said. "What do I look like, anyway? Some old guy?" With that, she leaned over and kissed him, first on the cheek, then on the lips. "There now, that didn't hurt, did it?"

Getting out, Kohl was shaking his head and grinning. "Your mom was right. You *are* a caution."

She laughed. "Don't I know it! Well, I'll see you around, Tom Cobb. Bye now."

She drove off, U-turning through the cul-de-sac and heading down the lane past houses she undoubtedly thought were filled with happy rich folk, instead of anxious debtors. As he walked up the drive, Kohl wondered if Diane would still be up, and if so whether she would notice that he hadn't come home in the Bronco.

The house was modern and glassy, its two stories built into the side of the hill like stairs, with the roof of the lower level serving as a deck for the three bedrooms upstairs, two of which were suites. Everything else was on the first floor, including Kohl's room, which Diane sometimes still referred to as the servant's room. The house was spacious and up-to-date, with every modern convenience a person could want, yet Kohl found it oddly uncomfortable to live in, probably because it seemed almost like a model home, had that kind of antiseptic emptiness, with just a few pieces of tasteful furniture here and there, and none of the junk and clutter Kohl was used to in his own home and in those of other farm families back in Illinois. And he imagined the reason for this was that he and Ken and Diane did little except sleep in the house and occasionally listen to music or watch some television. No one cooked, no one read, no one worked, no one did much of anything except come and go.

At the moment only the downstairs lights were on and everything seemed peaceful, which made Kohl wonder if Ken had succeeded after all in keeping the mess to himself, not dragging Diane into it. If so, she might already have gone to bed, and for once Kohl knew he wouldn't feel even a touch of disappointment in that fact. Better not to see her at all than risk involving her.

Entering by way of the garage, he made his way through the kitchen and down the hallway toward the game room, where the TV was playing. There he found Diane standing by the front window, just turning away from it, dressed in one of her handsome floor-length robes. In the four months he'd lived with her and Ken, he had never seen her smoke before.

"So you're back," she said.

"Where's Ken?"

"In the bathroom, vomiting for the tenth time."

Across the room, on the big-screen TV, Jonathan Winters was breaking up Johnny Carson. Though Kohl already knew that she knew, by the language of her body if nothing else, he still wouldn't let himself be the first to mention the accident.

"I've never seen you smoke before," he said.

She smiled icily. "Maybe that's because I've never been sucked into a hit-and-run before."

"Last I knew, we were gonna keep you out of it."

"Let's just say you didn't quite manage it." She took a shallow drag on the cigarette and flipped it into the fireplace. "And who was that brought you home? Ken said you took one of the bikes with you."

But Kohl had a more pressing question. "Have you heard anything yet? About the man?"

She looked at him in disbelief. *"You don't know?"*

He shook his head.

"I'm afraid the poor man didn't make it. Dead on arrival, as they say."

Hearing this, Kohl realized it was what he'd expected, virtually *known*, all along. "Did they say who he was?"

"No. The family has to be notified first—the usual statement."

Kohl hadn't forgotten about the briefcase or that its contents would undoubtedly identify the man. But since she hadn't mentioned it, he decided not to either. "Any word about the vehicle?" he asked.

"The Bronco, you mean? The murder weapon?"

He didn't like it that she'd been drawn into the thing, but he'd had enough sarcasm for the moment. "Just tell me what you goddam know, all right? I wasn't driving. I tried to make him go back."

"Not hard enough!" She practically screamed the words at him, as her eyes suddenly filled with tears.

"You don't know that," he said.

"The hell I don't! He didn't go back, did he!"

"Because he wouldn't. It was *his* decision."

"Then why didn't *he* ditch the goddam thing? Because *he couldn't,* that's why! Because he was wiped out and needed good old Tommy to lean on once more! You sure helped him this time, didn't you!"

Kohl had no desire to argue the point, since he didn't feel very good about it all himself. "You asked who brought me home," he said. "It was just a ride I hitched. I lost the bike key."

Just then Ken came out of the bathroom down the hall. Walking like a sick old man, he came straight over to Kohl and embraced him in the manner of a relative at a funeral. In his eyes Kohl could see that he had kept on drinking, vomiting or not.

"How'd it go?" he asked.

Kohl shrugged. "Okay, I guess. Could be days before they find it. Maybe weeks."

Ken looked relieved. He even smiled. "Good. Tomorrow I report it stolen, right?"

Kohl glanced over at Diane, who was looking at them as if they were regressing before her eyes, turning into a pair of lower primates. "I still haven't heard," he said to Ken. "The police looking for a Bronco or what?"

"The news just said a four-wheeler or a pickup—can you believe that? The eyewitnesses couldn't even agree on what they saw."

"Or the police could be snowing us," Kohl said. "Trying to give us a false sense of security."

Diane gave a sharp, mirthless laugh. "Jesus Christ, listen to yourselves! Have you lost your way or what? Ken said the accident wasn't his fault, that the man stepped right out in front of you. So tell me—I guess I'm stupid—I just don't understand. Why not get a lawyer and fight it? Why not do the lawful, rational thing? It's still not too late, you know."

"I agree," Kohl said. "It would've been better to do it sooner. But she's right, Ken—it's not too late."

Ken picked up the remote and switched to one of the music channels, getting four cadaverous youths singing about world hunger. He killed the sound, sighed, sat down. "I've already told you," he said. "Both of you. I had, what—five or six drinks before the accident? So, considering my last DWI, I simply didn't have any choice." He looked from Diane to Kohl and suddenly began to yell at them. *"Can't you understand that? Can't either of you get it through your fucking heads?"*

Looking disgusted and weary, Diane nodded in defeat. "All right, okay, you do it your way—the good-old-boy way. Just one thing, though—you keep me out of it, understood?"

"I already told you we would," Ken said.

"If the police arrive, I'm making a beeline for bed. I've been there for hours and I don't know one damn thing about the accident or the cover-up or anything else. Understood?"

Ken was already nodding. "Yes, yes—it's understood."

She looked at Kohl.

"Of course," he said.

She lit another cigarette. "And if I may—one little suggestion. Don't report the Bronco stolen for a couple of days at least. You report it tomorrow and they're gonna think, Wow, what a neat coincidence. A four-by-four's involved in a hit-and-run in Kirkland and the very next day a Kirkland resident reports his Bronco stolen."

"What's wrong with that?" Ken wanted to know. "The people who stole it, they could've been driving."

Kohl saw her point. "No, she's right, Ken. You don't want the police making a connection between the two. That'd just be inviting trouble."

"All right, then. We wait a couple of days," Ken said.

Diane started to give him a goodnight kiss but pulled away as if she'd been scalded. "My God, you still reek of vomit. You ever heard of mouthwash?"

Ken dismissed her with a wave of his hand. "Go on to bed, will you. And don't wait up."

"Don't worry. Listen, I'm gonna have to take a sleeping

pill—I've got an open house tomorrow at ten. So use the guest bedroom, all right?"

"*All right!*"

She turned to Kohl then, with a look of wry amusement. "And you, Tommy—I just can't imagine anyone picking you up at night looking like that."

"Like what?" he asked, just to hear what she'd say.

"Like a—I don't know—like a proletarian Hell's Angel." She smiled in triumph. "How's that?"

"Not bad. It's the mud-covered overalls you like best, right?"

"Of course. Just the right touch." Her smile faded and she reached out and lightly touched his forearm. "Look, I'm sorry for what I said earlier. I know you didn't have any choice— you did what you felt you had to do. I just hope it doesn't all blow up in our faces."

"Me too," he said.

She seemed to catch herself then, realize that she was being a bit too generous, and maybe even vulnerable. She withdrew her hand from his arm, turned, and headed for the foyer. But as she started up the stairs, she had one last thought to share. "Remember, I've been asleep for hours."

"Right," Ken said. "Goodnight already." When she was gone, he turned to Kohl and shrugged. "I just couldn't keep it from her, man. She knew right off something was wrong. You know how she is."

"It's all right," Kohl said. "Forget it."

"I wish I could forget the goddam accident." Ken held up his hands for Kohl to see. "Look at that—I'm still shaking. That's why I've had a couple more drinks." As he looked at Kohl, his face seemed to implode with anguish. "I'm wasted, man! I can't handle this! I just can't!"

Kohl put his hand on Ken's shoulder, and Ken sagged against him. And suddenly they were kids again. Ken's father had beaten him or he had gotten bad grades or lost a fight at school, and on the way home, going across Kohl's woodland, the break would come—Ken unable to handle his pain for another minute—and an embarrassed Kohl would put his arm around him as they walked along or pat him to still his crying or even this, hold him like a brokenhearted girl. But as always, Kohl could endure it for only a moment or two before pushing him back and gently shaking him.

"Ken, it wasn't your fault!" he said now. "The man stepped right out in front of us. You couldn't have braked any faster than you did."

Ken nodded eagerly. "That's true, isn't it! It really is true!"

"You bet it is."

"And not stopping—I didn't have a choice, Tommy. Honest to God. Some guys could make it in prison, but not me—you know that. Christ, they got fags in there as big as you. I just couldn't make it! *I couldn't!*"

"It's all right, Ken. Anyway, it's over and done. There's nothing we can do about it now—except get a grip on ourselves and tough it out."

"I know, I know! But doesn't it bother you? Don't you wonder who the guy was? Jesus, I can still see him holding that briefcase up—*Christ, the briefcase, Tommy!*" He clapped his hand to his forehead. "I been so busy pukin' I forgot all about it! Come on, let's see what's in it. At least we can find out who he was."

Kohl followed him down the hallway, stopping in the kitchen to get a pair of rubber gloves while Ken went out to the garage to retrieve the hidden briefcase. When he came back in with it, Kohl tossed the gloves onto the kitchen table.

"Here, you can get these on better than I can."

Ken placed the briefcase on the butcher-block table very carefully, still handling it as it were a bomb. "You really think we need gloves?"

Kohl shrugged. "For the contents anyway."

While Ken pulled the gloves on, Kohl opened the case, which was light and sturdy, aluminum covered with a grainy vinyl. "When we're done," he said, "I'm gonna punch some holes in it and deep-six the whole thing. After I clean up, I'll take it down to the marina." His idea was to row the Willi-waw's dinghy out to the middle of the lake and drop the case overboard, in two hundred feet of water.

But Ken was so busy going through the contents of the case that he didn't seem to hear. There were three cheesy por-nographic magazines featuring voluptuous nude women in bondage being whipped, burned, strangled, and sodomized by masked men. Ken took the magazines out and placed them on the table. Then he went through the other items very gin-gerly, as if they might infect him. There was a small spiral notebook and a book of matches advertising *TONY JACK'S, Seattle's Sexiest Ladies, 1st and Dix, Downtown.* There was a bottle of Rolaids and a stack of business cards stuck into a side pocket and a miniature baseball bat wrapped in a damp white towel that had a couple of light rust-colored stains on it. Ken picked out one of the cards and tremblingly held it up for Kohl to see. *Richard M. Giacalone,* it read. *Investments.* Then a Bellevue address and phone number.

"A businessman," Ken said. "I killed a businessman."

Kohl was looking at the baseball bat and the stained towel. "Some businessman."

Ken replaced the card and turned his attention to the re-maining items in the case: a gold signet ring with the letters RR engraved on the face, in the manner of the Rolls-Royce symbol, then some bank deposit slips in the name of Ricky Ross. And finally there was a Kodak envelope containing re-cently developed color photographs of three dark, burly men with wavy pompadours and—presumably—their wives and many children enjoying a backyard cookout. In a number of the photos there appeared to be a spaceship hovering just over the hedge that bordered the property.

"The Space Needle," Ken said. "House must be on Queen Anne Hill."

Kohl wanted to put it all away and hide the case again until he was ready to take it down to the marina, but he was also curious enough just to stand there and watch as Ken shakily opened the spiral notebook and thumbed through the first six or seven pages. At the top of each was a name, usually a nickname—"the wart," "Slimey," "Mr. RR."—then a round number—600, 1500, 1200—and finally date notations running down the page, next to more round numbers, these usually less than one hundred.

Ken sadly shook his head. "A businessman. A family man. Christ, why couldn't he have been a drug dealer or terrorist or something like that?"

"It's just our rotten luck," Kohl deadpanned.

And Ken gave him a look. "I guess I sound like an asshole, right?"

"You could say that."

"I'm shitless, that's why. I'm so scared I don't even know what I'm saying."

"I know the feeling, man." Bare hands and all, Kohl started to put everything back into the briefcase.

But Ken balked. "No, wait a minute, Tommy. I want another look." And he actually spread his arms out over the photographs, as though to protect them from Kohl's unfeeling touch. "Just another few seconds, okay?"

"No, it's not okay."

"I keep thinking about his wife and kids. I wonder which ones they are."

Kohl sighed. He was about to turn away and head for his room to clean up and change clothes when something caught his eye, something moving outside the kitchen window. Almost absently he looked up—and there she was, Bobbi-with-an-i, giving him a wistful, lost-puppy look and turning up the old pom-pom smile, both at the same time.

"Oh Christ!" he said.

Ken still couldn't tear himself away from the photographs. "What's the matter?" he asked.

"We've got a visitor."

2 Though it was over and done, both of them having made it together a second time, Bobbi continued to sit on Kohl, straddling his body, as if she found him simply too comfortable to dismount. Through the open glass hatch above her head he could see part of the Big Dipper, and he imagined she knew how softly the starlight sculpted her body in the darkness of the bow cabin, how very sexy it made her look even at two in the morning, with him feeling drained in just about every way a man could.

Smiling, she leaned forward and ran her fingers into his chest hair. "I ain't sure which was better—this or on the bottom."

"This. It was easier."

"Lazybones." She punched him playfully on the chin. "Just cuz you some kinda hunk don't mean you don't have to sweet-talk a girl."

Kohl cupped her breasts, then thought better of it and dropped his hands, not wanting to get her started again. If he didn't get to sleep soon he was afraid he was going to get cranky.

"Bet you think I'm easy, don't you?" she said.

"Why on earth would I think that?"

She laughed and he chuckled, about all he could do with her still sitting on him.

"How come only women get to be easy?" he said. "Hell, girl, I'll bet I'm twice as easy as you."

"I bet so too. And just as dumb."

"*Dumb?* Why's that?"

"You ever heard of safe sex?"

It was a thought that had crossed his mind earlier, that he was about to have sex not only with her but with her friend Rusty and God knew who else. But that was about all it ever did with him—cross his mind. Considering the way his luck had been running the last few years, there didn't seem to be all that many things worth getting scared about. And it wasn't that he tried to be reckless, only that he wasn't excessively cautious either. Seat belts, he thought, were for optimists.

"Do I look like I have AIDS?" he said.

"Not hardly."

"There you go."

Again they were both laughing, and this time Kohl managed to pull her down and roll her off him while distracting her with a kiss.

"I got a wild and crazy idea," he said. "Why don't we go to sleep?"

She pretended to pout. "You just a big old killjoy."

"And I'd better warn you—anyone wakes me up, I usually toss 'em overboard."

"Like you tossed that little old bike?"

"Something like that."

"Well, then," she purred, "guess I'm feelin' kinda sleepy myself."

"Attagirl."

Earlier, when she popped up at the house, Kohl had tried to motion her away from the window toward the back door, so he and Ken could shovel everything back into the briefcase unobserved. But she had been slow to move, was obviously interested in what they were doing. Then, while Ken briefly left the room to hide the case again, Kohl went over to the door and let her in. And she was nothing if not apologetic, explaining that her girlfriend's old man had returned home and that another "real close friend," a guy, had got married recently without even bothering to let her know—could Kohl feature that, wasn't it a bummer? And finally she informed him that she didn't have enough money on her for a motel room and wasn't in the mood to go to a bar and get herself picked up.

"So here I am, like a little old lost dog," she said. "You wanta give me a kick and send me on my way, I'll understand. I really will."

When Ken came back into the room, Bobbi immediately turned up the wattage, smiling brightly and touching her hair and thrusting her pert breasts a few more centimeters out into her Mickey Mouse T-shirt. Using only their first names, Kohl introduced them. He explained to Ken that she was the one who had picked him up in the mountains and that they were going to spend the rest of the night together on the Williwaw. This last seemed to mystify Ken as much as it did Bobbi, but at the time Kohl had no more explanations left in him. He took the girl by the hand and led her back to his room, to wait there while he showered and changed. The last thing he wanted was for her to spend even a few minutes alone with Ken, taking him in with her cornpone dumb-little-me act while she patiently grilled him to a turn, probably for no other reason than simple uncomplicated nosiness. But whatever her motive, no matter how innocent it might have been, Kohl still feared the outcome—that he and Ken could well end up having to take in a fourth co-conspirator, this one with agendas and allegiances all her own. So he planned on keeping her close, at least until he could get her out of the house.

For her part, Bobbi didn't seem to mind it at all, being

dragged off to his room. Lounging back on his bed, she asked why they didn't just stay right where they were instead of going off to "some dumb old boat somewhere," and Kohl explained that Ken's "wife" was very strict about such things and that he had to go along with her because it was her house. At the time he had peeled down to his shorts and was about to go into the bathroom to take a shower. And Bobbi wasn't missing a thing, least of all his uneasy, embarrassed smile.

She shook her head in mock sorrow. "I guess the bigger they are, the easier they pussy-whip."

"Ain't that the truth," he said.

Later, driving him down to Yarrow Bay, she took the same blacktop Ken had used in his flight from the accident. And when they reached Lake Street, she told him that there had been a fatal hit-and-run earlier in downtown Kirkland.

"Just north of here, on this same street," she went on. "I heard it on the radio. They said it was a four-by-four that hit this poor guy."

"No kidding." Kohl knew that he should have looked over at her, blandly met her mocking gaze. But he wasn't feeling quite that cool, especially as his words came right back at him now.

"No kidding," she said.

Since the marina was directly across Lake Street from where they were, he busied himself telling her where to turn in and where to park. Once they were out of the car, he unlocked the chain-link gate and led her on down the main pier past the moorage docks, the first four of which were covered, to Ken's uncovered slip near the end. Even for a landlubber like Kohl, the marina at night was a place of singular beauty, with the water lapping softly at the rough-hewn pilings and sleek white boats, and in the background the lights of Seattle coruscating across the dark lake. Yet all Bobbi seemed interested in was dollars: how much this boat had cost and what that one was worth and how many millions an average slip rented for.

In answer Kohl told her that he was a hick too and that all

he knew about yachts was that if you had to ask the price you couldn't afford one.

"Oh, that's bullshit," she said. "You telling me the people who own these here boats never asked the price?"

"Not according to J. P. Morgan."

"Well, what does she know? *Gong Show* make her some kind of expert or something?"

Kohl wondered if she was putting him on. "Of course it does," he said.

Not unexpectedly, the Williwaw disappointed Bobbi, the pleasures of teak and brass apparently not as obvious to her as those that inhered in fiberglass and stainless steel. In addition, the boat was still a mess, only partially restored, with tools and electric cords and sawdust and odd lengths of wood lying about, though not in the head or in the galley or the bow cabin—the areas Ken wisely had finished first, so he could work on the boat for days at a time, should the spirit ever move him to do so.

Now, as Kohl tried to will himself to sleep, the events of the last four hours kept going off like marine flares in his head, scenes that would burst into bright, scary life for a few seconds before slowly fading. And the one he finally took with him into the pit was Ken following him and Bobbi to the door as they were leaving for the Williwaw. While Bobbi went on out to her car, Ken shakily reached out to hold Kohl there for a few seconds longer.

"God, I hate to be alone tonight," he said, his eyes brimming.

"Diane's here."

"I really need you, Tommy. I really do. I'm not sure I can cut it here all night alone."

Kohl took hold of his shoulder so firmly Ken winced. "You've just got to, man. There's no other choice. I have to get her out of here—you can see that, can't you?"

Ken was crying freely by then. "I guess so."

"You have to get hold of yourself. It's that simple. Remember, this was *your* idea, not going to the police."

Ken nodded disconsolately. "I know, I know." And suddenly he was holding on to Kohl for dear life. "Listen, man, I ain't ever forgettin' what you did for me tonight. You're the best, Tommy. You always were, and you still are."

Kohl patted him on the back, then gently pulled away, feeling embarrassed. "Well, hell yes, old buddy," he said. "Everybody knows that."

Kohl was not used to summers that were dry, cool, and sunny all at the same time. He had asked the men at work if this kind of weather was unusual and they assured him that it was typical Northwest summer weather, including the happy fact that in comparison with other parts of the country, it was virtually insect-free. So Kohl decided that he'd just settle back and enjoy it, but there were still times when he found it hard to get used to, such as now, waking up cold and shivering under blankets in the middle of July. Fortunately a pillar of sunlight poured down through the open hatch onto the deep swell of Bobbi's hip, and Kohl took this as a sign that warmth and pleasure could be his even though she was still sound asleep.

Very gradually he worked the blankets down from her shoulder and over her hip so that her bottom finally was exposed to him as well as to the sun. And for a time he rested his head on that warm, plump pillow, rubbing it with his beard and nipping at it, hoping to wake her so gently she could not possibly be in anything but a receptive mood. And as it developed, that was indeed her mood, probably would have been anyway, cheek-nuzzled or not, since pom-pom girls were nothing if not accommodating. There was a priviso, however.

"Now, you just hold your horses, buster, cuz I gotta pee first." Smiling and slapping at his hands, she hopped out of the bed. "There any mouthwash on this old tub?"

"I sure hope so," Kohl said.

It was the middle of the morning before they finally made it to a nearby Denny's for a late breakfast. Because it was Saturday, the restaurant wasn't very crowded, and Bobbi had the waitress seat them in a corner booth where there was no one else around. At the time, Kohl considered this innocent enough, figuring the girl was merely trying to sustain the feelings of intimacy and affection that had developed between them overnight. Even on the way in, when she stopped to buy a newspaper, he thought nothing of it. But once they had their coffee and were waiting for their food, she quickly got down to business, turning to the local news section and finding exactly what she wanted.

"Why, here it is," she said. "Right on the front page—that hit-and-run I was telling you about last night."

Kohl still felt he had no choice except to play the innocent. "The one in Kirkland?"

"Right. The Bronco one."

"*Bronco?* That's what it says?"

Bobbi smiled brightly. "Well, a Bronco's a four-wheeler. And it says four-wheeler."

"So's a Jeep. Or a Jimmy. Or a—"

"I know that, silly. I was just talkin'." She turned back to the paper, carefully fashioning a look of amazement as she read. "Why, it says the guy was some kinda criminal, can you beat that?" She gave Kohl a conspiratorial look and pretended to shiver. "Sort of makes you wonder, don't it?"

"*Criminal?*" Kohl said.

"Sure, that's what it says. Here, look." She turned the paper sideways on the table, so they both could read it, a single-column story on the lower half of the page.

Tony Jack Brother
Killed in Hit-and-Run

Richard A. Giacalone, 36, brother of alleged crime figure "Tony Jack" Giacalone, was killed Friday night by a hit-and-run vehicle on Lake Street in Kirkland. Witnesses described the vehicle as a late-model Jeep or short-bed pickup truck with off-road tires.

Giacalone was thrown almost 80 feet by the impact and died of massive head injuries and general trauma, according to Medical Examiner R. L. Fleet. A police spokesman said that there was no reason to suspect that the incident was a so-called "mob killing." The victim and his brother, Tony Jack, have been linked to various alleged criminal activities in the Seattle area, including loan-sharking and the notorious L'Amour Escort Service, which the district attorney's office shut down as a front for prostitution. Convicted of pandering in that case, Richard Giacalone served a three-year sentence in the state prison at Walla Walla.

Tony Jack, who now owns a nightclub in Seattle, stated that his brother was an investment counselor and that if the police were slow in finding the hit-and-run driver, he and his other brother, Arnold Giacalone, would offer a reward and help the police in any way they could.

Richard Giacalone is survived by his wife, Anna, and their three children. A family spokesman said that funeral services will be private.

Bobbi repeated her observation. "Sort of makes you wonder, don't it?"

"Wonder what?"

"About maybe it wasn't an accident, you know? Like maybe he was doin' somethin' crooked and someone wanted to stop him real bad. Like that, you know?"

Kohl lit a cigarette. "You have a rich imagination."

"Oh, I know it. My mama always tells me that." She reached over and put her hand on his arm. "And you wouldn't believe what I'm imaginin' right this second, Tom, about this dumb old accident. You just wouldn't believe it."

Under his shirt Kohl felt a drop of sweat slide down his back. "Oh, I don't know—why not try me?"

She laughed and put her hand to her mouth, as though it embarrassed her, the nonsense she was about to spout. "Now remember, I don't believe any of this, cuz I know you're a real straight guy and all. But it's real weird, the way it all kind of fits. I mean, well, the thing did happen right down the street in Kirkland, didn't it—sorta between the downtown and Kin's house. And then the way you got rid of that Bronco—well, if somebody didn't know you, she might figure you was, well, sorta gettin' rid of the evidence, if you know what I mean. Makin' sure that if someone found the Bronco it was banged up all over, not just in front. Cuz someone rich, like your cousin, he'd have all kinds of ways to git money faster than tryin' some old insurance scam, right? And then him being kinda drunk like he was last night, and you two hidin' that briefcase when I showed up."

Kohl just sat there looking at her, wondering whatever had happened to that simple pom-pom girl with the beautiful sun-lit ass. "You about finished?" he asked.

She made a hapless, comical gesture. "That's it, I guess."

"Well, I said it before and I'll say it again—what big eyes you have, Grandma."

Bobbi laughed. "Don't I, though!"

Kohl said nothing for a while. He let his face settle into a solemn mask and he let his eyes grow cold as he sat there staring at the girl. He watched as she began to squirm; he listened to her giggle.

"I guess it doesn't matter," he said finally. "As long as you know I'm too straight to be involved in anything like that."

"Oh, I know it, I really do, Tom," she assured him, reaching for his arm again. "But even if you was involved—even if you was, I'd never say anything. Never a peep. You know that, don'tcha, Tom?"

Before he could answer, the waitress brought their food, a cardiologist's nightmare of bacon and eggs and pancakes and syrup and orange juice. And it wasn't until she had refilled their coffee cups and left that Kohl finally answered.

"Sure," he said, "I know that."

But the truth was he couldn't be sure what Bobbi's intentions were, any more than he could be sure whether she actually believed her scenario or was merely fishing in promising waters. He was fairly certain that she wasn't the type to go running to the police with her suspicions—that didn't seem to be her style at all. He would have given odds that she had a police record of her own somewhere, sometime, if not for assaulting a housemate like Rusty, then maybe even for prostitution, considering how casually she had mentioned not "being in the mood" to find a night's lodging as a bar pickup.

So all Kohl could do finally was guess, make a judgment. And common sense told him that she was only guessing herself, that the parts she had to the puzzle really didn't add up to anything unless a person desperately wanted them to. Which she apparently did. As to *why* she did, Kohl was inclined to give her the benefit of the doubt there too, figuring for some reason that it wasn't money she was after so much as friendship and security, possibly nothing more than an invitation to join their little conspiracy, since that might also mean joining their little household, for a while anyway, living what she considered the Good Life—or at least living it as Kohl did, as a poor relation.

But when they left the restaurant and headed in her car for Ken and Diane's, Kohl mentioned none of this, pretended that her scenario was only a flight of fancy already forgotten. He told her again of the problem with Diane, that if it weren't for her unsociable ways, he would have invited Bobbi to stay with him and Ken for a few days or at least until she worked things out with her boyfriend, Rusty. Meanwhile he had her detour past a cash machine in Kirkland, where he withdrew one hundred dollars out of his bank account and gave it to her.

"If you promise me it's only a loan, I'll take it," she said. "Otherwise I can't, cuz it'd make me feel like—well, kinda like a hooker, you know?"

"Okay, I promise—it's only a loan. If you don't pay me back, I break both your legs."

"That's more like it." She leaned over and kissed him. "I

appreciate it, Tom. I really do. You're okay, you know that?"

"That's what I keep hearing," he said.

Even though Diane's open house would last only three or four hours, Kohl knew she would be gone most of the day, Saturdays being what they were in the real estate business. And for a time he thought Ken was gone too—renting a car, visiting the scene of the crime, God only knew—but then he found him sleeping fitfully in his and Diane's king-size water bed in the master suite, which probably meant he hadn't turned in until after she left for work. Grateful for small favors, Kohl went out to the garage and began working on his truck, something he deeply regretted not having done on Thursday night, so he could have driven it to work on Friday. If he had, then Richard Giacalone would undoubtedly have made it across Lake Street and Bobbi-with-an-i wouldn't have Kohl by the short hairs and Ken wouldn't be asleep upstairs, having nightmares about the hit-and-run.

Kohl's truck was a 1979 Chevy four-wheel-drive pickup with an odometer that read twenty-three thousand and change, the first hundred thousand having already come and gone. And the poor old beast looked it. The only spiffy thing about it was its sheepskin seat covers, which concealed the considerable damage Kohl's heft had inflicted over the years. It also had a pair of truly awesome bumpers, steel I-beams his father had welded to the frame and fitted with two-by-ten oak plank insets so he could go out in winter storms and push or pull almost any vehicle out of the snow.

At the moment, though, Kohl's only concern was the carburetor butterfly, which kept sticking despite the liberal dousings of WD-40 he had administered. He knew he needed a whole new carburetor and that a new fuel pump wouldn't have hurt anything either, but he also knew from experience that by taking the carburetor apart and cleaning it in gasoline before reassembling it, adjusting a screw here and bending something there—that by doing no more than this he generally could coax the thing into working a while longer. And that was precisely what happened this time. In fact, gunning the engine, he thought he detected a sound out of its youth, a confident, understated roar he hadn't heard in years.

After cleaning up, he made a sandwich and got a cold beer and went into the game room to watch television, preseason football if he could get it. But a tennis match—Evert against Navratilova for the thousandth time—was the best he could do. As he was finishing the sandwich he heard Ken shuffling down the stairs, like an old man. And in his hooded robe he looked like one too, an old Capuchin monk holding on to the railing as he teetered into the foyer. Sighing, he came on into the room.

"Christ, what a hangover," he lamented. "I feel like death."

Kohl said nothing at first, wondering how the man would hold up under the news that Richard Giacalone was not your average businessman. "Maybe you ought to try staying sober today," he suggested.

"You think so?"

"Yes, I do."

"Your little hick—I take it you shed her by now?"

"Yeah, this hick shed that hick. For the moment anyway."

Ken sat down very carefully, as if he feared he might injure himself. "You got the truck fixed, uh?"

"Sorry if I woke you."

"You didn't. Anyway, I gotta get out of here today, Tommy. I can't just sit here and wait for the goddam police to show up. I'll go crazy."

Kohl shrugged. "I guess we could go for a drive."

"Good. You know that house in the pictures, where they were having the cookout?"

Kohl stared at his cousin. "Are you totally out of your mind?"

"I know, I know—it probably sounds stupid, maybe even sick, I realize that. But I keep seeing those kids. And for some crazy reason, I think it would help me to see where they actually live. To see where *he* lived. To sort of get it all straight in my mind, you know?"

"No, I don't know."

"We just drive by the place, Tommy—that's all. What could it hurt?"

Kohl watched Chris Evert try in vain to run down a cross-court smash and he too suddenly felt his age. "Just drive by, uh?" he said.

"That's all, man. Honest. I really think it would help me."

"And would it help any if I told you Richard Giacalone was an ex-con? And that his business—his *family* business—was loan-sharking and prostitution and neat stuff like that?"

For a time Ken said nothing. He just sat looking over at Kohl and frowning, as if this bit of news simply would not compute.

"I still want to go there," he said finally. "Just drive by. Okay, Tommy?"

Once again Kohl found it hard to believe what he was doing. Even worse, it seemed that was about *all* he'd done for the last sixteen hours or so—things someone else might do, some asshole like old Junior Gates, the jokester genius back home who one Fourth of July tossed a lit string of firecrackers out of his truck window while buying gasoline and burned down half of Blanton in the process. Now, Kohl knew he wasn't really in Junior's league, but he was definitely beginning to wonder about cousin Ken, because the man just wasn't behaving as your average hit-and-run fugitive would on the day after. Instead of staying in bed or getting drunk again or watching from behind the Levelors for the flashing lights of a police car, there he sat next to Kohl in the truck, a perfectly proper Saturday yuppie in designer jeans and Reboks and a peppermint-stripe shirt that probably cost more than Kohl's favorite sportcoat.

Yet Ken was not off to the races or going out on the boat—he was on his way to view his victim's home, or at least what he thought was his victim's home. Kohl had explained to him that the oldest of the Giacalone brothers—Tony Jack—apparently was the one who ran things and owned things, like the strip joint, so the house in the photographs was more likely his than his brother's. But Ken was not to be discouraged.

"Just drive by," he said. "What could it hurt?"

Kohl shrugged. "Nothing, I guess. But if I were you, I wouldn't be thinking about goddam Giacalone or his kids or his house—I'd have some other things on my mind."

"Like what?"

Like what? Kohl, driving, looked over at him. Like my little hick has put it all together, he wanted to say. But he had no idea how Ken would react to the news, whether he'd come totally unglued or just pass it off as something of no concern to him, a pesky mosquito compared to the rats of guilt and fear already feasting on him.

Kohl had agreed to the drive finally only because Ken promised that he would go over the Bronco story with Kohl until they had it letter-perfect, exactly what each of them would tell the police regarding the vehicle's disappearance. And that was what they were doing as Kohl drove his truck down Route 520 and out onto the world's longest floating bridge, with the lake stretching almost ten miles to the north and more than that to the south. Dazzling in the afternoon sun, the lake didn't even look crowded, despite the dozens of boats tacking and churning across it.

"We should get to the police station by eight tomorrow morning," Kohl said. "I don't want to miss any more work than I have to. And remember, you talk first."

"Right. I just report the Bronco missing, because I don't really know it's been stolen. They'll want my pink slip and all that. Then when they ask for details, I turn to you."

"Because I'm the one who was using it. My truck was down, so you let me drive the Bronco to work on Thursday. And after work I stopped off at the Sitting Bull—which I actually did, incidentally, in case they bother to check. After five or six beers I moved on to another bar, and then later a couple more. Only I can't remember which ones they were—it's all kind of vague. Anyway, I think I was in Bellevue somewhere when I met this divorced woman who took me home with her, in her car. She had a real nice liquor cabinet, so we partied most of Friday and Saturday. And I guess I forgot all about the Bronco."

"Which is where I come in again," Ken said. "I tell them I figured you had the damn thing with you all that time. Only you didn't and now you can't even remember where the hell you left it."

By now Kohl was grinning ruefully at the thought of what a pitiful figure he would cut at the police station: a typical lush with a bad memory and probably a dash of VD in the bargain.

"Right," he said. "And they naturally will ask why we don't check with the woman, since she might remember where she picked me up. But of course I can't remember her last name or even where her house was."

Ken laughed out loud at that, then assumed the exasperated expression of Kohl's imagined interrogator. "Well, what about her goddam first name then? Can you remember that at least?"

"Sure—Debbie." Kohl looked over at Ken again. "There must be at least a thousand Debbies trolling the Eastside bars, wouldn't you say?"

"At least. Anyway, you think after hearing all that the cops won't be putting out any APBs on the Bronco, right?"

"Hell, it probably won't even make their stolen list. They gotta figure it's sitting in a parking lot somewhere and that either we'll eventually find it or someone will call a tow truck and have it impounded. Either way, I can't see them wasting time on it."

"Excellent." Ken barely got the word out before he dropped out of the conversation like a stone into the lake. It was an old habit of his, a quirk from childhood. One second he'd be there with you, giving and taking, and the next second he'd be gone. There would be a sudden silence and Kohl would look over at him just as he was doing now, only to find this very quiet stranger sitting in his place. At the moment the stranger was staring straight ahead with eyes cobalt-blue in the bright sunlight and his wavy dark-blond hair blowing freely and his chin held slightly raised, as though to emphasize the chiseled perfection of his profile. But Kohl knew that he wasn't posing, knew that even as vain as he was, Ken wouldn't have wasted such silliness on him. More likely, he was going through the accident again in his mind, throwing his head back as he laughed at Kohl's batting eyes and wolfish grin and then too late looking back at the road again, at this man from out of the blue absurdly holding up his briefcase to ward them off, and then *that sound,* the terrible finality of it. Or perhaps he was merely lost in contemplation of what mattered most to him just then, which apparently wasn't staying out of jail but rather what lay ahead, beyond the freeway and around another lake and up on a high hill, something he probably thought of as expiation.

Kohl accepted the fact that his hometown and the flatlands surrounding it didn't really compare with Seattle, with its steep hills and dazzling views of skyscrapers and blue waters and distant white-capped mountains. Yet from where he sat, parked in his truck, he knew he wouldn't have minded at all if the view wasn't of all that but of rows of corn running straight back to the eighty acres of oak woods that had been part of his family's farm. And he wondered if the only difference was possession, ownership, in that while he'd erroneously thought of all that as his, he found it impossible to think of anything he saw now as ever being a meaningful part of his life.

Giacalone's street, handsome as it was, had no real character other than affluence. It was a mélange of the old and the new, the beautiful and the ugly. There were two huge old Victorian wood houses and a Georgian mansion made of dark-orange brick with white wood trim, and all three were beautifully maintained and beautiful in themselves. But in among them were a modern apartment building and a number of condominiums, all glassy boxes with cramped little balconies—or decks, as the locals called them—so the poor souls trapped inside could at least look out at the Sound and the mountains and pretend that was where they really lived.

And then there was the Giacalone house at the end of the street, small in comparison with the other three and of mixed parentage as well, looking both Spanish and neoclassic, with narrow Greek columns holding up a slanted roof of red tile. Kohl, who considered himself anything but an aesthete, nevertheless knew enough to recognize a bastard when he saw one, and the house was definitely that, albeit an expensive bastard, considering the view and proximity to the city's downtown. In addition, there was the intriguing presence of that visitor from another world—the top of the Space Needle, which looked less like a revolving sky restaurant than it did a flying saucer hovering just over the backyard hedge, narrowly visible between the house and three-car garage.

After a brief argument, won by Ken's trembling hands and moist eyes, Kohl had agreed to park for a few minutes—at a spot about halfway down the block-long street, which sloped from the connecting avenue to the Giacalone house at the very end.

"I don't know what the hell you're getting out of this," Kohl said.

"I already told you—I just want to see where the man lived. And his wife and kids. Get it straight in my mind, you know?"

Kohl groaned. "Look, if you're thinking of turning yourself in and this is just your weird way of working up to it— fine, I'm with you. Like Diane said, it's not too late."

But Ken wasn't listening. Before Kohl could stop him, he had thrown open the door and slipped out of the pickup, heading for the gate of the Georgian mansion. Kohl started to scramble after him, then thought better of it, realizing that all he could do was draw attention to them, especially if someone saw him dragging Ken back to the truck by the ear. By way of compromise, he punched the dashboard so hard it broke in two, thereby sharply diminishing his net worth. And it didn't help matters at all when he saw what his cousin's goal was: an old oriental gardener working just inside the gate. What on earth, Kohl wondered, was Ken going to say to the man? *Hi there, fella—I'm the guy who ran over your neighbor's brother. You think they'd let me see his wife and kids? Sort of pay my last respects?*

Whatever he said, it was brief. Within seconds Ken was back on the sidewalk, only headed in the opposite direction now, down the street toward the Giacalone house. And Kohl had to admit that his cousin looked perfectly at home, a virtual paradigm of the successful man about town, casually dressed, casually handsome, casually strolling down this elegant little street of the urban rich. Watching him, no one would have dreamed that he had accidentally killed a man the previous night—wouldn't have dreamed it for the very good reason that he looked as if he'd forgotten about the incident himself. But for Kohl this further irrationality was simply one more indication that the man was about to break. In fact, Kohl wouldn't have been surprised if it happened at any moment, if not right at Giacalone's front door, then on the way home, or *at* home. And Kohl suddenly realized how very much he wanted that to happen, how desperately he wanted to be out from under the whole goddam mess. So he felt no special anxiety as he watched Ken come to the end of the street and turn left, passing by the Giacalone house. Nor was he surprised when Ken about-faced and started back. Nevertheless Kohl's hands—what Diane called his "big mitts"—began to sweat as he tightened his grip on the steering wheel. And not all that unexpectedly, Ken began to walk like a kid on the way to school, just dawdling along as he started past the house again. He gazed absently up at the trees and he peered down the street at Kohl in the pickup, and then he wandered on a few more steps, until finally there he stood, facing the open gate in the wrought-iron fence that edged the property.

Jaunty as a vacuum-cleaner salesman, he entered through the gate and skipped up the front stairs, moving past the Greek columns to the front door, where he stabbed at a doorbell. The porch was shaded and dark, and when the door finally opened the house's interior looked darker still. Kohl couldn't see who had answered the door. Whoever it was, he or she obviously wasn't what Ken was looking for, because the door went shut almost immediately and Ken was on his way back down the walk.

When he reached the truck, he was shaking his head in disgust and disappointment. "Just a maid," he said, getting in. "She did tell me who lived there, though. It's like you said— the brother, Tony Jack."

Kohl was resting his head on his hands, which still gripped the steering wheel. "And if it was the widow, what then?" he asked. "Would you have confessed?"

Ken shook his head. "I don't know. I really don't." Then he looked over at Kohl as if a bright idea had just occurred to him. "I guess I don't even know what I'm doing anymore. Is that what you think, Tommy? You think I've gone over the edge?"

Kohl didn't answer.

On the way home Kohl wished that they were ten-year-olds again, because then he would have parked the truck and clamped a headlock on dear old Ken and dragged him out into the grass for a thumping. At the very least he would have thrown him down and sat on him, held him there on the ground until he cried and said he was sorry and wouldn't act like a stupid fuck-up ever again. But they were three times ten, and for some reason this meant never doing anything the easy, natural, effective way.

60

Then too Kohl was just as angry at himself as he was at Ken, because he knew how keen his disappointment had been when nothing came of Ken's bizarre little foray into Tony Jack's domain—no sudden confession, no call to the police, no blessed end to the ever-expanding nightmare. And Kohl had to ask himself what kind of man—what kind of best friend—would risk seeing his own cousin carted off to prison rather than carry on as they had agreed, covering up a crime that was really not a crime at all but an *accident*—an accident caused by the victim as much as by anyone. And Kohl's answer wasn't to his liking: A spineless friend, he told himself. A man without loyalty. It was an answer that galled him yet firmed his resolve to see the thing through. There would be no more talk of going to the police, at least not on his part.

Later that afternoon, when Ken began to drink again, Kohl suggested that they go down to the marina and work on the boat. Ken thought about it for a while, sipping at a scotch. Finally he shrugged.

"Yeah, why not? What could it hurt? Be better than moping around here waiting for the police to show up."

In fact, he found the idea so much to his liking that by the time they reached the marina, it had become *his* idea. "I always say, a little hard work never hurts, Tommy. Especially when you're at loose ends, right?"

"Right."

The most important part of the work on the Williwaw—rebuilding the wooden hull—had been done at a boatyard, by professionals, months before Kohl arrived. As a result, there at least was no immediate danger of the thing sinking. But before it could be operational there was one other major job yet to be done: the boat's ancient twelve-cylinder Chrysler engines had to be either rebuilt or replaced. But since Ken knew nothing about engines and didn't have the twenty or thirty thousand dollars it would have cost to replace them, this was a subject that seldom came up. And anyway there were dozens of other jobs—*doable* jobs—yet to be finished.

For instance, on this day Ken decided that he wanted to

install the mahogany control panel he'd had a woodworker cut out for him, with precise slots and holes for the boat's gauges and controls. Unfortunately he hadn't figured out ahead of time how the panel would slide in *over* such controls as the two throttles, which were much larger at the outer end than they were at the base. And this frustrated him so greatly that he finally tossed the panel aside, changed into a pair of swim trunks, and went out to the bow to lie in the sun.

Kohl had little affection for finishing Ken's work for him, but it had been his lot off and on since they were kids—doing the chores, baling hay, whatever—and he eventually picked up the panel and set to work. It proved to be a job any twelve-year-old could have solved if he put his mind to it. Essentially all Kohl had to do was disconnect the throttles, clutches, and gauges, fit the panel into place, and then reconnect everything from underneath, working on his back. It was delicate, tedious work, and it took him over an hour to finish the job.

By then Ken had roasted himself on all sides and was sitting back in the shade, working on his third or fourth scotch and scowling through a pair of Vuarnet sunglasses at the lake as the sun began to slip down behind Seattle. When Kohl got a beer and joined him, he thought the man would at least ask about his precious mahogany panel, but he didn't.

"Guess you think I'm pretty much a flake, uh, Tommy?" he said.

Kohl tipped up his beer bottle, hoping that if he ignored the question, it would go away.

"Well, do you?"

"You're sure as hell acting like one," Kohl said finally. Then, against all his instincts, he couldn't help mimicking his cousin's voice. " 'We'll just drive by, Tommy. What could it hurt?' "

"I know, I know," Ken said.

"Any minute the law could come down on us, yet you go ahead and pull a stunt like that. It's hard to figure, Ken."

Ken shook his head, as if it puzzled him as much as it did Kohl. "I don't know—I just can't seem to get my head straight since the accident. I know it was the guy's fault—more than mine—but it doesn't seem to make any difference. My head just keeps going, *You killed a man, you killed a man.* And I guess I figure I can't get away with it. It's all gonna come down on me."

Then you should go to the police, Kohl wanted to say. But his own feelings of guilt were still fresh in his mind. "Not if you get a grip on yourself," he said. "Remember why we're doing all this—because you said you couldn't cut it in prison."

Ken's eyes had filled with tears. "Yeah, I know. But it seems I can't handle this either."

Kohl didn't know what to say to that. And he was afraid that if he touched him, even just patted him on the shoulder, Ken would break down completely. Fortunately just then Kohl saw Diane coming down the dock toward the boat.

"Diane's here," he said, with relief.

Ken didn't even look up. "Big deal," he muttered.

For Kohl, though, it *was* a big deal, and not only because she looked so good and had gotten him off the hook, but also because she was carrying two bags of leftovers from her open house that day. Most of it was finger food, cute little sandwiches and meatballs and such, but there was a lot of it, and Kohl gratefully dug in while Diane lamented her day.

"Lookyloos mostly," she said. "Three hours sitting in this perfectly awful little house—nice view, though—and not one legitimate prospect shows up. I hope you two had a better day." Hearing herself, she laughed and shook her head. "I mean, *considering.* Me, I've been jumpy as a cat."

"Mostly, we've been waiting," Kohl said. "But so far, the other shoe hasn't dropped."

"Maybe it never will." Smiling, Diane turned to Ken, obviously expecting him to say something, at least acknowledge in some way that she was there. But he kept staring out at the lake. She glanced at the drink in his hand. "Maybe you ought to eat some of this stuff," she said. "You don't want to get sick again tonight, do you?"

The Vuarnets swiveled slowly, taking her in. "I'll do what I fucking want," he told her. "You can count on that."

For a moment she looked surprised and hurt. Then she turned back to Kohl, smiling almost gaily now. "My, but you have a nice cousin," she said. "He has such a sweet personality."

Kohl shrugged. "I'm not my cousin's keeper."

It was an opening Diane couldn't resist. "Wish I could say that."

And that was enough for Ken. Getting to his feet, he held his hand out to Kohl. "Give me your keys—I'm going home."

"A capital idea," Diane said.

Kohl tossed him the keys. "You're not going out, are you?"

Ken gave him a bored look. "Just don't worry about me, okay? I'm a big boy now."

Again Diane couldn't resist. "That's so true," she said. "And listen, *big boy*—be sure to drive carefully, okay?"

Diane let it be known that she wouldn't mind if some "tall, strong fella" would offer to row her around Yarrow Bay while there was still some light left. Kohl said he knew just the dolt she had in mind, and soon the two of them were out in the Williwaw's dinghy, a ten-foot fiberglass craft with a single foot-wide seat running from stem to stern, causing them to sit with their knees practically touching, denim to denim, Lees to Calvin Kleins. Kohl was so conscious of this, of her spread legs so dangerously close to his, that he wouldn't let himself even glance down at them. Nor was he unaware of how the lake breeze played in her hair or how her eyes and smile seemed to grow brighter still as the light failed.

At first they talked about the accident, their dubious good fortune that the police hadn't shown up yet. Diane agreed with Kohl that this probably meant that he and Ken hadn't been recognized, that no one had got their license-plate number.

Kohl also explained to her what he and Ken would tell the police Monday morning, when they reported the Bronco stolen. Diane asked how long he thought it would be before the vehicle was found and he said there was no way of knowing, that a troop of Boy Scouts might stumble upon it the very next day or it could remain lost for months. He was tempted to tell her about Bobbi and her uncanny scenario, but he didn't want to involve Diane any more than she already was. Also, he wasn't particularly anxious for her to know about him and Bobbi, especially that he and the girl had spent the night together on the Williwaw.

"Ken is so damned hostile," Diane said now. "You'd think I was to blame for the accident."

"He's that way with me too. And it's not surprising. It must be a heavy thing to deal with, knowing you killed someone, even if it wasn't your fault."

"I realize that. But he's been almost this bad for weeks. I guess it could be wounded pride—that he's ashamed I'm keeping him. Well, I don't like it either. But I don't know what to do about it. I keep hoping he'll give up this crazy charter-boat idea and get a job again." She gave Kohl a long, searching look. "Sometimes I think we're both dreaming."

"You and Ken?"

"Of course, me and Ken. Who else?"

Kohl smiled uneasily. "I don't know. It was just your look. I thought maybe you figured I was dreaming too."

"About what?"

"Who knows?"

She smiled and touched his knee, patted him, much like a grown-up with a child. "No, I never think of you as a dreamer, Tom. I'd say you've got those big feet pretty firmly planted in the real world, anyone does the kind of work you do."

Kohl reminded her that he didn't do construction labor by choice.

"I know that." She looked as if it actually pained her, the thought of him doing work that he disliked. "You know, I think that's part of Ken's problem too—your losing your farm. He blames his father, you know. He says the old man really put it to you and your parents."

Kohl laughed softly, shaking his head. "Uncle Ralph isn't exactly my favorite piece of work, but he didn't lose us our farm. We managed that all by ourselves."

He didn't talk about it very often, partly because it wasn't that uncommon a story, especially back in the Midwest. Kohl's mother and her brother, Ralph, Ken's father, each inherited a farm when their father died of a stroke at sixty. Uncle Ralph, of course, got the better of the two farms, the original Ryder homestead, which over the years had expanded to 360 acres, while Kohl's mother inherited the adjoining tenant farm. And though she and Kohl's father loved it dearly, they came to realize that it simply wasn't large enough—only 240 acres—to give them and Kohl and his young wife much of a living. So when land prices went over three thousand dollars an acre and Ken's father was astute enough to want out at that price, the Kohls persuaded themselves—and were fervently encouraged by the local bank and the FHA—to snap up the old home place for a cool million dollars, almost all of it borrowed, with their own farm and machinery as collateral.

Ken's father then banked his money, paid his taxes, bought a little house in town, a lakefront cottage in Wisconsin, and a thirty-foot motor home for wintering in Florida. And the ensuing farm depression—the sharply falling grain and land prices—touched him not at all. As Kohl and his parents sank hopelessly into debt, Ralph never offered to help them, and they knew better than to ask. The man after all still had his wife turn the collars on his shirts. He was a tightwad and a skinflint, but he was in no way responsible for the Kohls' misfortunes. And Ken knew this as well as anybody. In fact, Kohl imagined that his cousin's real brief against his father was that the old man refused to share the wealth with his only son.

"Don't worry about me," Kohl said to Diane now. "Soon as

I get enough money ahead, I'm gonna quit my job, shave off the beard, buy a three-piece suit, and become a yuppie."

Diane laughed, and Kohl thought of being on the shore and hearing that laugh, like the jingle of a very small, very perfect bell.

"I can just see that," she said.

Kohl smiled. "You just wait."

She sat there looking at him in the failing light. "You know, I feel so safe with you, Tom. Like nothing bad could ever happen to me."

Kohl had no idea what to say to that.

"It must be nice to be so big and strong," she went on. "To go through life and not have all the normal little fears."

That made *him* laugh. "What are you talking about? I'm probably afraid of more things than you are."

"Like what?"

He wondered whether to say it. "Like *you*. Like the first time I met you."

"Oh, come on," she said. "What's to be afraid of?"

"Disapproval."

"Aha! So even Hercules has a heel." Then she added, "Like Achilles."

Kohl smiled wryly. "You know, you didn't have to add the footnote. It so happens I'm a renowned classical scholar."

"Sorry about that."

"And what about Diane? Or should I say Diana?"

Her smile flashed in the darkness. "Oh, she has her heel too. And his name is Ken."

Kohl didn't laugh. "It's almost dark," he said. "We'd better head in."

3 Sunday passed without event. Neither the police nor Bobbi showed up at Diane and Ken's doorstep, and Diane as usual went off to work looking like the million dollars she was so hell-bent on acquiring. Ken divided his time between the toilet, the front windows, and the laundry room, where he now kept the briefcase and photographs of Richard Giacalone and his family. Meanwhile Kohl watched television and read the Seattle and Eastside newspapers, none of which ran a follow-up on the hit-and-run. In midafternoon he and Ken went down to the boat and worked for a few hours, after which they took the dinghy out into the lake and went swimming in the still numbingly cold water.

In the evening they and Diane went to a nearby restaurant on the lake and by ten o'clock had spent twice as much on wine and liquor as they had on food, and as a result almost had a good time. Diane told Ken that Kohl was going to become a clean-shaven yuppie soon, and Ken laughed at the idea.

"Oh no you don't!" he said. "It would be a sacrilege. Why,

it would be like bearding the lion. Didn't you know that Tommy's a lion? In fact, he was our Most Valuable Lion two years in a row."

"What *are* you talking about?" she asked.

Ken then explained that their high school football team, the Blanton Lions, had named Kohl their most valuable player in both his junior and senior years.

"He was a linebacker," Ken went on. "The scourge of central Illinois."

"I can believe it," Diane said.

"So please don't beard him!" Ken begged, laughing so hard now that other patrons looked over at the three of them and smiled, evidently wishing that they too were having such a fine time. And thanks to the alcohol, the trio's high spirits endured even after they got home. Later, Kohl was not surprised when he heard the sounds of lovemaking coming from the master bedroom suite. He thought of covering his head with pillows but knew that it wouldn't do any good, since it wasn't just the *sound* that bothered him.

By the way of escape, he thought about their conversation in the restaurant and what a laugh it was, the idea of his being voted the Most Valuable Lion in high school. As he remembered those brisk Friday nights under the lights, there was only one lion out on that field, and it was *fear*: fear of the coach and the crowd, fear of failure, and fear of success—fear of *life* finally. So Kohl had no qualms about shaving again someday. He knew that whatever he uncovered, it wasn't likely to be a lion.

The next morning, after calling his boss and telling him that he would be late, Kohl drove with Ken to the Kirkland police station, which was located in the city's municipal building, a glassy edifice sitting on a hill above the town. It seemed like a typical modern office building—until they entered the police station's lobby, which looked as if it belonged in Fort Knox. On either side were clerks working behind large expanses of bulletproof glass, with two-way radios for speaking with the public and narrow window slots for conducting business. Occasionally a locked steel door would open and a tall, slim female officer carrying papers would cross the tiny lobby and, unlocking the opposite door, enter that part of the station.

"Christ sake," Ken muttered. "What are they afraid of?"

"Us," Kohl said.

Finally their turn came and they were able to state their business to the clerk, who then called someone on the phone. Eventually the locked door opened again and another officer appeared, this one female also but much shorter and heavier than the first. A stolen or missing vehicle obviously didn't excite her very much, and she sighed wearily as Kohl and Ken followed her rolling hams through the locked door and back to her desk, where she sighed again as she began to fill out a form titled, simply, Vehicle Report. Ken had his pink slip and insurance papers with him, which gave her some pleasure. And when Kohl recounted his story of how he came to misplace the Bronco, she looked over at him with a spark of interest, as though she might have remembered something out of the distant past about sex and partying, but she quickly lapsed into boredom again and finally had Ken sign the report.

"We'll call you if anything turns up," she said.

And that was that. Outside, Ken was elated at how it had gone.

"Just what we figured—*indifference!*" he said. "The last thing they're gonna do is go out looking for the goddam thing! And if it falls into their laps, they'll probably just pick up a phone and give us a ring. We're home free, man!"

Kohl smiled grimly. "That's good to know. Now I can stop worrying."

"I didn't mean *that*," Ken protested. "Of course there's still plenty to be concerned about. I just meant we're home free about the Bronco, that's all."

As Kohl drove on to his job site, he wondered whether to say anything about what was really worrying him: that he had no idea what Ken would do once he was on his own, whether he would merely go home and get drunk or set out for Tony Jack's again or return to the police station and confess all.

"Just promise me one thing," Kohl said. "No more suicidal missions to Queen Anne Hill—okay?"

Ken shook his head in disgust. "Jesus Christ, Tommy, not that again! Yeah—*okay!*"

"I know—it's an old refrain by now. But you earned it, don't forget."

"Don't worry. All I'm gonna do today is check out car rentals. But you know, that's really gonna run into money. I still can't see why not buy some new wheels right now—I mean, what the hell does Diane know? *Houses!*"

Kohl had pulled up in front of the foothill house he was working on. "You know as well as I do," he said. "You buy a car before they start looking for the Bronco, it could look bad later, if they ever begin building a case against you."

"So I'm told." Ken was looking at the house, which was already framed and roofed but still a long way from completion. "You guys really slap 'em together, don't you? A good wind's all it would take."

"Right," Kohl said, getting out. "Have a nice day."

Ken smiled. "And fuck you too."

Kohl was surprised to find two crews at work on the house. When he asked about it, one of the carpenters gloomily gave him the bad news: their employer, J. C. Allen & Sons, had lost its credit line at the bank and as a result they were all going to have to work twelve hours a day in a mad rush to finish the house by the coming Friday. The idea seemed to be that once the house was finished, J.C. would be able to borrow on it again, since it would then be a more liquid asset.

"And what if he can't?" Kohl asked. "We still get paid?"

That, he was told, was the sixty-four-thousand-dollar question.

Despite the solid-sounding company name, J. C. Allen was essentially a working stiff just like his employees. He lived in a house trailer, his wife worked in a supermarket, and the sons in the company name were two little boys in grade school. J.C. often reminded Kohl of himself in his last years on the farm, a jack-of-all-trades workaholic, a man shoveling against a flood. And just as in Kohl's case, the flood was economic, costs that kept rising faster than income. Though his crews were nonunion, even a laborer like Kohl earned over ten dollars an hour. And having a small outfit—currently building only three houses—J.C. paid almost retail for lumber and borrowed money. The banks hadn't lost a cent on Kohl's farm, and he figured they weren't about to lose one on J. C. Allen & Sons either, since they usually reserved that privilege for more important debtors, the lucky few whose red ink ran into the millions.

In any case, he didn't mind at all giving his employer a full day's work for a full day's pay. And as a laborer, unloading all the lumber and other items and hauling them where they were needed, *when* they were needed, he had no choice but to work hard. One of the other laborers in fact was fond of pulling out his penis on the job, claiming that as long as he worked like a horse, he might as well look like one. Predictably, he was told that he resembled a pony more than he did a horse.

During the day Kohl phoned home and told the recorder that he would be working late and no one had to pick him up because he was going to hitch a ride with one of the carpenters. And after stopping off at the Sitting Bull for beer and supper, he finally got home at eleven, relieved to see that Ken had indeed rented a car, a bright-yellow Chevrolet Corvette, which he'd parked just outside the garage, under the floodlights, presumably to keep the neighbors up to speed on the state of his wheels.

Inside, Kohl wearily exchanged a few words with him and Diane, most of them about the Corvette: Diane pretending outrage at the rental fee while Ken waxed enthusiastic about the car's acceleration and handling. Diane then gave Kohl the good news about a new client who had flown in from L.A. that day, a very rich, very gay retiree and his handsome young lover, who insisted on a lakefront house no matter what the price. Kohl congratulated her on her good fortune and Ken on his sports car, then he showered and went to bed. The next day he again put in twelve hours of work, not getting home till after dark. And because no one else was there, he headed straight for bed, pausing only to shower on the way. He knew he probably should have read the paper or watched television in case there was any further news on the hit-and-run, but he doubted that there would be any, considering that there had been no follow-up on Sunday and Monday. Regardless, he was much too tired to care about anything except sleep.

Wednesday was more of the same, at least until five o'clock, when J.C. showed up with paychecks for everybody along with the melancholy news that the banks weren't going to lend him any more money, even if the house was finished. For the time being anyway, he was out of business and the men were out of work. Kohl expected that everyone would want to stop for a few drinks and talk things over, but they all had more experience as wage-earners than he did and headed straight for their banks, to get their money while the checks were still good, *if* they were good.

Following their lead, Kohl went through the drive-in at Seafirst and arrived home with a little over six hundred dollars in cash for his last eight days of work. He showered and changed and took a beer out onto the side porch, where he lounged back on a cushioned chaise. Because of the trees and the neighboring houses, he could see only a small part of the lake. Still it was something to watch, all the sails barely moving on the smooth blue water.

For days the muscles in his neck and shoulders had felt as

if they were being slowly knotted up, but he sensed a certain loosening there, an easing of tension. He figured that the main reason for this was simply because the police still hadn't shown up, and the conventional wisdom was that the longer it took them to solve a case, the less likely it was *ever* to be solved. But, strangely, he imagined that losing his job also contributed to his feeling less tense. Admittedly, he didn't look forward to hunting for another job, but at the same time the prospect of not having to do construction labor for the immediate future made him feel almost like getting up and dancing. More important than that, though, was the fact that he would be free now to spend more time with Ken—in effect, sit on him, keep him from blowing the cover-up on an *impulse.* Of course this still left Bobbi to worry about, but Kohl was reasonably confident that the girl was not the kind to go running to the police with her suspicions. With any luck at all he might never even see her again.

Ironically, even as he was thinking this he saw the two cars coming up the street: Diane's Cadillac followed by the yellow Corvette. And as Diane pulled up to the front door, Ken drove around to the garage—*with Bobbi sitting next to him.* Kohl immediately felt his neck and shoulders snap to attention. With a feeling of dread, he got to his feet and went back into the house just as Diane came into the foyer, looking coldly furious. At the same time Kohl heard a familiar voice, soft and cornpone, coming from the kitchen. "Well, it's up to you, Kin. Whatever you say."

"What's *she* doing here?" Kohl asked.

Diane's smile was withering. "Oh, you know the little woman, do you?"

Diane tossed her purse onto the dining-room table and went on into the game room, heading for the bar. Then Ken swept past Kohl too, evidently with the same goal in mind. But Bobbi detoured over to the dining-room table to pick up Diane's purse. Holding it with both hands, as if it might fly away, she came on into the foyer.

"Boy, have we got problems," she said.

"Like what?" Kohl asked.

She looked into the other room at Ken, as though for permission to go on. But he was more interested in the drink he was hurriedly putting together. "My boyfriend Rusty," she explained. "You remember that crazy theory I had, the one I told you about at Denny's. Well, I told him the same thing, just as a kinda joke, you know? But he up and took it serious, he really did. He even went all the way down into that ravine and checked on Kin's Bronco—and, well, to make a long story short, he wants ten thousand dollars or he's goin' to the police, he says. Ain't that a crock?"

Kohl stood there looking at her, wondering where on earth she got the gall that allowed her to come on so sweet and innocent *while* she was picking your pocket and reading your mail.

"Of course, you didn't put him up to it," Kohl said.

"No, I did not!" Looking hurt, she went on into the game room and carefully placed Diane's purse on the bar. Then she got a beer out of the refrigerator, casually, as if it were something she'd done before.

Kohl followed her in. Diane was standing near the fireplace, looking at the three of them over the rim of her drink as if it were a gunsight. Ken had sagged into one of the leather chairs, his look and slouch proclaiming that he was not about to cope.

"Well, what about it?" Kohl asked. "You two actually gonna let this sweet young thing shake you down?"

Ken roused himself. "She's not a part of it."

"Like hell she's not," Kohl said. "Tell me then—who delivers the money to her boyfriend? Federal Express?"

"Actually, it won't be her, Tom," Diane put in. "Could be she trusts her accomplice. Anyway, I'm afraid Ken's been elected for that little task. Eight o'clock tonight at the Bellevue Mall parking garage."

"So you *are* going to pay?"

"What the fuck choice do we have?" Ken yelled, only to look

cowed by the sound of his own voice. He brought his free hand up and covered his eyes, as though he couldn't bear to look any longer upon such a perfidious world.

Bobbi had no such problem. "Well, I sure can understand why y'all feel the way you do. I really can. I mean, you got no reason to trust me. But it kinda puts me out too, you know, cuz all I'm tryin' to do is help Kin. I know Rusty real good, and lemme tell ya, he's real bad news. He really is. If he says he's goin' to the police if ya don't pay, then that's what he's gonna do. You can put that in the bank."

"I'll remember that," Diane said. "Be nice to put something *in* the bank for a change."

Kohl felt like sagging into a chair himself. "You've already got the money, then?"

Diane nodded. "Easy come, easy go."

"Like hell," Kohl said.

And Bobbi seemed to know just what he was thinking. "It wouldn't be smart to cross Rusty. It's like I said—he's real bad news."

"And is that why you tried your little theory on him?" Kohl asked. "To see what old Bad News would do?"

"Well, it was real stupid of me—I guess there's no two ways about that. And I'm sorry. I really am."

"I can imagine." Lighting a cigarette, Kohl asked how all this had come about. The last thing he knew, Ken and Bobbi had barely been introduced. Ken sighed as if he found the question oppressively boring.

"Bobbi came by Monday afternoon," he said. "Looking for you. And since you weren't here—"

"He took me along to help him find a car," Bobbi cut in. "And then he let me stay on the boat one night. And we just been drivin' around together since. You know, sorta killin' time."

Diane smiled. "How sweet. Isn't that sweet, Tom?"

Kohl suggested to Ken and Diane that the three of them talk in private. Diane shrugged agreement, but Ken would not go along.

"Why bother?" he said. "We gotta pay, it's that simple."

Picking up her purse, Diane led the way through the foyer and into the dining room. From there they could watch Bobbi without being heard.

"I'm glad you're here," Diane said. "As you can see, Ken's wiped out."

"When did you find out about all this?"

"Around four. I'd just shown a place to my two gays when Ken called on the car phone. I had to drop them off and run. If I lose this sale, I'm gonna kill somebody."

"And Bobbi—this the first you've seen of her?"

"Fortunately, yes. But as I understand it, not everyone here can say that."

Kohl stood there and took it, the way she was looking at him. "I had no choice," he said finally. "She saw me dump the Bronco. She picked me up, and didn't have any place to go. I knew you wouldn't want her staying here, so I took her down to the boat."

"I'm sure she was grateful."

"Not that much, it would seem."

"You have a point."

"You sure you want to go through with this?" he asked. "Till now you had deniability."

"Just like a president."

"This is *your* money, Diane. There's a record. A paper trail. You could be dragged in."

She affected a look of childlike innocence. "How? My boyfriend asks for money, naturally I give it to him. I don't ask why. It's just the way I am."

Kohl sighed. "It's your decision."

"Yes, it is."

"And you've got it all—the full ten thousand?"

She patted her purse. "One hundred hundreds. A neat little package."

Kohl asked her what she and Ken had agreed to, exactly when and where they were to make payment. And after she told him, he tried hard to smile.

"Maybe we can work something out," he said.

"Like what?"

"A couple of things. The way Bobbi described this guy, I think he'd settle for less. A lot less. And then we have to give him a good reason not to try the same thing again later. Or get cute and tip off the police anyway."

"And how do we manage all that?"

"I could talk to him," Kohl said.

Bellevue, which bordered Kirkland on the south, was the largest of the Eastside bedroom communities, a kind of mini-Seattle complete with its own stand of modern skyscrapers—buildings that reminded Kohl of the time he and Ken had sat in the Bronco outside the downtown McDonald's, Kohl contentedly devouring a Big Mac while Ken picked at a salad and scowled up at one of the new high rises.

"You know what really pisses me," he said. "All the skyscrapers in the world, and I don't even own one."

Kohl had agreed that it was a sorry state of affairs, but he thought now that if it was ever given him to own any building on the Eastside, he would choose not one of the skyscrapers but the Bellevue Square Mall, which covered a couple of city blocks and housed scores of shops, plus four large department stores, ranging from plain old Penney's to the pricey Frederick & Nelson's. Of the mall's three large parking garages, Rusty the Blackmailer had chosen the one at the southeast corner, next to the Nordstrom store. It was an open-sided poured-concrete building, with four levels of parking, including the roof, which was the level Rusty—or possibly Bobbi—had selected for the meet. And their reasoning was not that bad, Kohl had to admit. For one thing, it was an open public place in which an overt act of violence would almost certainly be observed. At the same time, it was not so crowded that one couldn't carry out personal business with a reasonable degree of privacy. To ensure this, Kohl had parked far from any other car, with a number of empty spaces on either side of him.

Rusty's instructions were that Ken bring the money in his new Corvette, with Bobbi as a passenger, that they be there by eight and wait for him to show up. If the police met him instead, Rusty would simply tell them about the hit-and-run, and that would be that. It was all up to Ken, Rusty supposedly had told Bobbi. Ken could choose to keep his ten thousand or he could choose freedom. Bobbi said that Rusty "swore on his mama's grave" that he would never ask for more money.

"For him, ten thousand's an awful lotta bread," she went on. "I'd trust him if I was you."

But Kohl did not trust Rusty, any more than he did Bobbi, who at the moment was sitting next to him in the cramped cockpit of the Corvette, looking east over the parking garage's parapet at some of the skyscrapers Ken didn't own. And she was not very happy.

"He spelled it all out, just how he wanted it," she fretted. "And now you go and change everything. Why, he'll probably see you and just drive right on outa here, straight to the police. And if he does pull in and finds out he's only gettin' half what he wanted—well, God only knows what he'll do."

Kohl hadn't bothered to tell her that the envelope in the glove compartment contained nothing but paper and that what money Rusty would get—*one* thousand dollars—was folded up in Kohl's shirt pocket. Kohl and Diane had agreed that if Bobbi knew the true amount, she might not even go along for the meet, and without her sitting next to Kohl in the Corvette, Rusty would probably drive on by. Kohl's plan, if it could be called that, was simply to have everything appear as screwed up as things usually were in life, and especially in the life of a man like Rusty, who, according to Bobbi's own description of him on that first night, was a bum, a boozer, and a pothead. And Kohl had to believe that for a man like that the supposed five thousand dollars would be more than enough incentive for him to put up with a few changes in plan.

When Rusty pulled in, Bobbi was to get out of the car and

explain to him that Ken wasn't there because he was sick—which was true, Ken's anxiety already having brought on another bout of vomiting and diarrhea—and that in order to get the money, Rusty was going to have to do things Kohl's way. First he would have to get out of his pickup and show that he was unarmed—by taking off his jacket or sweater, if he was wearing one, and by raising his arms, by slowly turning around—and then he was to get into the Corvette with Kohl and promise him—somehow *convince* him—that he wouldn't be asking for more money in the future. Supposedly, Kohl would then unlock the glove compartment and give him an envelope containing the five thousand dollars, and it would all be over.

The reality, however, was to be somewhat different. But Bobbi wasn't aware of this, just as she didn't know that Kohl had his father's old army .45 automatic slipped in next to his seat, in case things started to get out of hand. Nor was she aware that they had an audience, that Diane—against Kohl's wishes—had followed them in her car at a considerable distance and was parked on the other side of the garage, on the same level, facing them. And Kohl was surprised to see in his sideview mirror that Ken was with her, a living testament to the effectiveness of Kaopectate.

As it got closer to eight o'clock Kohl could feel the knot tightening at the back of his neck. And as he nervously fingered the gun next to him on the floor, he kept telling himself that he wouldn't even have to pick it up, that everything would come out all right, because it was in Bobbi and Rusty's own self-interest to settle for what they were offered, take what they could get. To ease his tension, Kohl forced himself to talk some more with Bobbi.

"I just can't figure you, lady," he said. "Why you'd cook up a mess like this."

"I didn't cook up anything," she insisted. "I already told you that."

"All the time you and Ken have been spending together,

you must know why he took off after the accident, right? Because he figured he didn't have any other choice. So I keep asking myself how the hell you can justify this, making money off a friend's misery."

She gave him the pouting look again. "I ain't talkin' to you no more. You sure are different than the other night."

"You too, kid."

At that moment, he saw movement in his peripheral vision and turned to watch as a battered old Ford pickup—more gray primer than any other color—came up the ramp and turned down the outer row, Kohl's row.

"Oh Jesus, he's here!" Bobbi cried.

Kohl took her by the arm. "So he is. Now remember, take it slow. If he gets excited, you stay calm. And make sure he knows he's won—that I'm here to give him a lot of money. But he's got to be unarmed, you hear? If he's carrying, I split."

Bobbi angrily pulled her arm away. "Jesus! You want to rip it off?"

Rusty parked three spaces down, on the right side. As Bobbi got out and walked toward him, Kohl was wound so tight he almost giggled at the man's appearance, how closely he duplicated the mental picture Kohl had already formed of him: around forty, tall and gaunt, with long thinning hair, a wispy beard, and an Adam's apple the size of a chicken egg. Though dark glasses hid the man's eyes, Kohl could sense his fear and anger as Bobbi spoke with him. Then he stepped out of the truck and pushed her aside, scowling as he raised his wiry arms slightly, so Kohl could see that in his stovepipe jeans and armless sweatshirt he carried no concealed weapons.

"All right, get in," Kohl called over to him.

And Rusty did so, bringing with him an almost chewable effluvium of sweat, bourbon, and marijuana smoke. He left the passenger door open.

"I don't like any of this," he muttered.

"Tough shit," Kohl said. "But before there's any money, we gotta talk."

"She already told me—yeah, I give ya my word this is it. You pay me, it's done. It's over."

"All right. But we ain't paying what you want."

"She told me that too."

"You'll settle for half, then."

Rusty was agitated. "Yeah, yeah—let's have it!"

Kohl inserted the key into the glove-compartment lock, as if he were about to open it and hand over the money. But instead he swung his elbow back into Rusty's stomach as hard as he could, and the man buckled, gasping. And in Kohl's mind, that was it, that was all he would do to him. He was about to take the thousand dollars out of his pocket then and give it to him, along with a solemn warning that if he went to the police or tried for more money, *this* was what he would get, only more of it. But Rusty wasn't that easy. Even with the wind knocked out of him, he pivoted on the seat, one hand holding on to the open door while his spindly legs kicked out at Kohl, who by then had opened his own door and was scrambling outside, catching hard shots on his shoulder and hip before he finally got hold of Rusty's left ankle and hauled him yelling across the gearshift and the driver's seat and on out the car door, dropping him hard onto the concrete floor. When the man went right on yelling—*"Hey! Hey! Hey!"*—Kohl stomped on one of his bony knees, hoping some real pain would shut him up. But all it did was produce a high, keening squeal that left Kohl no choice but to punch him in the face, quiet him down by busting up his nose and mouth and probably giving him another chicken egg, this one on the back of his head as it bounced off the concrete.

Kohl then took out the ten bills and stuffed them into one of Rusty's pockets. "This is all you get," he said. "And you tip off the police, I'll be looking you up, understand?"

By then he was more afraid of spectators—other parkers, shoppers—than he was of Rusty. So he pulled him to his feet and practically carried him back to his truck, where he propped him up behind the wheel. Though the man looked barely conscious, he managed one furious word:

"Fucker!"

Still standing between the two vehicles, Bobbi had her hands over her mouth, as though to keep from screaming.

"Go on, get in with him," Kohl said. "This is your show, remember?"

But she didn't move, and Diane's car suddenly braked behind them. Ken immediately jumped out and ran to Bobbi, taking her by the hand.

"You come on with me!" he bawled. "You don't belong with that crook."

As they both scurried into the Corvette, Kohl turned and headed for the Cadillac. The door was already open and Diane was motioning frantically for him to hurry. And he barely got inside before she took off, burning rubber at first, then catching herself and slowing down, driving on at the posted speed.

"What the hell you doing here?" he said. "I thought we agreed."

She ignored that. "Christ, Tom, did you have to kill the guy?"

Kohl realized that he had gone too far, but it all had happened so quickly, so unexpectedly.

"No one got killed," he said. "He might limp for a while, though."

"He sure might."

And suddenly Diane began to laugh, from the release of tension, Kohl knew. Whatever the source, it was an infectious laugh, and by the time she pulled out of the parking garage and headed home, they were both howling.

Their mirth did not last, however. A few blocks farther on, the two of them lapsed into a stunned silence that was even more infectious than their laughter had been. Kohl's original intent had been so much less than the reality turned out to be. He had wanted only to intimidate the man, not beat up on

83

him, not injure him. And he had thought Bobbi would remain there with Rusty, drive off with him. After all, she was the architect of the whole mess, was she not? Yet now she was in the Corvette with Ken, on her way home with him, as if she were one of them, an ally instead of their blackmailer. Meanwhile her hapless accomplice was probably still in the parking garage, crumpled over the steering wheel of his pickup, with a dislocated knee, a broken nose, loosened teeth, and God knew what else. What if he wasn't able to drive? And when mall security finally checked on him and called in the police, would he tell the truth? Would he implicate them all?

Diane gave voice to Kohl's thoughts. "This is getting out of control, isn't it? We're really losing it."

"We lost it Friday night," Kohl said. "You were right—I never should've gone along with Ken."

"He didn't give you much choice. What were you supposed to do, turn him in?"

"I could've done nothing. I could've let the Bronco sit in the garage."

"Well, as my grandmother would say, it's all water under the bridge." Diane smiled fleetingly and looked over at Kohl. "I still can't believe he's bringing that little tramp home again. How can he believe she isn't behind all this? She's the one that saw you. She's the one who put it together."

"Aw, come on—Bobbi's all sweetness and light."

"So's my ass."

It was Kohl's turn to smile. "I could believe that."

She gave him a wry look. "You'll have to. Anyway, if he does bring her home, what do I do? Kick her out?"

"Well, Christ yes. It's *your* house."

"But she's Ken's friend, whatever that means."

"His blackmailing friend."

"Good point."

They were back at the house by nine o'clock, and Kohl judged that Diane felt pretty much as he did, as if the sky were already falling. He wasn't surprised when she, an occasional wine-sipper, joined him in having straight scotch, on ice. They went out on the porch to wait for Ken and Bobbi. Dusk was settling over the lake basin, and since it had been a hot, still day, there was a good deal of smog as well. It was a smog not totally without benefit, however, for it gave the fading sunset a warm, rusty hue that, reflecting off the water, made the lake look like a sheet of beaten copper.

Neither of them had much to say. The words that had flowed so freely out in the dinghy Saturday evening seemed scarce as sapphires this night. Kohl sensed that Diane did not feel any more discomfort over this than he did. In a way, there was just too much to say, at least on his part. He wanted to tell her how lousy he felt about his beating of Rusty and how uncharacteristic of him it was, violence of that kind. He wanted to tell her just how far out cousin Ken's mind was wandering the last few days and therefore how dangerous it was for them to go on "aiding and abetting" him. And above all, he wanted to tell her that she was a fool to let anyone walk all over her the way Ken did, because as far as Kohl was concerned, she could have had just about any man she wanted. But since he knew how self-serving all that would have sounded, he made do with silence and waiting—and Ken's Chivas Regal.

He made a second drink for himself, a double this time, and Diane let him freshen hers. As night fell and the drinks disappeared and nothing happened and no one showed up— no police, no Ken, no Bobbi—Kohl asked Diane if she wanted to go down to the boat with him.

"That's probably where they are," he said.

She shook her head. "No thanks. What would I do? Scream and holler? Scratch her eyes out?"

"Why not?"

"Weird thing is, I'm really not that jealous of the girl. Other than her being a blackmailer, what really pisses me about her is I don't know what the devil is going on. I mean, if Ken's having an affair with her—if he really wants a change—I can live with that. Matter of fact, a good part of the time lately I *dream* of that."

"I don't think Bobbi has affairs," Kohl said.

NEWTON THORNBURG

"What—just lays? Well, I guess you ought to know."

Kohl groaned. "Diane, I didn't seek it out."

"But you didn't resist, did you?"

"Men don't."

"No, I guess not." In the darkness her lovely green eyes appeared gray and sleepy as she looked down at the lake. "You join them if you want. I think I'll just go to bed and dream of my two gays from L.A. I've probably lost them by now." She smiled wistfully. "Among other things."

As he was leaving, Kohl reached out and touched her shoulder in a casual gesture of parting, and unexpectedly her hand came up and brushed his own, leaving it scarred for life.

"I'll see you later," he said.

Because there were no lights burning on the Williwaw, Kohl thought at first that no one was aboard. But there was some movement up on the command bridge and he saw the two of them in dark silhouette, peering down at him over the gunwale like soldiers behind a battlement. Then he heard Bobbi's easy laugh.

"It's only Tom, Kin—like I told ya."

"I can see that, for Christ sake," he groused. "I'm not blind, you know."

In the marina's dim lights Bobbi stood up, carrying Ken's ghetto blaster, which she for some odd reason turned on now. As Kohl climbed up onto the rear deck, the girl and Ken came down from the bridge. Ken was holding a near-empty bottle of scotch and a glass of ice.

"I been wondering when you'd show up," he said, over Willie Nelson's heavy twang.

Since Kohl could remember a teenage Ken trapshooting his sister's country-music record collection, he assumed that Bobbi's poor-dumb-me routine was working just fine. "We were wondering the same thing, back at the house."

"You mean we were expected?"

86

"Yes—expected."

"*Both* of us?"

"That's what I said."

Ken poured some more scotch into his glass. "Expected maybe, but not particularly missed, right?"

"Whatever you say."

"Yeah, I guess maybe I should've gone straight home and kissed ass, now that I think about it. I mean, after all, it was Diane's money and your muscle that saved my skin, right?"

Kohl was already wishing he'd stayed at the house. "Right," he said.

"But this little girl here," Ken went on, putting his hand on Bobbi's arm, "this girl who really put herself on the spot for me—I'm supposed to just kiss her off, is that the way it is?"

"You do what you want," Kohl said.

"Well, just don't fucking worry about that, okay, Tommy? I usually do what I want."

"That's for sure."

Kohl by now was almost as weary of the conversation as he was of Willie Nelson being on the road again. He looked at Bobbi. "Will you turn that goddam thing off, please?" he asked.

Bobbi shrugged. "Sure thing. All you had to do was ask, you know."

She turned the radio off and set it down on a work table. Sexy in white shorts and T-shirt, she sauntered over to the other side of the twelve-foot-wide deck and stood there facing Kohl, with her arms folded. "In case you been wonderin' about Rusty," she said, "we got to worryin' about him after we left. So we went back and had a look-see. I had to drive him home. Kin followed in the Corvette."

Kohl thought about that for a moment, unable to keep from grinning. "*You drove him home?* Jesus, this has got to be the coziest, friendliest blackmail operation of all time."

Ken gave a nervous laugh. "The *friendliest?* You couldn't tell it by Rusty."

"I'm just sorry as all hell about that," Kohl said. "If I'd

known the three of you were going home together afterward, I might have been more gentle."

Ken knocked off some of the scotch. When he brought his hand down, the ice in the glass rattled. "But Jesus, Tommy," he complained, "did you have to lean on him that hard? And shortchange him *that* much—just a thousand dollars. Now he's got it in for me too. Wasn't it enough I got Tony Jack and the police on my case? Did I really need Rusty too?"

"What do you mean, he's got it in for *you*?" Kohl asked. "I'm the one who ruined his day."

At that, Ken suddenly flipped his glass out into the water, probably to keep it from rattling. His eyes had filled; and as he spoke, his voice broke. "All I know is everybody's after my ass! And I got nowhere to turn! It's like I'm on death row or something! All I can do is wait to get it!"

His terror was almost palpable, like a sudden whiff of smoke. Kohl wanted to help him in some way, calm him, but before he could think of what to say or do, Ken turned and hurried into the cabin.

"Jesus, not again!" he bawled, disappearing into the head.

"The trots," Bobbi said. "He's had 'em off and on all day long."

Kohl looked at her. "No kidding."

While Ken was gone, Bobbi gave Kohl another of her pouting looks. "I sure wish you'd believe me, Tom," she said. "I didn't plan the blackmail thing—honest."

"All Rusty's idea, uh?"

"It sure was. 'Course, if I hadn't ran off the mouth like I did, he wouldn't a thought it up."

Kohl stood there staring at the girl, wondering if she could possibly be telling the truth. Common sense told him otherwise, but then common sense didn't have spaniel eyes and a pouting little-girl mouth.

"You could do me a favor, Bobbi," he said.

"I could?"

"If you're alone with Ken and he decides to do something

drastic—like call the police or Tony Jack—talk him out of it if you can. Ask him to talk with me first."

She smiled and shook her head. "Just who do you think I am—Diane? Hell, he don't listen to me. No one listens to me—you oughta know that, for heaven's sake."

"Just try, okay?"

"Sure. Why not?"

Ken came back out of the cabin. "Why not what?" he asked.

Bobbi laughed. "Look after you."

"Lucky you." He sat down heavily in one of the canvas deck chairs and looked up at Kohl with eyes that appeared red even in the darkness. "You've got to help me, man."

"In what way?" Kohl said.

"In the *money* way," Ken answered, not without an edge of sarcasm. "We were talking before you got here, and we think Rusty's so pissed he might go to Tony Jack and sell what he knows—sell *me,* in other words. So our thinking is we've got to give him the full ten, like he asked for in the first place. That's the only way I'm gonna feel safe, Tommy."

Kohl didn't respond immediately. He had formed a mental picture of the temporarily disabled Rusty—Bobbi's "chicken-thief kinda guy"—going to a mob figure like Tony Jack and offering to sell him information about his brother's death. And the picture almost had him grinning, despite Ken's look of desperation.

"Are you serious?" he said finally. "A mob guy like Tony Jack? A wiseguy? You don't *sell* people like that information, Ken. They find out you have it, they just pull it out of you, along with your teeth and fingernails."

"You don't *know* that," Ken snapped. "And we sure as hell don't know that Rusty knows it."

"Rusty's real dumb," Bobbi put in.

"And he's also real banged up," Kohl said. "I figure he'll remember my promise—that any more trouble out of him and I pay him another visit."

This infuriated Ken. He jumped up out of his chair,

knocked it over, and finished by kicking it against the bulk-head. *"You don't know shit!"* he cried. *"When are you gonna wake up? After they've killed me? Is that when? Is that what it's gonna take?"*

Kohl reached out to put a calming hand on his shoulder, but Ken pulled away.

"All right, okay," Kohl said. "Relax. I'll talk to Diane. But what I can't figure is why you don't talk to her yourself. She's your girl, not mine. You could go home right now and ask her."

Bobbi didn't like the idea. "For once, couldn't you just do what he asks?" she said. "Does everything always have to be your way?"

Kohl was as tired of her as he was of Ken. And in a way they scared him too, for suddenly they seemed to him almost like children, creatures with needs and fantasies and rages he couldn't begin to comprehend.

"All right, I'll ask her," he said again.

Ken nodded in sullen agreement. "And give the money to me. We'll get it to Rusty."

"Sure." As he left the boat, Kohl raised his hand slightly, as if it were too heavy for a normal wave. "You two take care," he said.

Because Diane was already in bed by the time Kohl got home, he didn't mention Ken's request until the next morn-ing, when he caught her as she was about to leave for work. She had paused only long enough for a stand-up cup of black coffee—her power breakfast, she called it—and it was obvious that on this day Ken's needs were going to run a poor second to those of her new clients, the "two gays" from Hollywood.

"If he's serious about it," she said, "he can ask me. My God, have he and I reached the point where you have to serve as our go-between?"

Kohl smiled slightly. "I don't think so, Diane. For one thing, I don't want the job."

"Good." She finished her coffee, checked her hair in the dining-room mirror, and flashed him a smile. "I'm off. Wish me luck."

"Good luck," he said, feeling like an obedient servant.

Kohl spent most of that day at the state employment office, first filing for unemployment compensation and then being interviewed by an employment counselor. Each of these tasks required hours of standing in line and filling out forms and in general being dragged about by the system. The counselor, an asthmatic man in his fifties, went through his routine with all the verve of a robot during a brownout. At the end, though, he did rouse himself sufficiently to offer Kohl advice: that because he had two years of college, there were all kinds of jobs available to him, not just construction labor.

"But only if you're serious," the man wheezed. "Get rid of the beard, cut your hair, buy a suit."

Two of Kohl's fellow workers also were at the employment office, and later they all stopped off at the Sitting Bull for an hour or so of beer and sympathy. Kohl told them about his counselor's advice, and the men had a lot of fun with that.

"You shave off that beard," one laughed, "and you might find Woody Allen underneath!"

"I could do worse," Kohl said.

"Or he might find a coupla chicken bones. Or a used Tampax."

Kohl went along with them. "Actually that's why I grew the damn thing in the first place. Cuts down on certain kinds of chafing."

"Yeah—that old ailment, pussy burn!"

Kohl had little affection for these blue-collar bull sessions. Men who one-on-one would have been sober and reasonably intelligent for some reason turned into filthy little boys when they were drinking in a group of three or more. Nothing would serve but crudity, and after a while Kohl often found it tiresome—and especially so today, because he was worried that Ken and Bobbi might have returned to the house and that Diane, taking off from work early, might come upon them— doing what?—soaking in the hot tub as they discussed their pressing need for more of her money? Though Kohl knew that Diane could handle almost anything that came her way, he still wanted to be there. Maybe they could all sit down together and sort it out, come to some kind of understanding. Sure thing, he thought. And pigs would soon be taking wing.

In any case, he was back at the house by midafternoon, and he wasn't sure whether he was more relieved or disappointed at not finding Ken and Bobbi there. On the one hand, it meant he didn't have to deal with them; on the other, it meant he was free to do a lot of wondering—and worrying— about where they were and what they were doing. As for Diane, she didn't come home till after six, and even then her feet barely touched the floor. Once again she had homered with the bases loaded, had not only regained the confidence of her California gay couple but had sold them nothing less than the "McDowney place," which she said was a huge old waterfront house on Mercer Island. She didn't say how much the property had sold for and Kohl didn't ask, but her considerable joy—in the face of all their problems—led him to believe that it was a substantial sum.

She didn't have time to talk because she was in such a hurry to shower and change. She was going to take her marvelous new clients out for a night of what she called "grazing" in Seattle's best restaurants.

"I'd invite you along," she said, "but the old guy would probably try to jump your bones. He just loves butch, according to Jason. And of course I don't want you breaking his knees, not yet anyway."

"Who's Jason?"

"The younger one. The *kept* one."

"Well, good luck," Kohl said. "I'm glad it's you and not me."

Her smile was not altogether sweet. "Me too," she said.

***

Kohl drove down to the marina later and checked out the Williwaw, but Ken and Bobbi weren't there. He then did some "grazing" of his own—on peanuts and popcorn—in four different bars during the course of the evening. And, shades of Ken, he drank mostly scotch instead of beer. He won some money at eight-ball in a beer tavern; and later, in a cocktail lounge, he pretended for some reason not to notice the subtle hints at sexual availability of an attractive Asian woman of indeterminate age. Instead he found himself blubbering on about his life as a farmer in Illinois, and when she asked why he would ever leave something he loved so much he pretended ignorance and even indignation. He hadn't said one word about "loving" anything, he told her. In fact, he wasn't even sure what the word meant and didn't particularly care to find out. She turned away from him as if he'd slapped her.

When he got home, Diane was already in bed and he had to fight against a drunken urge to tiptoe upstairs and peek into her bedroom. For some reason, he was certain she would be asleep and the idea had fixed in his mind that she would not have any covers on and that she would be lying naked on her side, facing away from the door, so that he could see in perfect detail if her ass was indeed a thing of sweetness and light. But he was not *quite* that drunk and instead spent an hour in the hot tub, sipping at a bottle of Courvoisier.

Waking late the next morning, he found himself alone again in the house, with a hangover that seemed the perfect physical equivalent of his mood, the sense of anxiety and foreboding that had been building in him steadily since the night of the accident. And realizing that he had been fool enough to enter into it all willingly—the cover-up, the "handling" of Bobbi, the meet with Rusty—didn't make it any easier. But it was Ken's absence, his *continued* absence, that made Kohl feel like a man about to have quadruple bypass surgery, because he had absolutely no idea what his cousin was up to. And when he factored in the influence of Bobbi, the wide-eyed conniver, the reckless innocent, he could only grind his teeth at the possibilities that lay open before him. Ken's terror the other night would have seemed to preclude any more bizarre forays over to Queen Anne Hill, and Kohl had a hard time picturing Ken and Rusty working together at almost anything. All he was left with was the shaky surmise that the two of them—Ken and Bobbi—were off hiding somewhere, staying lost until the whole thing blew over or at least *seemed* to blow over. But that, Kohl feared, was probably only wishful thinking.

Oddly, the thing that worried him the most was his deepening involvement with Diane. And the problem there wasn't only that she was Ken's girl—housemate, lover, whatever— but also that she was virtually the antithesis of what he'd always thought he wanted in a woman. His ex-wife and the four other women he'd had affairs with over the years had all been pretty and feminine and softly sexy, with an almost brooding quietude about them, a tranquillity that invariably became for him a kind of therapy, something to which he could bring his occasionally wounded spirit much as one would carry a run-over dog to the local vet.

Though he realized that none of those relationships had lasted, he felt that they at least indicated a certain consistency of taste on his part. And it didn't make much sense to veer so sharply in the opposite direction. Not that Diane wasn't attractive and sexy—she definitely was, but in a hard-edged, hard-assed, high-fashion sort of way. She was caustic and flippant and at times condescending. And if she ever spoke to him the way she often did to Ken, Kohl would have walked in a minute. But then, unlike his cousin, he hadn't been living off her for a couple of years.

Nevertheless, the attraction was there, and getting stronger by the day, at least on his part. He would have thought that he already had enough on his mind, just being Ken's cousin and trying to stay out of jail at the same time. Besides, as an out-of-work ex-farmer who looked like a mountain man, he figured his chances with Diane were zilch. More and more, he felt like a total fool.

To clear his mind, he decided to get something done this day: if not bring his cousin solidly back to earth, then at least find him and talk to him, lead him back into the fold of the family, such as it was. He started at the marina, once again vainly checking out the Williwaw before driving on across the lake and into Seattle, parking for a while at the top of Tony Jack's street on Queen Anne Hill. And though the glassy spaceship still hovered just over the backyard hedge, Ken and Bobbi and the yellow Corvette were not to be seen.

After driving back to the Eastside, Kohl went into the foothills beyond Issaquah. He passed the spot where he had dumped the Bronco and continued for another mile or so, following the narrow mountain road until he came upon a small house trailer sitting amid a mini-junkyard of old cars and refrigerators and other detritus. An Okie evidently, Rusty had brought his environment with him. But since it was an environment that didn't include Ken's car or Bobbi's old Buick, just the gray-primered pickup truck, Kohl turned around and left, figuring that he wouldn't get anything from Rusty alone, except a possible blast of buckshot.

That evening Diane was in a perverse and reckless mood. She came home from work with her feet not only touching the floor but practically dragging across it. Life was the pits, she said. Her two fags—not "gays" now—had backed out on her, withdrawn their offer on the McDowney place.

"And you want to know why?" she said. "Though our food here is *adequate,* according to the old queen, the night life is—and I quote—'an absolute yawn.'"

"How dare he?"

"And you know what else he said? That a person couldn't even get AIDS in this burg."

"No wonder he backed out."

Diane sighed. "Three whole days shot in the ass."

Kohl told her that Ken had not been home and wasn't down at the boat either, which elicited little more than a shrug.

"So what else is new?" she said.

She suggested that Kohl phone out for pizza, adding that she was going to celebrate with champagne and that he could join her if he wished.

"Celebrate what?" he asked.

"Why, having champagne," she said. "That's reason enough, isn't it?"

"So long as mine comes in a Budweiser bottle."

"Peasant," she said, handing him a bottle of Mumm's to open.

When it came to drinking it, though, she proceeded at a very modest pace. Nevertheless she was soon acting a little high, and after a while she suggested that Kohl shave off his beard. He had to do it sometime, and what better time was there than the present? Also, he would never get a better audience, because she "just loved" to watch men shave—which turned out to be something of an understatement. For as soon as he began, she took up a position that put her only a few inches from him, staring raptly as he chopped away at the thicket with a throwaway Bic.

"You didn't have a beard when you came here," she said, "but I can't even remember what you looked like."

"Like this?" he suggested, finishing up.

She laughed. "Could be. Though without the two-tone look."

And indeed that was what he had: white skin where the beard had been, tan elsewhere. But the deed was already done and Diane seemed to approve. Taking hold of his chin, she gave him a stern reprimand.

"Now, don't you ever do that again. You've got a nice strong jaw. Why hide it?"

"Sorry, Mom."

"Well, you'd better be. And now, guess what. *It's haircut time!*"

Kohl resisted at first, figuring that a haircut by a less than sober real estate agent wasn't something he needed at this point in his life. But Diane assured him that he couldn't do better in any barbershop in town, that she'd cut Ken's hair for years and didn't cut it now only because he insisted on having it done every week or two. And once again she took Kohl's chin in hand.

"And you must know this," she said. "If I was good enough for Ken—"

"You're good enough for anybody."

"Right."

Kohl obediently sat down on one of the kitchen chairs while she pinned a towel around his neck. She began by using a comb and barber's shears and finally a pair of thinning shears. And there were times when she leaned against his shoulder as she worked, unaware that this innocent contact was causing a certain turmoil under the towel. She observed that his hair was like "curly steel" compared to Ken's "silken tresses."

"And so thick," she added. "You'll never go bald."

He told her that his barber back in Illinois, Doc Wilson, never talked about hair, only the Chicago Cubs.

"Football's so boring," she said.

"How about baseball?"

"That too."

Finally she was finished, and Kohl had to admit she'd done a good job, making him look nothing like a mountain man, in fact downright presentable.

"What do I owe you?" he asked, just as if he were in Doc Wilson's.

Smiling, she turned her cheek up to him. "A wet one," she said.

But a dry one was all he dared, a mere peck on her elegant cheek. She pretended to sulk at the meagerness of it.

"I worked a lot harder than that," she complained.

Since he knew she was only teasing, he didn't try to improve upon the kiss. She poured herself another glass of champagne and Kohl hit Ken's horde of Chivas Regal again, making a double scotch and soda. The two of them went out onto the game-room porch then and sat watching as the light failed, turning the huge lake into a pool flecked with a confetti of sails. Kohl tried once more to talk about their problems, reminding her that if everything suddenly came undone all she had to do was plead total ignorance and he would back her up. But she didn't want to talk about any of that.

"Tonight's for *champagne*," she said, giving it the French pronunciation. *"Et la musique."*

After putting a golden-oldies LP on the stereo, she pulled Kohl out of his chair and the two of them began to dance to Andy Williams's "Moon River." The wood floor was not an ideal surface, however, so they went inside and danced in the dark, anticipating one of the songs to come. Some of them were big-band instrumentals, others were vocals—"Stardust," "Blue Moon," "Tennessee Waltz"—songs that made Kohl think briefly of his father, who had loved them dearly. But most of the time all he could think about was the woman in his arms, the clean and subtle smell of her, the softness of her hair against his face, the feel of her strong slim back under his guiding hand. And once again he was unable to control a part of himself, just like a kid at a high school dance, and he knew that she felt it too, through her cotton slacks, this intruder rising between them. But all Diane did was pull back slightly and smile at him.

"The ultimate compliment," she said.

And soon they were kissing, hesitantly at first, as if they feared they might bruise each other's lips. But then something gave way in them, the rock and mortar of some deep restraint, and suddenly her tongue was in his mouth and his hands were pushing up her blouse and sliding under her panties onto her buttocks, pressing her against him. They didn't undress each other so much as tear at the other's clothes, as if pants and shirts had become an obscenity. And when they were naked, Kohl took her in his hands, that sweetness and light he had yearned *to see* just the previous night, and lifted her onto his body and carried her that way to the couch, where they fell, kissing still, Kohl already plunging in her, holding her as if all he wanted out of life were the next few moments.

And then it was gone and the two of them lay there in each other's arms, stunned and breathless but alive, much as if a violent storm had ripped through the house. Diane's eyes had filled with tears, and in the growing silence Kohl wondered what her next words would be; certainly not the words of a lover. At the same time he was desperately searching his own mind for something to say, the *right* thing to say. Then suddenly it was too late, for he heard a car swing into the driveway and head for the garage, the muffled roar of its engine unmistakably that of a Corvette.

"Christ, it's Ken!" he said, reaching for his pants.

After touching her face, Diane was just lying there on the couch, staring at her wet fingers.

"You want him to know—great," Kohl said. "So do I."

But she had come out of it by then, was already scrambling for her clothes. "*No! No!* You stall him, all right?"

Kohl had his pants on and had picked up his shirt, was hurrying across the foyer toward the hallway that led to the kitchen, confident he would get there in time—when Ken suddenly came tearing around the corner, his face white and eyes panicking. And Kohl saw him take it all in—Kohl's unbuttoned shirt and Diane behind him in the game room, sighing in futility as she sank back on the couch, wearing only her panties and uselessly holding her blouse up to her naked breasts. Kohl saw him take it all in—and put it aside.

"*They're here, Tommy!*" he cried.

"Who?"

"*The police, for Christ sake! They're parked out in front! They've come for me!*"

Kohl looked out through one of the door's slotted windows and felt himself go weak, for there was indeed a police car parked out in front, one of Kirkland's dark-blue Ford LTDs. Two uniformed officers had gotten out of the vehicle and were coming up the walk toward the house.

"They must have pulled up just before you got here," Kohl

said. In the game room, he saw that Diane had her slacks back on and was hurriedly buttoning her blouse.

"It's all over," Ken said. "I'm finished."

And the way he said it, the way he began to move toward Kohl—shuffling, head down, face crumpling—Kohl knew what was expected of him. He held him, patted him.

"Hey, man, we're gonna be all right," he said. "It was an accident. We'll get a good lawyer. We're gonna be okay, understand?"

Ken nodded desperately, like a little boy.

4 In the first few moments after Kohl opened the door and the two policemen entered, Ken practically held out his hands to be cuffed. He said something to the effect that he was glad it was all over and that maybe he could sleep now, but fortunately he was shaking and snuffling as he said it, and the police apparently didn't understand him.

"He's had the flu and just had a fight with his girlfriend," Kohl explained, making a face of benign exasperation, openly inviting the policemen to ignore Ken.

The older of the two officers introduced himself and his partner, but before he could state his business Kohl interrupted, introducing himself and Ken and Diane, who had come to the game-room doorway but no farther, as if to make it understood that whatever the problem, she was not really a part of it.

"Who's the owner of the yellow Corvette?" the officer asked.

"I've been driving it," Kohl said, "though Ken's the one

who leased it. Why? What's the problem?"

The officer sighed. "Oh, some clerks up in the Bellevue Mall claim they saw some kinda altercation on the top level of the parking garage. And they took down the license number— the Corvette you rented."

Kohl smiled wearily. "Oh, *that*. More domestic problems, I'm afraid. I've been seeing this woman who's separated from her husband, and he doesn't like it much. So we met up there to talk it over. Only he started getting a little rough, so I got out of the car, but he kept coming. I guess he did fall down."

Being average-sized men, the officers looked somewhat dubious as they surveyed Kohl.

"This guy got rough with *you*?" the older one said.

Kohl nodded. "He's a feisty little guy. Not a lotta sense."

"I'd say not. Can you give me his name and address?"

"I just know him as Rusty—Rusty Means. Lives up in the mountains somewhere, in a cabin. I don't think he works very regular."

"And how about you, Mister Kohl? Where do you work?"

Kohl gave him J. C. Allen's number and told him that he hoped to be back at work soon and that he and Ken would be happy to sign a statement or help in any way they could. But the officer had already closed his book.

"Naa, there's no reason to bother. Kinda thing we normally wouldn't even look into, only there were three witnesses and they all seemed to think something big was going down."

Kohl shrugged. "Well, it was big to me. I'd hoped the fella would just accept things the way they are. But no such luck."

"That's par for the course," the officer said.

After the two of them had left, Ken folded onto one of the decorator chairs in the foyer. "Jesus, I almost blew it," he said. "I was sure they were here for me."

"Next time remember the first commandment," Kohl told him. "Never volunteer."

"You got it, man. I won't forget."

Considering how Ken had walked in on them, Diane obviously did not want to encourage any more conversation. "I'm going to bed," she said.

Ken looked up as she swept past him. "Where do I sleep?" he asked.

"Not with me."

Ken turned to Kohl, smiling slightly, even sheepishly. "I kinda figured that," he said.

Though the next day was a Saturday, Diane didn't rush off to work. Instead she brought her coffee and a microwaved croissant out onto the deck, where Kohl was pretending to read the morning paper—pretending because the events of the previous night, especially the lovemaking with Diane, were about all his mind could handle. So he had sat there in the morning coolness, reading words and turning pages, learning nothing.

"Ken's still asleep," she said. "I think we should talk, don't you?"

"About last night?"

She smiled at his little joke. "Yes, about last night. I just wanted to say—I don't know what happened. The champagne and music, I guess. But I don't think we ought to read too much into it."

"You mean I shouldn't."

"No, I mean *we* shouldn't. Everything's been in such a turmoil. I don't know anymore how I feel about anything. Or anybody."

Kohl sat there trying very hard to read her, to see beyond her fine clear eyes and their look of sincere, urgent concern. "I know how I feel about you," he said. "Just about like I did last night."

She smiled, almost wistfully. "No, you don't. Last night was a kind of dream, Tom, something outside our normal lives. And I won't soon forget it, believe me. You really—" She shook her head, as though in embarrassment. "You really got to me. But it was wrong for us. You know it was. And I don't think we should expect it to happen again, okay?"

As she said this last, her eyes grew moist and she reached out and touched his hand, the same hand she had seared the night before. Kohl's desire to please her was such that he almost nodded agreeably and said, Okay, never again. But it would have been a lie.

"I think it was right and good," he said. "I think it should happen again, and again."

She withdrew her hand and turned from him. She finished her coffee and got up, her look of warm concern suddenly gone, frosted over. "Would you do me a favor?" she asked.

"Of course."

All business, she needlessly explained to him that the Williwaw was draining her financially and that it was very important to her that the work on the boat be finished as soon as possible.

"You see, I don't think the charter thing will fly," she said. "And the sooner Ken tries it, the sooner he'll give up and I'll be able to sell the boat and get some of my money back."

Kohl couldn't help smiling. "Diane, I know all this—what are you getting at?"

"I was wondering—before you look for another job, would you work for me? Finish the boat, I mean. I'd pay you, of course—the same as you've been making, or more. You just tell me how much."

"How about a thousand a week?"

She was not amused. "I'm serious."

"Yeah, I kinda thought you were. But Diane, do you realize it would cost a good fifteen thousand just to replace the engines—and that's with *used* engines? And the entire job—you're probably looking at thirty thousand altogether. That is, thirty on top of what you've already got into it."

The figure made her wince, but it didn't change her mind. "Even so, I'd like to go ahead with it. I've checked around, and the consensus seems to be that if the Williwaw were ship-shape, it would bring over a hundred thousand."

In the end Kohl agreed to work for her until the boat was finished, but he also suggested that they make Ken a part of the package—tell him that she would hire Kohl only if Ken worked right along with him—and Diane readily concurred. It would be one way, she said, of keeping Ken on a tight leash, away from Bobbi and other mischiefs.

"Yeah, that too," Kohl said, with a straight face.

Later that morning, when Ken finally got up, Kohl steeled himself for at least a verbal showdown over what Ken had seen the night before—his lover and cousin caught almost in the act, *flagrante delicto*. But Ken apparently had no more stomach for the showdown than Kohl did, and there was no mention of the incident. Kohl told him about Diane's job offer and explained that it all depended on him, whether he would work full-time right along with Kohl. To Ken, this added condition was an insult.

"Well, Christ yes, I'll work along with you," he said. "It's *my* goddam boat, after all! Just because I still owe her some money on it—that doesn't mean she calls the goddam shots!"

"You don't want me working on it full-time?"

"I didn't say that, man. After all, you're the carpenter and mechanic and all that. But I'll sure as hell be right there with you." Ken's look of exasperation hardened into bitterness. "I suppose she figures I won't stay the course, right? That once the boat's finished, the charter service will be *finito* too. Am I right?"

"She didn't say."

"She didn't have to. But we get the boat in shape, Tommy, and I'll show her—I really will. I'll pay her back every blessed red cent."

Down at the marina, Kohl made a list of the things yet to be done on the Williwaw, including the parts and tools he would be needing. As he worked, he asked Ken what had happened since the night he talked with him and Bobbi on the boat. "You were pretty worried about Rusty then," he said. "But no mention of him now—how come?"

"What good would it do? I haven't seen any money forth-coming."

"You mean the ten thousand?"

"That's what I mean, all right."

"Did you ever ask Diane for it?"

"And a fat lot of good it did me too. But that doesn't mat-ter now anyway. According to Bobbi, Rusty doesn't want to have anything more to do with us. Told her he's got his own fish to fry."

"Which means?"

"What the hell you think it means? He's going to Tony Jack and sell me, that's what it means."

"You're sure of that? Is that what Rusty told Bobbi? Or are you only guessing?"

Ken laughed ruefully. "If I knew for sure, you think I'd be sitting here talking with you? I'd be down at the police sta-tion with Giacalone's little briefcase, that's where I'd be."

"And I wouldn't blame you," Kohl said. "But honest, Ken— I can't see a flake like Rusty doing it, going to a mobster and trying to *sell* information. He'd be scared shitless, and with good reason. I really don't think we've got anything to worry about there."

"*We!*" Ken scoffed. "What the hell's this *we* shit? I'm the one they'll be coming after."

Kohl held up his hands. "Okay, then—*you* don't have any-thing to worry about. At least I don't think you do."

"Wow, what a relief that is!" Ken mocked. "I get the same assurances from Bobbi. So how come I keep shaking, uh, Tommy?"

"Bobbi tells you the same thing?"

"Oh, yeah—she's real upbeat lately. She's with you. She fig-ures I'm home free. Rusty hasn't got the balls to talk, she says, so what have they got to work with, Tony Jack and the police? Zilch, that's what Bobbi says."

Kohl grinned. "The astute Bobbi-with-an-i. Tell me, where's she keeping herself these days?"

"At her mother's in Seattle. I guess the old lady got her fill of baby-sitting."

"One would."

"But Bobbi will be around, don't worry about that."

"I wasn't."

If Kohl had any worries about Bobbi, it was that she *would* be around. At the moment, though, he had other things on his mind, such as whether to try to rebuild the boat's ancient Chryslers or replace them with purchased rebuilds. After phoning a couple of boatyards and talking with the marina's shop mechanic, he confirmed his initial opinion that the Chryslers had to go. Diane could probably have bought a pair of brand-new *diesels* for what it would have cost to rebuild the Chryslers, largely because there were almost no parts available and Kohl would have been forced to have them custom-made, not unlike parts for a NASA space shuttle.

Kohl knew that if and when he acquired the necessary engines, he couldn't very well rebuild them on the boat or in Diane's garage, where the only tools she had on hand were a hammer and a couple of screwdrivers. So his first step was to line up a workshop of some kind, and for that he contacted one of the older carpenters he'd worked with, Harry Boldt, who had a reputation as a first-class backyard mechanic. As it turned out, Harry not only had an excellent auto shop in his garage, but was inclined to take a month or two of unemployment compensation before seriously looking for a new job. Consequently, it would be "right up his alley," he said, to hire out both his shop and himself for a modest twenty an hour if Kohl was interested. Which he was.

"Soon as I find the motors," he said. "I'll be in touch."

But finding what he wanted proved to be difficult. He and Ken scoured the classifieds and started driving all over the Seattle area looking for used V-8s that were good enough to rebuild and cheap enough to buy. Considering that Seattle was the per capita boating capital of the western world, there were surprisingly few engines available, probably because the re-buildable ones were already back at work, powering boats, while the others had been junked. Then it dawned on Kohl that there were literally hundreds of them available if one knew where to look—*inside* the engine compartments of unsalable old boats. Since the boats themselves were virtually worth-less—there being little call for rotted wood and cracked fiber-glass—the boats' only value was their engines and other mechanical accessories. With that in mind, Kohl and Ken went boat-shopping and within a few days turned up a thirty-two-foot SeaRay that had been maintained so poorly and left out in the rain so steadily that its twin Volvo 225-horsepower en-gines were in danger of falling through the bottom of the soggy craft. After checking with Diane, they bought the boat and the trailer it sat on for five thousand dollars, then phoned Harry Boldt and told him they were coming. With Ken's help, Kohl towed the huge craft to Boldt's garage in Bellevue, where they winched the engines out of the hull, putting one of them on a block holder so they could begin work on it as soon as they were ready. Next, Kohl and Ken towed the poor, gutted craft to Joey's Boat Graveyard on a scenic country lane twenty miles south of Seattle. Kohl asked Joey to make an offer on the boat, and the man did—one dollar, "just to make everything nice and legal," he said.

Throughout these busy days and hours—most of them spent on the road, in Kohl's truck—Ken continued to avoid the sub-ject of catching Diane and Kohl in postpartum disarray. Fi-nally his silence on the matter was more than Kohl could handle.

"Ken—aren't we ever gonna talk about it?"

"About what?"

"About Diane and me, for Christ sake! You practically caught us in the act—you know that. So what's going on? Why the big silence? Are we all just gonna go on pretending noth-ing happened?"

Ken, in the truck's passenger seat, didn't even bother to look at Kohl. "It's between me and Diane," he said.

"The fuck it is! Who the hell am I, some stranger who just happened by? The thing keeps eating at me, but nobody wants to talk about it. Not Diane. Not you—"

"Because it's between *us*, Tommy. Between her and me."

Kohl almost laughed. "Jesus, I could've sworn I was part of it. Sure felt like it anyway."

Ken didn't even get mad at that. Suddenly a great fan of newstalk, he switched stations on the truck's old AM radio and turned up the sound. But Kohl still had a few words that he felt needed saying.

"Okay, we'll drop it for now. But it won't go away, and you know it. Or maybe I should just pack up and leave. That's probably the only thing that makes sense."

Ken shook his head thoughtfully. "No, I wouldn't want you to do that, Tommy. I don't blame *you*. I know you didn't force her. The way I see it, it was *her* fault. And that's why it's between her and me." He said this matter-of-factly, much as if he'd memorized the words and now was only reciting them.

Kohl looked over at him, expecting to get some idea what was going on inside his handsome head. But for once his cousin was inscrutable.

One night, after they had been working late at Harry Boldt's garage, Ken asked Kohl to swing by Kirkland's marina park, and Kohl wondered if his cousin wanted to revisit the bar where they had been drinking on the night of the hit-and-run. But no, all Ken wanted to do was wander out onto the docks there, the public moorage near which the two of them had skinny-dipped in March. Handsomely maintained and lit by soft globe lights, the docks were a favorite haunt of evening strollers. But now, after midnight, only one couple and a solitary man were in evidence, sitting on benches as far from each other as they could get.

Since Ken seemed to know exactly where he wanted to go,

Kohl followed him out to the very end of the dock and sat down next to him on the flooring, with his feet hanging over the water. Ken got out a pack of cigarettes, gave one to Kohl, and took the last one for himself. Surprisingly, he then crumpled the empty pack and returned it to his pocket.

"Sometimes you just gotta get near water," he said. "A lot of it."

"Well, you got it, kid." And indeed the lake looked massive at night, also a touch forbidding in its blackness, despite the lights sparkling across it.

"I'm so fucking depressed lately," Ken said. "I don't think I'll ever come out of it."

"The fix you're in—that doesn't help matters."

Ken looked puzzled. "But that's just it, Tommy—things aren't all that different now. I mean, you spend all your life being afraid of this or that—worried something's gonna happen or something else isn't gonna happen. Just ordinary shit, you know? And all of a sudden here I am, with something to really be scared about—and you know what? It isn't all that different. It's just more of the same old shit." He shook his head. "When you get right down to it, Tommy, life's a fucking drag. Don't you think?"

Kohl took in a lungful of cigarette smoke, wondering what he did think. "Yeah, I guess so," he said. "A lot of it *is* a drag. But it's got its moments."

"Like what? Sex, booze, a snort now and then?"

Kohl barely smiled. "No. As a matter of fact, I was thinking of all this water here. How cool it is. How clear."

Ken groaned. "What the hell difference does that make? The water and the mountains and the sky, they may look great—but my hands are still shaking." He held them out for Kohl to see. "See? Look at that."

Kohl thought of his mother and his father and his farm, which was someone else's now. "Yeah, I see. But think of it, Ken—out of all time we're alive for what amounts to a second or two."

"So why not make the most of it, uh?"

"I don't see we've got any other choice."

Giving him a quizzical look, Ken took a last drag on his cigarette and flipped it out into the water. "Sure we do," he said. "The same one I gave that cigarette. I could go on smoking it—or I could snuff it out."

At that, Kohl got to his feet. "Come on, let's go. I've got some serious sleeping to do."

Ken held up his hand, and though he was roughly pulled to his feet, he came smiling. "You just can't face it, can you, big guy? Sometimes people just reach the point where—"

"Where they snuff it, right?"

"Right."

Kohl put his hand on his cousin's shoulder and shoved him along as they headed back up the dock toward the parking lot. "You ever try it," he said, "and I'll kill you."

Ken nodded wearily. "Yeah, I was afraid of that."

Much of the next week Kohl spent in Harry Boldt's d..rk and greasy garage, working on the first engine, resurfacing the crankshaft and putting in new rings, pistons, and valves. It was work that old Harry loved and Kohl tolerated and Ken could not abide. The first few days he would stand around and watch, handing Kohl or Harry an occasional tool before announcing finally that he had to leave. There would be an errand he had to run or some job he wanted to finish on the boat, and he'd come back for Kohl later. On the fourth day he stayed in bed, claiming that he was coming down with a virus. And after that he simply went his own way again, not bothering to tell anyone where he was going or why. Kohl reluctantly reminded him of his promise to Diane to work closely with Kohl during this period, but the reminder was not appreciated.

"Christ sake, the lady doesn't own me, Tommy. Lincoln freed the fucking slaves, remember?"

Diane was gone at the time, attending a three-day seminar

in real estate law at Evergreen College in Olympia, which left Kohl on his own with Ken, without any real leverage against him, no way to keep him underfoot and out of trouble.

Kohl and Harry Boldt finished the first engine and started on the second; and when Diane returned home, Ken made it a point to drive her over to Harry's garage to see what her money had bought. Looking at the finished engine, power-sprayed and freshly painted, she playfully told Ken that she was impressed by how much he'd accomplished in so short a time.

"It was a group effort," he assured her.

"I'm sure it was," she said.

When the two of them left, Harry Boldt told Kohl that he wasn't sure which of them frosted his balls more, that it looked to him like a dead heat.

"I can tell you one difference between them," Kohl said. "She pays the bills."

When he returned home that evening he assumed that Ken and Diane had gone out together, since the Corvette was missing and there was no sign of anybody in the house, no sound coming from upstairs. But after he had showered and changed clothes, he heard water running and he called upstairs to see if anyone was there. When no one answered, he went up and knocked on Diane's door, which was slightly ajar. Through the opening he saw her coming out of her bathroom in a long white terry robe and holding a wet facecloth against her cheek. Her eyes were red from crying. Without knocking again, he entered.

"What the devil happened to you?" he asked.

"Well, come right on in," she said. "Don't stand on ceremony."

"What happened?"

She removed the facecloth briefly, letting him see the left side of her face. Though it was red, it didn't appear particularly swollen.

"I've had ice on it," she said. "And as for what happened—your cousin happened. We finally had our little chat about you and me—and the night he walked in on us."

"I'll kick his ass."

Diane shook her head. "No, you won't. I can take care of myself. I scratched his pretty face and kneed him where the sun doesn't shine."

Kohl grinned. "It's *don't* shine," he said. "And I'm not sure you've got the right place."

"Whatever. I also told him to clear out. And he said he would—as soon as his boat is finished."

"*His* boat?"

"That's how he sees it." Still holding the cloth to her face, she sat down at her dressing table. "And he scored his points too, I must admit. He said his thing with Bobbi was meaningless, only sexual, whereas what I did was calculated and cruel. He thinks I seduced you and that my motive was simply to get even with him. To *hurt* him."

"Did you set him straight?"

"You don't think he was right?"

In his confusion, Kohl smiled uneasily. "Diane, I was there, remember?"

She looked at him in the mirror. "So was I, but I'm not sure. It seems I'm not sure about anything anymore."

"Why do you complicate everything?"

"Because everything is complicated."

"How about what we felt?" he asked. "How complicated was that?"

She gave him her grown-up look, fond, indulgent. "That was passion, Tom. Sex."

He came up behind her and put his hands on her shoulders, lightly, halfway expecting her to pull away. Instead she inclined her head, laying her face against his hand.

"When it's just sex," he said, "I don't feel that kind of passion."

Still looking into the mirror, she regarded him thoughtfully, as if he were a reluctant client. "We're *so* different—don't you know that?"

"In what way—because I'm a laborer and you're a tycoon?"

"*Tycoon!* That's a laugh. No, Ken has my number. Phony bitch, he calls me. And he's right—I'm as phony as he is."

"Is that a fact."

"Yes, it is." She sounded almost proud of it. "For instance, you say when it's just sex you don't feel that kind of passion. And you mean it. You're so sure of yourself."

"So?"

"So we're very different, Tom. You're a real person. You're all in one piece. You know who you are and what you want and what you feel. But I don't. I really don't. So how could we possibly relate, you and I? We might as well be from different galaxies."

This little speech struck Kohl as so stupid, so uncharacteristic of her, that the only way he could deal with it was through humor—by getting down like a baseball catcher and gazing up at her, much as a dwarf might have regarded his queen.

"Maybe I could make a real 'perthon' out of you too," he said. "It'd be hard work, but I'd be willing to try."

For a moment she looked as if she were about to laugh—at herself as much as at him—but then her eyes did their little thing again, abruptly frosting over. "I wish you wouldn't patronize me," she said.

"I wasn't."

"Oh yes you were. You think of me as some kind of silly, stylish business freak who couldn't survive five minutes out in the world you know. But every so often I stir up something between your legs or ears and you figure you'll do me the honor of being nice to me so you can get me into bed and give me the greatest gift of all—your schlong. Well, thanks, but no thanks."

Kohl felt as if an Illinois copperhead had sunk its fangs in him. He had stood up by then, had even backed away a few steps, until he hit the corner of her bed and sat down, barely aware that he had done so.

"Jesus, woman, why all the hostility? I thought we—" He didn't quite know how to say it. "I thought we got kind of close the other night."

"Well, we didn't!"

"All right. Okay." He got up from the bed and started for the door, but she reached out to stop him.

"No, don't go yet, Tom. I'm sorry. I'm such a basket case lately. I don't even know what I'm saying half the time."

Feeling both a fool and a weakling, Kohl turned back and took her outstretched hand. She got up from the dressing table and sat down on the edge of the bed, gently pulling him down too, having him sit next to her.

"You work too hard," he said.

"It keeps me from thinking."

"About what?"

"About what?" Though her eyes had filled, she smiled brightly. "About my perfect life, of course. Do you realize I'm twenty-seven years old? I've given him my four *best* years—best-looking anyway—and what do I have to show for it? A swollen face and a fifty-thousand-dollar wooden scow he uses for humping his cowgirl. And on top of that, I'm now an accessory to a fucking felony—*his* fucking felony."

"You've told him to leave," Kohl said. "And maybe you'll be able to sell the boat soon."

"That doesn't get me back my four years."

"No, it doesn't."

She gave him an almost pleading look. "You know, I'm not like I seem, Tom. I mean, I'm not this cold-hearted yuppie who thinks only about money and status. I'd like to be married. I'd like to have kids. I really would."

Kohl wondered if she meant it. "Well, you're a woman," he said. "A beautiful woman. You *should* be married. You *should* have children."

"Someday I will." Her voice broke and she leaned against him.

At the same time, her robe fell open, revealing her bare legs. And Kohl felt a strong urge to stroke them, to run his hand up the inside of her thighs, but he was afraid that if he touched her there, made the moment at all sexual, she would pull away altogether. So he compromised. He put his hand on her knee and suggested that he give her a massage.

"And *only* that," he went on. "Just to relax you. Make you feel better."

She looked up at him. "You mean it?"

"Of course I do."

"You're a nice man, Tom," she said.

"I'm a prince."

She smiled again. "If I kiss you, will you turn into a frog?"

"Could be."

"I'll just have to take my chances, won't I?"

In the days that followed, Kohl would think often about this second time they made love and how eerily different it was from the first time. He realized that the circumstances were not the same, that it was daytime instead of night and they were both cold sober and she had to be careful of her face. But those conditions, he felt, would have explained differences in *degree*, not in the very nature of the thing. Yet that was how he felt about their lovemaking that afternoon, as if it were a different act performed with a different woman. He imagined that his own lack of ease also played a part in it, the fact that for days he'd taken her at her word, believing that their first time together had also been their last, that it had been merely a moment of weakness on her part, an aberration she would not likely ever repeat. And now to have her submit so easily, so casually—it probably did throw him off at first, for a few minutes anyway. But none of that explained how *she* was, her utter want of passion, the fact that she just lay there like a woman who actually expected nothing but a massage. He kissed her breasts and sucked on them and after he went down on her she made no move to reciprocate. He even had to take her hand and place it on him, as if she were blind as well as paralyzed. She did stretch languidly and she sighed and even kissed him, but gingerly, as though to remind him of the tenderness of her face. And when he was ready to enter her she reached up into the bed's bookcase headboard and magically produced a condom, which for a few moments rendered him almost incapable of even needing it. As for why it was required this time and not the other, Kohl didn't bother to ask.

When he finally left the room he felt as if he'd just scrimmaged with the Chicago Bears. And for days afterward he felt emotionally battered, wondering why on earth the woman had so casually let him into her bed—for nothing. He wondered if it had been a kind of object lesson, a bedroom show-and-tell session designed to teach him beyond all forgetting that the two of them shared nothing but an occasional sexual urge, and a very weak one at that, on her part anyway. In his pain and confusion, Kohl began to work all day and half the night on the Williwaw's second engine, to the point where even Harry Boldt had had enough of his garage.

"I don't quit soon, the old lady's gonna have me certified," he said.

During this time Kohl also arranged for a marine salvage company to take the Williwaw's old engines, and on the day the company's bargelike craft chugged into the marina even Ken was on hand—with Bobbi at his side. By then relations between Kohl and Ken were not very cordial anyway, Kohl having warned his cousin that if he ever laid a hand on Diane again he would wind up in the hospital. And now to have Bobbi flouncing into the picture once more, all smiles and tight white shorts, did nothing to improve Kohl's mood. At the same time, he wasn't able to work up any real hostility toward the girl, probably because she knew her way around him just as surely as she did around every other man she'd ever met. In his case, there was a kind of subtle conspiratorial thing she put into her smile, as if to say, Yeah, I know you're on to me, big guy, but have a heart, okay? And he did, up to the point anyway of returning her smile, which was a little beyond him.

Instead he concentrated on the job at hand, the first step

of which was to help the salvage boat tie up to the stern of the Williwaw. The boat was a forty-foot steel flatbed with a pilot-house at one end, a winch in the center, and a swiveling twenty-foot-high A-frame at the other end, through which the winch's cable ran, over a pulley. The two men aboard the craft appeared to be father and son, judging by their looks and the way the older one kept shouting orders and abuse at the younger one and shaking his head in disgust at virtually every move he made. Though Kohl's own father had never been like that, in fact had contentedly given his son every responsibility he could handle, father-son conflict was something Kohl had seen far too much of back in Illinois, especially during haying and harvest time, when it filled the air like chaff.

Ken and his father—the future millionaire—had been prime examples of the syndrome. On the one hand was this humorless, perfectionist martinet and on the other his daydreaming, girl-pestered sybarite of a son. Their battles in the fields and in the barn were legendary, with man and boy screaming at each other and Ken usually losing it in the end, speeding off with a loaded haywagon or stabbing a hayfork into the barn wall before running home to shower and change clothes and get on with his love life. So Kohl wasn't surprised to see Ken's immediate hostility toward the salvage-boat operator—the father.

Having already unbolted the old Chryslers from their mounts, Kohl considered the job at hand to be simple enough: securing the cable around each engine in such a way that it wouldn't shift and accidentally take out the side of the boat when the winch hoisted it up. And this was the son's job, something he obviously had done many times before, yet still couldn't perform to his father's satisfaction.

"No! *Under* the goddam corner, Billy, for shit's sake! You don't want it to slip, do ya?"

Though the kid seemed able to take this in stride, Ken could not.

"Why don't you just get off his back for a change?" he yelled. "He knows what he's doing!"

The father, a burly, balding man in his forties, didn't appreciate Ken's advice. "And who the fuck are you? You want me to do this job or not? I don't *need* these fuckin' old engines, you know."

"You're getting them for nothing!" Ken shot back.

"The fuck I am! What a candyass! You think somebody just *give* me this rig, do you?"

Kohl stepped in then, afraid Ken was going to scuttle the deal entirely. He took him by the arm and walked him into the cabin and patiently reminded him that while the boat might one day be his, right now it was Diane's, bought with *her* money, and she had hired Kohl to make sure it was soon in running order. The old engines *had* to go.

Ken was briefly indignant, claiming the boat was his alone, that all Diane owned of it was an unsecured debt, which he would pay off one day. Then he hit Kohl where it hurt.

"You just don't give a damn about that kid because you never had to eat your old man's shit! He was so fuckin' lazy, he didn't care what you did."

Kohl walked out on him. He gave the father the okay sign, and within an hour both of the huge, rusty old Chryslers had been winched out of the Williwaw and deposited gently as eggs onto the salvage boat's deck. After Ken and the son threw off the lines, the salvage boat backed out of the marina and started for home.

Almost immediately Bobbi came out of the cabin carrying a six-pack of Coors beer. "Time to cool off," she said, smiling as if she were in a television commercial.

And Kohl had no problem with that: a pretty girl bringing out cold beer after a job was finished and the sweat was still running. He figured that the advertising mavens had done their homework on that one. He took two cans and opened one, even smiled a little as he thanked Bobbi and sat back against the gunwale to cool off. But Ken was not as easily satisfied.

"You know I don't drink that piss," he said to her.

She responded with an ironic shrug. "Well, excu-u-se me. Sorry I can't fix a drink to suit you."

"That's for damn sure." Sighing, he got up and went into the cabin, apparently to mix a proper scotch and soda.

Bobbi shook her head. "He's really worried. Did he tell you that Rusty's missing?"

Kohl took the beer away from his mouth, even set it down. *"Missing?"* he said.

"Sure looks like it. I went up to his place a couple days ago to get some clothes I left, and he was gone. His truck too. And—"

"Christ sake, the man comes and goes, doesn't he?"

"Well, if you'd just lemme finish. His precious hound dogs didn't have no food or water, and lemme tell you, he loves them dogs more than he ever did any woman, includin' me. And git this—the door was unlocked, the TV was on, and guess what I saw on the dresser."

"Just tell me, okay?"

"His little can of Copenhagen and his Buck knife. And he don't go nowhere without them. Absolutely nowhere."

While she was telling Kohl this, Ken had returned with his scotch. As he listened, he nodded solemnly, almost in resignation. "Didn't I tell you, Tommy?" he said. "The asshole went and did it. He sold me to Tony Jack. Only instead of gaining some cash, he loses his life. Jack probably cemented him into his ratty old truck and dropped them both out in the Sound."

Kohl wasn't buying. "Oh, come on, you two. Rusty's into all kinds of illegal shit, right?"

Bobbi shrugged. "He deals a little weed and acid now and then. But mostly he steals stuff and sells it. Junk, for the most part."

"And who does he deal with?"

"Bikers and cowboy types. Guys like him mostly."

"So maybe he crossed one of them," Kohl said. "Maybe—"

"Maybe bullshit," Ken cut in. "Maybe we'd better find out."

***

Kohl never did understand how Rusty managed to keep his house trailer in an area so undeveloped it had to be either a state park or a timber tract. Yet there the thing sat, at the high end of the mountain road, a gaudy plastic box set back in the firs like something that had dropped from the sky, a piece of extraterrestrial garbage.

As the three of them pulled up to the trailer in Kohl's pickup, Rusty's hounds were so overjoyed at seeing human beings again that they practically came through the windows of the truck. They calmed down very quickly, though, especially after Ken kicked one of them.

"See, it's just like I told you," Bobbi said. "His truck ain't here, and he ain't here."

"Is the door locked?" Kohl asked.

"Well, sure. I locked it when I left the other day." As she produced the key, Bobbi explained that because there was no well or spring on the property, Rusty had hauled in what little water they used. "So it ain't too clean inside," she warned. "Be careful where you sit."

"Who the hell's gonna do any *sitting*?" Ken groused, still in a dog-kicking mood.

Going inside, Kohl saw what Bobbi meant: the place was filthy and cluttered and so oppressively small he had a hard time believing she and her babies had actually lived there, with the missing Rusty. On the bedroom dresser Kohl saw the pocketknife and the can of chewing tobacco, but they told him nothing he didn't already know. Elsewhere, if there was any other clue to the man's disappearance, the three of them weren't able to recognize it. And since there wasn't a telephone in the trailer, there were no messages jotted down, no listing of numbers, nothing. About all they learned was that Bobbi had been correct: Rusty was not there.

As they left, she said that she knew a couple of his hangouts. "Maybe we could check them out," she suggested. "See if anybody there has seen him or knows where he is."

"Might as well," Kohl agreed. "And we'd better check back

here in a couple of days too—we can't leave his dogs alone."

"That's a real good idea," Ken said. "I'll bring my four-ten."

Bobbi laughed uneasily. "Oh, Kin, you don't mean that!"

"Don't bet on it," he muttered.

She brightened suddenly. "Listen, I know the names of a couple of his cronies too. We could phone them and see if they know anything."

"Why not?" Kohl said.

Ken was grimly shaking his head. "I'll tell you why not. Because Tony Jack's the only one who knows where old Rusty is. Just like he's the only one who's gonna know where I wind up. My *body*, that is."

"That's the attitude," Kohl told him. "No sense being a pessimist."

Ken didn't even look at him. "Tell me about it," he said.

The two bars they checked out were onetime country places surrounded now by suburban sprawl. In each the music was country-and-western and the clientele was largely blue-collar, with a smattering of bikers and other rebels, including a few scraggly outcasts from the same litter as Rusty. With Bobbi at his side, Kohl made the rounds, buying beers and asking about the missing man; but most of the patrons didn't even know Rusty, and the few who did had no knowledge of his where-abouts.

Later, when Kohl and Bobbi tried to find telephone numbers to go with the names Bobbi remembered—cronies of Rusty's—they were equally unsuccessful. And Ken seemed to take a perverse pleasure in their failure.

"Look, if you two ever decide to get serious about finding Rusty, all we gotta do is drive over to Tony Jack's house and ask the man. Or better yet, we could wait a couple of days—ask him when he comes gunning for me."

They were driving home at the time, and though Kohl wanted very much to contradict Ken, reassure him in some way, he couldn't think of anything to say. He knew he couldn't keep repeating the same old bromide that he *believed* Rusty wouldn't go to Tony Jack; he was getting tired of hearing that one himself. Bobbi didn't have anything reassuring to say either, so the three of them drove on in silence, heading north on the freeway toward Kirkland. In time, Ken got out a cigarette and lit it, and Kohl couldn't help noticing that his cousin needed both hands to get the job done. Even then, it was a shaky enterprise.

The next night, as Kohl was working with Harry on the second engine, Ken phoned and asked Kohl to stop off at the boat on the way home.

"I've got something real interesting to show you," he said.

By the time Kohl got there it was almost midnight and the marina was eerily quiet, the only sounds those of lapping water and the creaking of a few wooden boats. As before, there were no lights burning on the Williwaw, and when Kohl saw the double barrels of a shotgun peering down at him from the bridge, he didn't have to wonder where Ken was.

"Hey, it's me!" he called. "I'd take it as a favor if you didn't shoot my ass off."

"Funny man," Ken muttered, coming down from the bridge as Kohl boarded the yacht. "I'm taking the night watch," he explained. "Bobbi's gonna spell me in the morning."

"Jesus, has it really come to this?" Kohl said.

Ken gave him a murderous look. "What do you think—I'm gonna blithely turn in while a bunch of wiseguys could show up any minute?"

Kohl followed him into the cabin. "You feel that way, why don't you stick with me—work alongside us at the garage and sleep at home. You'd be safer than here."

"Yeah, but I wouldn't have Bobbi that way, and she's got more smarts than all of you put together."

"Is that a fact?"

Ken took a folded piece of paper out of his pocket. "You bet it is. She's always thinking. Always trying to figure the angles."

"I kind of sensed that," Kohl deadpanned, sliding into the dinette booth across from Ken. "But what am I doing here? What's this big thing you wanted me to see?"

Ken unfolded the paper, a torn-out section of newspaper, and laid it in front of Kohl. "A little something Bobbi found in the newspaper. Sort of an insurance policy for me."

"Insurance against what?"

"Against Tony Jack," Ken said.

While Kohl read, Ken explained that Bobbi had come across the item in the local paper that evening, three column inches about the late Ricky Ross, founder of the Deli-Deli chain of delicatessen stores. It seemed that his will had been found improper and his estate was headed for probate court—nothing much to get excited about there. But the last paragraph of the story, recapping the circumstances of the man's death—*that* caught Kohl's attention just as it had Bobbi's, for the lakefront condominium in which Ross's decomposing body had been found was located in the same block where Richard Giacalone had been run down four days earlier—a connection that the newspaper, and evidently the police too, failed to make.

"You see what it says," Ken offered. "They think the guy walked in on a burglar who beat him so badly he died of a heart attack. But Giacalone's the one with the guy's ring and bank deposit slips. So it had to be him, right? Collecting on a loan, right?"

Kohl gave the clipping back. "That's how it looks."

"You see how it can be my insurance," Ken said, excitedly lighting a cigarette.

"Yeah, but go ahead anyway. Spell it out for me."

"Well, it isn't very complicated. We just give Tony Jack an

anonymous tip that the guy who accidentally killed his brother wound up with his briefcase, with all the incriminating evidence about Ross's murder. And that's what it'd be, right? Murder—heart attack or not."

"Far as I know."

"Right. Anyway, we tell Tony Jack we've got all this evidence but that he's perfectly safe so long as nothing happens to the guy who accidentally ran over his brother." As he spoke, Ken kept watching Kohl. "Well, what do you think? Is this insurance or is this insurance?"

"Yeah, I suppose so."

Ken was indignant. "You *suppose* so! That's all you can say?"

Just then Bobbi joined them in the cabin, coming up from the bow stateroom like a little girl, yawning and rubbing her eyes, wearing only panties and her Mickey Mouse T-shirt. She complained about having been awakened so late, but when Ken told her what he and Kohl were talking about, she brightened immediately, happy to recount the tale of her marvelous discovery.

"You just never know what you're gonna find in the papers," she said, "long as you don't bother with the front page and all that political junk. The best stuff's in the personals, I always say—though I didn't find this story there, of course. This was on the obitchry page." She wrinkled her nose and laughed. "Like a li'l old diamond layin' right there in the mud."

Kohl asked her about Ken's idea: using what she'd found as insurance against Tony Jack. "You think it's a good idea?"

She gave Ken a look of mock reproval. "In the first place, it wasn't exactly *his* idea."

"The hell it wasn't," he bristled. "Anyway, who gives a goddam—it's the obvious thing to do. The *only* thing to do." Looking pugnacious and defensive, he turned to Kohl. "But of course *you* see something wrong with it, don't you? What else is new? I should've known that. Anything that makes sense to me ain't gonna wash with wise old cousin Tom."

Kohl looked from one of them to the other, wondering

whether they were serious about the idea or were just testing it out on him, hoping they wouldn't have to go through with it. "How would you contact Tony Jack?" he asked. "By letter, by phone, or what?"

"We haven't decided yet," Ken said.

Kohl lit a cigarette and dragged deeply. "Well, you're right, Ken," he said. "I do have a problem with it. One of these days the Bronco will be found, and maybe—just maybe—the police will connect you to the hit-and-run. What happens then?"

"Then I bargain with the briefcase. I keep it stashed somewhere, and I deal. If they let me walk free, I feed 'em Tony Jack on a murder charge. Or conspiracy anyway. Something like that."

This was not the sort of thing Kohl expected from his cousin, a plan this devious and hardball. And though it made a kind of sense, he couldn't see Ken bringing it off, not in a thousand years.

"It'd be kind of risky, wouldn't it?" he said.

"So what?" Ken shot back. "It's kind of risky just walking around, knowing that people are out there selling you."

That puzzled Kohl. *"People?"*

Ken made a face. "Yeah—Rusty's not the only one who knows what happened. There's also Bobbi's mother."

Kohl felt as if the deck had suddenly pitched under his feet. *"Bobbi's mother?"* he said.

The girl laughed and shrugged. "Yeah, wasn't that smart of me, though? Miss Big Mouth of the Month. That was before I knew Kin, though. 'Fact, it was the same day I did all that talkin' to you, Tom, at Denny's."

Kohl looked at her. "In other words, the same day I gave you a hundred dollars."

She nodded ruefully. "Yeah, and that's how I repay you, right? Me and my big mouth. But listen, Mama won't tell nobody. I already warned her. She knows this ain't small potatoes. Her lips are sealed."

"No doubt." Kohl got a bottle of scotch out of the cupboard and poured himself a sizable drink.

"Me too," Ken said.

Kohl gave him the bottle.

"What do you think now?" Ken asked, smiling coldly. "You still think you know just what I should do?"

Having no answer, Kohl looked over at Bobbi. "How can you be sure your mother isn't blabbing it around? Like over the back fence?"

Bobbi nodded gravely. "I told her she'd never see the babies again."

"And that's a threat?"

"For her it is."

Kohl sat there nursing his drink, uncomfortably aware that the two of them were watching him, expecting something from him: if not a solution to the problem, then at least his concurrence in Ken's solution. But he couldn't give it.

"Why don't we wait another day or two. See if Rusty turns up."

"You don't think I ought to contact Tony Jack, then?" Ken said. "Warn him off?"

"Why take the risk?"

"To stay alive—I guess that's a pretty silly reason, huh?"

"I didn't say that."

Even though Ken had had a long and difficult day, his hair wasn't mussed and his suede jacket and chinos were spotless. And at the moment, as he leaned back in the red leather booth, with his handsome head framed by teak and brass and tiny windows through which the lake and marina sparkled in the darkness, Kohl found himself idly wondering if that had been his cousin's motive all along in choosing a classic yacht as his latest project—because he looked so splendidly at home in it. But all of a sudden the picture had gone bad. The yachtsman's eyes had filled with tears.

"Okay, Tommy," he said. "You win. I'll just sit here and wait for it, like any other asshole on death row. And one of these days the door clangs open and in walks Tony Jack. What do I say then? 'Hey, you're not supposed to be here—my cousin promised'?"

Kohl groaned. "What is it you want me to say—go ahead and make contact? I can't do that."

"Why not?"

"Because I think you're assuming something that isn't true."

"What?"

"That the reason Rusty's missing is because he went to Tony Jack and sold you."

"You know different, do you?"

"No, Ken, I don't. But you're figuring that once Tony Jack got the information he wanted—either by paying Rusty for it or by squeezing it out of him—he couldn't let the poor devil live because of what he knew. I mean, if you were suddenly gunned down, who could tie Tony Jack to it? Who would know that he even knew you? Rusty—right?"

"Exactly—and that's why he's missing. Tony Jack's a wise-guy, and wiseguys don't like loose ends."

Kohl shook his head. "I disagree. I think they play the percentages, like everyone else. They're businessmen. And Rusty's testimony wouldn't *prove* anything, only that Tony Jack knew about you. And second, Rusty would be scared shitless. Nobody likes to testify against mobsters, and that would go double for a small-time thief like Rusty. Tony Jack would *know* he had nothing to fear from him."

Even before he was finished, Kohl could see the anger rising in Ken. And in the end it pushed him out of the booth and onto his feet in the middle of the cabin, where he stood like a cornered animal, turning one way and then the other. Finally he brought his fist smashing down against the tabletop.

"Then where the fuck is Rusty?" he yelled.

"I don't know."

"Right! You don't know! So what the fuck am I supposed to do—relax and take things easy because you say so? Because you got a *theory?"*

Kohl put out his cigarette. "I don't know, man. I'm only telling you how I see it. How it looks from here."

"Yeah? Well, let me tell you how it looks from *here!*" But Ken seemed to lose his train of thought at that point. Looking rattled and scared, he stood there for a few moments before he finally continued. "Maybe I better get my ass back on top. No sense buying it in my sleep, right?"

On his way to the cabin door, he picked up his shotgun and told Bobbi to make him some fresh coffee and bring it up to him. "And bring a bottle of scotch too," he added.

After he was gone, Bobbi smiled and shook her head. "Him and his precious scotch. You'd think it was holy water, the way he carries on about it."

"Or scotch," Kohl said.

Bobbi laughed, much too hard. But she grew solemn immediately, almost as if she'd passed her hand in jest over her face, changing personalities. "Listen, Tom, I've been wantin' to apologize for some of the things I said here the other night. I know all you're tryin' to do is help Kin, and he knows it too. He really does. It's just that he's so darned sensitive, you know? He needs people like us to lean on." She laughed again. "Good old country people."

Kohl didn't even smile. "He been leaning on you, has he?"

"Oh, not that way, silly. I mean like *support,* you know?"

"Sorry."

"No reason to be. You know what?"

"No, what?"

"I ain't forgot my first night here on the boat. *With you.*" She waited a few moments, obviously expecting him to say something. When he didn't, she nonchalantly went on. "You was awful nice to me that night. I'm real sorry how I paid you back."

Kohl looked back at her as he left. "Me too," he said.

5 Kohl hadn't seen Ken for two days when Bobbi phoned, late in the afternoon, saying that she was at the Westwater Café in Seattle, that Ken had left her there and was supposed to return and pick her up. But he hadn't and she was worried.

"Why?" Kohl asked. "What's he up to?"

"It's kinda hard to explain."

"Try it anyway."

"Well, I guess he sorta made contact with Tony Jack."

Even though Kohl had been halfway expecting this, he came close to punching out the nearest wall. "What do you mean, sort of?" he asked.

"Well, he didn't tell 'em who he was, of course. And he made it kinda like a treasure hunt, you know?"

"Treasure hunt?"

"That's just what Kin called it, yes." And suddenly Bobbi sounded as if she were crying. "Oh, I don't know—it's all so crazy. Listen, Tom, please come and git me, okay? I think he's in real trouble. I really do."

"I'll be there soon as I can. And you stay put, understand? Even if he comes back. I want to talk with him."

"Okay, but hurry, all right? Please hurry."

Kohl was in his bathrobe at the time, having just stepped out of the shower, after a long day aboard the Williwaw, welding new engine mounts into place. He dressed hurriedly and picked up his father's .45 automatic before running on out to his truck—just as Diane pulled in. He went over to her and told her what had happened and asked her to move over, so he could take the wheel of her car, figuring she would want him to drive. But as usual, she had a different agenda.

"I can't go now, Tom. I'm in the middle of a sell, for God's sake—a place up on Somerset. I'm taking the client to dinner. We'll probably close after."

Kohl frowned, as if he had trouble seeing her. "Well, sure—first things first, I guess."

"Oh, don't look at me like that!" she demanded. "You know Ken—it's probably just a wild-goose chase! He'll be all right. He always is."

Before she finished, Kohl was already hurrying back to the truck. And as he roared down the driveway, he knew that she was out of her car and heading toward the house—not that he bothered to look. He didn't figure she'd be waving goodbye.

The Westwater Café was one of a half-dozen or so very successful restaurants owned by a pair of local Greeks who seemed to know exactly what their fellow Seattleites wanted. Kohl had been in the place twice and both times had found it rickety, loud, and reeking of fish. But it was located on the lakefront, with a fine view of the Eastside and the Cascades, and obviously appealed to its yuppie clientele, most of whom looked to Kohl as if they had come there straight from tennis or sailing. Though Kohl found the food tasty enough, he got the feeling that the Greeks could have served garbage without suffering any great drop-off in trade.

To get there Kohl first had to crawl along with the afternoon bridge traffic and then had to wind his way through the university's mile-long arboretum. When he finally pulled into the café's parking lot, Bobbi hurried toward the truck, trailing wolf whistles from three college-age boys sitting at one of the outdoor tables.

"Where to?" he asked her. "Where you think he is now?"

"I don't know. But the last place we were together was right next to here, in the park."

Leschi Park was a grassy strip of lakefront stretching north from the café and a few other businesses. There was a breakwater of gray boulders and a path running the length of the park, wandering under the shade trees. Between the grass and the road were a half-dozen cars scattered along a narrow parking lot—solitary salesmen and lovers enjoying the lake view. Kohl joined them now, breaking sharply in the gravel.

"Okay, let's go over it from the beginning," he said. "*Everything,* Bobbi—but not too slow, okay?"

She nodded dutifully. "Like I said—he called Tony Jack and said he had these items, you know, from the briefcase. Kin said they was his bony fides or somethin' like that and that if Tony Jack wanted to see 'em, all he had to do was pick 'em up where Kin stashed 'em—the cookout picture right under that trash can over there." She pointed toward a tall green can anchored near a tree. "And one of Ross's bank-deposit slips. We hid that at the art museum, right next to that big black doughnut out in front."

Knowing Ken as he did, Kohl tried to fill in the rest. "Then you and Ken parked somewhere along here and watched, to see if anyone picked up the photo, right?"

Bobbi didn't seem at all surprised that he knew this. "Right. It was two people, a chunky guy with a red flattop—God, I hate them flattops, don't you? And then a real good-lookin' black chick, skin like coffee with cream and straight black hair, not kinky, you know? And legs up to her boobs."

"Maybe a stripper at Tony Jack's."

"You know, she could be—I never thought of that."

"And they knew right where to go?"

"You bet. They pulled up in a light-blue hardtop—one of them old-time Caddies, about a block long. And the guy went straight for it. He tipped up the can and found the picture, right where Kin told 'em it was. The black chick got out but she just sorta hung around the car."

"And you and Ken were in the Corvette watching them."

Bobbi nodded. "But up the street a little, you know? And we was kinda scrunched down, so they couldn't see us."

"Flattop and the black girl?"

"Sure. Who else?"

Kohl sighed. "That's the question, all right."

"What do you mean by that?"

"I mean someone might have been watching you watch them."

"Who?"

"Who do you think?"

Bobbi suddenly went pale. "Oh, Jesus! You mean *he* mighta been watchin' us—*Tony Jack?* Watchin' *me?*

"Why not?"

"Oh God." Bobbi brought her hands up to her face, as if to shield herself from a suddenly very ominous world.

"And when the couple left," Kohl said, "Ken followed, right?"

Coming out from behind her hands, Bobbi nodded slowly. "Yeah. But first he takes some money out of his billfold and then gives me the billfold. Also the car-rental stuff."

"Why? Did he say?"

"For safekeeping is all he said. But I figure he was scared that if they got hold of him—and if Rusty told them his name—he could pretend he was someone else. Give them some other name."

Kohl felt weak. "Oh Christ," he muttered.

"And that's when I started gittin' antsy," Bobbi went on. "I mean, everybody knows about these mob guys and what they do to you, right? So I didn't want to follow. I kept yellin' at Kin, but he wouldn't listen. I opened the car door then and he slowed down some." She gave a sharp laugh and shook her head. "But the car was still movin' when he kinda pushed me out, can you believe that? I hit the road runnin', I really did."

"He said he'd come back for you."

"He said to wait at the café—kinda yelled it, you know?"

"And he just kept on driving, following the Cadillac?"

Bobbi nodded wearily. "That's what I said, didn't I? And lemme say I woulda stuck with him too, if it wasn't for the mob thing. You know, the mafia. You always see it on TV, how they can find *anybody, anywhere*. You just can't hide from them. They put out a contract on you and that's that. Bang bang, you're dead."

Kohl had no illusions about the danger Ken was in and which he himself seemed so hell-bent on sharing. But as usual he didn't feel that he had much choice in the matter, probably no more than Tony Jack felt he had. The one thing he was certain of was that every second counted. He had to find Ken— reel him in—before Tony Jack did. And even if he failed at that, even if the mobster already had Ken and had wrung him dry of every bit of information he possessed—even then Ken might still be alive. Till nighttime anyway. Kohl *had* to believe that.

For a few moments, he thought seriously of pulling over and phoning the police. But when he considered what he would have to tell them, he kept on driving. His first stop would be the art museum; and if Ken was not there, then the house on Queen Anne Hill, then Tony Jack's strip joint downtown. And he soon found that without Bobbi along it would have been a much longer journey, since most of Seattle was still alien country to him.

From the freeway, he knew how to get to the Queen Anne Hill house, and he had been downtown on a number of occasions, but he had seen the museum only once, at well past midnight, with Ken driving and neither of them rigorously sober at the time. Located in a park on Capitol Hill, the museum looked out over a reservoir toward downtown Seattle and, on a clear day, Puget Sound and the Olympic Mountains. Between the museum and the view there was a piece of modern sculpture commonly called "the doughnut," but which looked to Kohl much more like a tractor tire: huge and black and unevenly worn. On the night they visited it, Ken claimed that all true Eastsiders believed that if a man could piss through the doughnut without getting a drop on it, he would live long and die rich. But as he was unzipping his fly, a museum guard came hurrying toward them and they reluctantly retreated to Ken's Bronco and sped away.

This was the spot where Ken had hidden the second item from the briefcase: one of Ricky Ross's bank-deposit slips. Bobbi said that Ken had buried the slip, all but a protruding corner of it, between the sculpture's marble pedestal and the surrounding grass. When they finally reached the museum and saw neither Ken nor his car, Bobbi got out of the truck and ran over to the doughnut, checking the area where Ken had secreted the deposit slip. Coming back, she held out her empty hands.

"No sign of it," she said, getting in. "Tony Jack's got it now. And Ken too, I bet." Her eyes had filled with tears.

"How do we get to Queen Anne Hill from here?" Kohl asked.

He felt bad about putting the tiny oriental maid through five minutes of terror, but he couldn't see that he had any choice in the matter. When she answered the door he asked if Tony Jack was there and the woman said, "Nobody home. You reave prease. Come back nudder time."

As she began to shut the door, Kohl moved fast, catching it just before it closed and pushing it open, seizing the woman by her small hard arm as she turned and started to run. When she began to scream, he covered her mouth with his other hand and then walked her through the house that way, room by room, each crowded with about twice the furniture and bric-a-brac it was meant to hold. Kohl kept trying to reassure the woman, but when he felt his ridiculously heavy .45 start to slip sideways in his belt, under his shirt, he took his hand off her mouth in order to straighten the gun, and she immediately began to scream again.

"I said you're gonna be all right!" he told her, covering her mouth again. "Just the downstairs now. We check that out and then I leave."

It was a remodeled basement, totally carpeted, most of it taken up by a posh game room with cork walls and an antique pool table in the center, under Tiffany lamps. Like the other rooms he'd checked, it was unoccupied. Not until he came to the very last door did he see anyone besides the maid: an old woman sitting in a rocking chair, facing a console television on which a rock video was playing soundlessly. The room had been converted into a small apartment, with a kitchenette and adjoining bathroom. Though Kohl could not be sure of it, he believed he had just seen the mother of Tony Jack.

Turning back, he led the maid toward the stairs, gradually releasing the pressure on her mouth.

"All right, I'm leaving now," he said, "unless you yell again."

She nodded in desperate agreement.

"Just tell me where I can lock you up. With the lock on the outside."

"Wine cerrar," she got out. "Udder side." She pointed beyond the stairs at a heavy wooden door. He turned the inside light on for her and then closed and locked the door.

When he finally reached the street, he thought for a moment that Bobbi had run out on him, but then he found her stretched out on the truck's seat, hiding. "Not there, uh?" she said, sitting up.

"Not there."

"I still feel cruddy about not going in with you, Tom. But I just couldn't of, no way. I'd of spent the whole time peein'. I really would."

136

"It's okay. You're my lookout, remember?"

"I don't think they got him anyway," she said. "He probly didn't tail them all the way to the museum. He probly just cut out and went back home, and that's where he is now, waitin' for us."

Kohl was already driving back up the dead-end street. "And he just left you at Leschi, uh?"

Gripping her head, she began to bounce up and down on the seat. *"I don't know! I don't know! I don't know!"*

Kohl put his hand on her leg, to keep her from bouncing. "Look, Bobbi, I'm scared shitless too. I don't do this for a living, remember? But we *have* to go to the strip joint. He could be there."

"And I stay in the truck again?"

"Right."

She drew up her legs and hugged them. "I know Kin's got his faults," she allowed, "but you know, I really got it bad for him anyway. And you know why, Tom? Cuz he's the only classy guy who was ever nice to me."

Though Kohl's mouth was ashen with fear and anxiety, he couldn't help smiling. "Thanks," he said.

As far as Kohl knew, the upper part of First Avenue was probably the only seedy area of downtown Seattle. Even then it was a mixed bag, with the popular farmers' market and tony restaurants and high-rise condos squeezed in among the peep shows and soup kitchens and wino bars. He and Ken had knocked around the area a number of times, twice with Diane, usually after a movie or dinner. Yet he had never been inside Tony Jack's before, probably because Ken was not one who enjoyed rubbing elbows with the "windbreaker set," as he called blue-collar working stiffs, seemingly oblivious of the fact that Kohl—the man he was talking to at the time—was undeniably one of them. Then, too, there was sophisticated Seattle's curiously puritanical attitude toward sex and alcohol, decreeing that the two should not mix, that strip joints could serve only soft drinks—a prohibition that undoubtedly dampened Ken's enthusiasm for tits and ass as much as it did Kohl's.

After pulling into a parking lot, Kohl took the gun out of his belt and put it on the seat, under a window rag.

"You just wait here," he said to Bobbi. "Give me a half hour, and if I'm not back by then, start yelling for a cop. Understand?"

Bobbi nodded, but said nothing. She was still hugging her legs.

"The gun's too big," Kohl told her. "It'd show, so I'm leaving it here. Remember, thirty minutes."

Again she nodded. "Boy, I don't know about this, Tom."

He closed the truck door very quietly for some reason and walked out of the parking lot, joining the flow of pedestrians on the sidewalk.

Tony Jack's was located on the corner, less than a block away. And it seemed to Kohl that he was there in an instant, taking in the cheaply liveried black barker making his spiel to the passersby.

"Twenty—count 'em—twenty gorgeous gals dressed the way you like 'em, gents! Yeah, this is the hottest show in town, fellas! So come on in and live a little! Twenty—count 'em—"

After paying the five-dollar price of admission, Kohl entered through a vestibule into the showroom, which was large and dark, quaking with the sound of hard rock. From the stage a T-shaped runway extended out among the tables, where the patrons—almost all of them men—sat in the gloom, looking bored as four or five girls danced to the recorded music, one of them spotlighted on the stage while the others performed for tips at the individual tables, giving a close-up, hands-off view. Overhead a pair of revolving glitter domes, reflecting spotlights, raked the room with varicolored points of light.

Kohl took one of the banquette tables along the wall and ordered a Coke from a waitress with dark-red hair and milk-white skin—one of the dancers, he judged, looking at her lissome figure. When she returned with his Coke, he asked if his "old friend Tony Jack" was there. She gave him a bored look and moved her head about a quarter inch in the direction of the open doorway at the far end of the bar.

"He could be back," she said, "but who knows? He don't zackly check in with me, ya know."

Kohl overtipped her and she almost smiled. "Ketch ya later," she said.

Checking his watch, Kohl saw that six minutes had already passed. But he remained in the booth awhile longer, studying the soft-drink bartender and another man who stood off to one side, doing nothing—the bouncer, apparently. Neither man was as large as Kohl, not that it mattered, considering that there were two of them and that miniature baseball bats were probably standard equipment for employees of Tony Jack.

Kohl was afraid that if he asked to see the boss he would get the brush-off, which left him with no option except to go straight toward his goal and trust to luck. He waited until the stage dancer began to peel off her G-string before he got up and started for the doorway at the far end of the bar. Since the rest rooms were just this side of the doorway, he knew the bouncer and bartender wouldn't even notice him—until he passed the men's-room door and kept going. Casualness was the key, he told himself. He was just a big guy who needed to take a leak, that was all. The walls were shaking with music and the girl onstage, nude now, was pretending to copulate with one of the stage posts. The bartender, indifferent, had his back to both the stage and Kohl, who kept right on walking, through the doorway and down a narrow hallway made even narrower by the cases of soft drinks stacked along it. Almost immediately he came to an open doorway to a dingy little vestibule office where an elderly blue-haired lady sat working at a cluttered desk, totaling a column of figures on an ancient adding machine. Next to her was an old Royal manual typewriter, and Kohl had no doubt that if she kept Tony Jack's books, she did so in a bound ledger, with a fountain pen and

Parker's permanent blue-black ink. Beyond her desk was another door, closed.

"Who're you?" she asked.

"I'm here about a job," Kohl said. "Tony asked me to drop by."

She looked dubious. "He didn't tell me nothin' about it."

Kohl made no response to that and finally she shrugged and thumbed at the door.

"Well, go ahead then. He's in there."

The woman's presence eased Kohl's mind considerably. He couldn't very well imagine Tony Jack carrying on a baseball-bat interrogation of Ken while a blue-haired lady sat outside the door, adding up the day's take. Yet as he knocked once on the door and then opened it, he couldn't help wondering where Ken might be, if not here. If Tony Jack or his henchmen hadn't abducted him, then where in the hell was he? Why hadn't he returned to the café for Bobbi? Why hadn't he at least phoned?

Tony Jack was not alone. Standing at his elbow, checking something on his desk, was a gaudily beautiful young black woman with café au lait skin, bouffant hair, and legs that did indeed seem to run almost up to her small, high breasts. While she exhibited only mild interest at this large stranger coming in unannounced, Kohl saw a momentary alarm pass like a strobe light across Tony Jack's beefy face. Simultaneously he slid open one of his desk drawers and unobtrusively reached inside it, and Kohl didn't doubt that the man's hand had come to rest on the butt of a gun.

"Who the fuck are you?" Jack asked.

"I'm looking for my cousin. He said he'd be doing business with you today."

"What's his name?"

"George Orwell."

"Don't know him. And that still don't tell me who the fuck you are."

"Tom Orwell."

Tony Jack was on the short side, but husky and bull-necked.

The hand Kohl could see was round as a mallet, the stubby fingers bright with diamonds. He was wearing a French-cuffed pink shirt, a maroon silk tie, and the vest of an expensive gray pinstripe suit. Above such finery was the face of a butcher with, paradoxically, an evangelist's head of hair, a wavy gray pompadour, sprayed stiff.

"Yeah? Well, people don't just walk in here off the street, Thomas. You stand very still now, you hear me?" He motioned to the black girl. "Pat him down."

"Be my pleasure," she said, smiling wickedly. "And since we gonna be so close, my name is Heather." She came around the desk, moving as if she were nude on a stage. "My, but ain't you one big mother, Thomas," she went on, running her hands along his body, feeling for a weapon. At his groin, she was especially diligent. "But only average where it counts."

"Forget that shit," Tony Jack said. "Is he clean?"

"He ain't packin' nothin', if that's what you mean."

Jack breathed easily then. He withdrew his right hand from the drawer and leaned back in his executive chair. "Can't be too careful these days, Thomas," he said. "All kinds of head cases runnin' loose. Assholes get a hard-on for one of the girls and then blame me when they don't find true love. Go figure, uh?"

"Must be a grind."

"You bet your ass it is. Anyway, since you're already here, why don't you just speak your piece. Then you can be on your way. Fair enough?"

Looking down at the man, at his impassive, slotted eyes, Kohl wondered if he should even bother to say a word. But, as it had just been pointed out, he *was* already there. "Well, it's like I said. My cousin claimed he told you on the phone about certain items you might be interested in. And he said he told you where to find them."

Frowning comically, Jack looked up at the girl. "You got any idea what the fuck Thomas is talkin' about?"

Heather shook her head. "Not a clue."

"Oh, I think you do. I think you both do." Kohl felt cool sweat sliding down his chest. "And I can promise you, anything happens to my cousin, I'll give you all you can handle. Maybe more."

Tony Jack was enjoying himself now, affecting a look of earnest consternation and holding out his hands in a gesture of bafflement. "What the fuck?" he said to Heather. "Who the fuck is this guy, anyway?"

Behind him was a large window that looked out into the showroom. Soundproofed and probably mirrored on the other side, it gave Kohl a fine view not only of the dancers but also of the bouncer, who had turned suddenly, glancing at the window as he headed toward the doorway at the end of the bar, apparently signaled by some sort of alarm Tony Jack had tripped. For a few seconds Kohl just stood there gazing at the glitter domes' reflected lights, which kept crawling across the window like luminous roaches. He decided it was time to bail out.

"Look, maybe I made a mistake. My cousin is kind of flaky and I guess he gave me a bum steer."

"I guess so," Jack said. "But what about that threat you just made? What about that, huh?"

"I guess I was out of line."

"You sure was, Thomas. You was *way* out of line."

At that moment the door flew open and the bouncer rushed in, carrying not a miniature baseball bat but a piece of bamboo as long as his arm and almost as thick. His job apparently was to persuade, not maim. Nevertheless Kohl found himself moving to the side, backing away from both men.

"Whoa," he said. "Hold it. I'm on my way. You let me pass and no one gets hurt. I obviously made a mistake, and I'm sorry about it. I apologize."

Tony Jack gestured for the bouncer to hold off. "Well, what do you think, Henry? He barges in here and shoots off his mouth like some kinda real tough guy. And now he starts whimperin'. So what do we do?"

The bouncer was holding his club at the ready, but he didn't look very anxious to use it. "I don't know, Tony," he said. "You tell me."

Running his hand along the black girl's hip, Jack wagged his head thoughtfully. "What do you say, babe? You think he's sincere? You think he's really sorry?"

Kohl had the feeling that the girl had spent most of her life learning to look cool and indifferent, even when her knees were shaking. So though her smile was pure insouciance, he could see the other thing in her eyes, the tiny lick of fear. She after all had been there, at the park.

"Don't ask me," she said. "You the boss, Tony."

Tony Jack laughed. "Yeah, that's the God's truth, ain't it? So I say—well, okay, we let Mister Candyass walk on outa here—*this time.*" His smile had faded and his eyes narrowed into slots again. *"Capische,* asshole?"

"Yes," Kohl said. "I understand."

Jack mocked him. *"Yes, I understand."*

Heather and the bouncer laughed dutifully as Kohl edged toward the door, his body tightly coiled, ready to strike out against the bouncer if the man made the slightest move in his direction. Hurrying through the outer office, he saw that the blue-haired lady had disappeared. As he headed down the hallway toward the showroom, he could hear Tony Jack's laughter clattering behind him, like a tail of tin cans.

Though a cold rage was building in him, Kohl was bathed in sweat by the time he reached his truck. Bobbi was lying down in the front seat again and wouldn't even look up or unlock the door until he banged on it. As he got in, she sagged back against the seat.

"God, it was already over twenty minutes, Tom!" she protested. "I been goin' crazy!"

Gripping the steering wheel, Kohl lowered his head onto

his hands. "Yeah, I know the feeling. It wasn't all fun in there either."

"Why? What happened?"

"I ate shit."

"Why?"

"Seemed like a good idea."

"But what happened?"

Straightening up, Kohl got out a cigarette and lit it. Bobbi took the pack from him and lit one for herself.

"The black girl was there," he said.

"The same one?"

"Or one just like her. But I didn't have any leverage. I had to eat shit and walk."

"That's not so dumb, you know. That's smart."

"Yeah, I know." Kohl rolled the window down and tried to wave some of the smoke out of the cab. "But what now?" he said. "What the hell do we do now?"

Just then a huge car passed behind them, a light-blue early-eighties Cadillac hardtop. Kohl stopped breathing as it pulled into a reserved spot at the end of the row, next to the alley. Two men got out, one of them burly and potbellied, with a full head of light-red hair, brush-cut.

"Hey, that's him!" Bobbi said, in a whisper.

"Yeah, I figured." Kohl thought of taking the gun with him, just for protection, but decided again that it was too damned large, almost impossible to conceal. And anyway the two men didn't know him—he would have the initiative. As he scrambled out of the truck and headed for the alley, Bobbi yelled at him.

"Hey! What about me?"

Kohl gestured for her to stay in the truck, but didn't say anything—the distance between the parking lot and Tony Jack's was much too short. Reaching the alley, he called to the red-haired man.

"Hey, Red! Hold up—it's me!"

Both men turned and looked at Kohl, who realized suddenly that the second man was probably Tony Jack's other brother, a pale imitation: smaller, balding, not as well dressed, in fact absurdly dressed, wearing a plaid jacket and red pants, with a white belt and white shoes—the same sort of outfit farmers wore to church when Kohl was a kid. And the red-haired man was no easier on the eyes, with his splotchy white skin and flattened nose and a mouth that appeared locked in an open sneer, the better to show off his snaggly brown teeth.

"Tom Orwell—remember?" Kohl said, almost upon them. Ignoring the brother, he directed his words at the red-haired man. "Tony said I should drop by and see about a job as a bouncer."

The men looked at each other, as though in the expectation that the other would know who Kohl was. In that moment Kohl moved in on them, casually reaching out as though he intended to shake the redhead's hand but instead kicked him hard between the legs, then swung his outstretched hand sideways, chopping the brother in the neck. The brother wobbled but didn't fall. And when he reached unsteadily for something inside his coat, Kohl hit him again, hooking his left fist into the man's groin, which put him down and out, rolling among the trash cans.

Kohl turned back to the redhead, who was on his knees now, gasping at the waves of pain rolling through him. He made a slight, crawling move, trying to get up, and Kohl kicked him in the stomach this time, hard enough to pitch him over into some other cans and boxes, which dribbled eggshells and coffee grounds and rotted vegetables onto his hound's-tooth jacket. He was still conscious, however, and when he made a feeble move to get something out of his side pocket, Kohl pushed his hand away and reached into the pocket himself, drawing out a pearl-handled switchblade knife. Flicking the blade open, Kohl turned the man onto his belly and straddled him, pulled his head back as far as it would go before placing the blade against his throat. And Kohl reminded himself that he had to keep going just as he was, that this was not a time

145

for niceties, that at that very moment Ken was probably tied up somewhere, blindfolded, beaten, or worse. He could be dying. He could be dead.

"Where is he?" Kohl demanded "You lie, I cut."

The man made a desperate, whimpering sound, and Kohl eased the pressure on his neck so he would be able to talk. And he did.

"I don't know, man! I really don't! I—"

Holding the back of the man's head now, Kohl slammed him facedown into the pavement, more in frustration than anything else. A crowd was already gathering at the end of the alley, watching the carnage. And in the distance Kohl could hear someone calling for the police. Leaning down over the brother, he whispered a warning.

"If my cousin dies, Tony Jack dies. You tell him that, understand?"

The brother managed a nod of sorts.

"That's a good fella," Kohl said.

As he got up and started back, he saw Bobbi waiting for him down the alley. Holding her fists above her head, she was jumping along like a football cheerleader, as if she thought body English might get him there faster. Together, they sprinted for the truck, and within a minute they were out on Pike Street, heading for the freeway. Kohl told her that he hadn't learned anything, that it had all been for nothing.

"That's okay, Tom," she said, patting him like a proud mother. "I'm just glad I'm on your side, that's all."

Late that night, in the game room at the house, Kohl and Bobbi sat like a pair of backward school kids, pretending to listen as their teacher—Diane—held forth, pacing the room, smoking, thinking out loud. Bobbi, nursing a beer, seemed as much awed at being there, tolerated by Diane, as she was daunted by their shared predicament: still not knowing what had happened to Ken or what they should do about it. As for

Kohl, he'd already had his say, deciding finally that they had no choice left except to call in the police, and the sooner the better. Diane had asked him for just a few minutes more, and that was what he was giving her. At the same time, it allowed him to fortify himself with one more Chivas on ice, from Ken's very last bottle. He knew this was hardly the time to have even one drink, but he'd gone ahead anyway, mostly out of frustration, knowing that so far that day—cold sober—he hadn't exactly set the world on fire. Unhappily, this was his fourth drink and he still didn't feel a thing, certainly not any release from tension.

His father's .45 lay only inches from his hand on the lamp table next to where he was sitting. A loaded .410 shotgun was stuck like a bumbershoot into the umbrella stand in the foyer, and Ken's six-shot automatic twelve-gauge was strategically stashed in the kitchen. In addition, all the outside lights were on. If Tony Jack had Ken, that meant he also had Ken's home address and anything else he wanted to know, despite Ken's pathetic master stroke, leaving his rental contract and wallet with Bobbi. So if Jack decided to come after his brother's briefcase or after Kohl himself, for dirtying up his alley, Kohl was ready for him. But this was not going to happen, according to Diane. She'd spent her college summers working as a Girl Friday in her uncle's Portland law office, she said, and as a result knew a little something about criminal law.

"And I can tell you right now," she went on, "that the briefcase—and everything in it—is absolutely useless as legal evidence. Because it's tainted. The principle involved is what they call chain of evidence or something like that. And it's got to be unbroken. It's got to connect directly from the suspect—Giacalone—straight to the courtroom, without anyone except the police touching it. But my God, in this case the police have never even had it. Why, you and Ken could've invented the whole thing—found the guy's briefcase and put in it all that stuff you took from Ricky Ross's, after you robbed him and beat him."

Bobbi missed the point. "After *they* robbed him! What the

devil are you talkin' about? It was Giacalone did all that! He's the one had the business with Ross, not Kin or Tom!"

Diane smiled wearily. "You know that, and I know that, and even the police would know that. But they still couldn't act on it, because the evidence is useless. If we call them and say Tony Jack has abducted Ken and might harm him—to avenge the hit-and-run—the police will ask us how we know this, and we'll trot out the briefcase. And even though they'll probably believe us, they know that if they raid Tony Jack's home and his strip joint or whatever and come up with zilch, then they're gonna get slapped with a harassment suit, because they didn't have probable cause."

Kohl was struggling against a strong desire to get up and carry Diane over to a chair and drop her into it. Instead he drained his glass and lit a cigarette. "Of course, Tony Jack's a legal scholar too," he said. "Naturally he'll know the briefcase is tainted. That it couldn't possibly hurt him."

"Well, how could it?" Diane shot back. "Even if it was allowable as evidence, none of it implicates him—just his brother, who's dead. After all, anybody can pick up matches at a strip joint."

Bobbi did not quite follow this. "So what does it all mean?" she asked.

"It means," Diane told her, "that if we call the police in, they won't come down on Tony Jack—they'll come down on us, as accessories to a hit-and-run."

"So what do we do, then? Just sit here and wait for Kin's body to turn up?"

"Good question," Kohl said.

But Diane did not agree. She shook her head, as if both of them had just failed bonehead math. "I've already told you— Ken has countless friends from the past, friends neither of you know. Unfortunately for me, most of them are *girl*friends. And I'd bet this house that he's with one of them now—that he just chickened out at the last minute and dropped in on her, flashing his pearly whites and asking if she'd put him up till all this blows over. And he's just dumb enough to think it will."

Bobbi's mouth fell open at that. "Kin *dumb!*" she bawled. "Jesus H. Christ, woman, I don't think you even know the man. Kin's just extra-sensitive, that's all, like a thoroughbred. And if you wanna know the truth, I can't figure what he ever saw in a cold bitch like you."

Diane stopped pacing long enough to stare at Bobbi. Then she turned to Kohl, her face virtually expressionless. "Look, Tom, I let her come in because she was with you. But I won't be insulted in my own house. Please take her down to the boat or dump her on the freeway or at McDonald's or wherever—I don't give a fuck. Just get her the hell out of here, okay?"

Bobbi was looking at Kohl as if she expected him to do just what he was told. She after all was the one who once observed that the bigger they are, the easier they pussy-whip. But in this instance she was wrong.

"No, I don't think so," Kohl said to Diane. "I don't want her alone on the boat, in case Tony Jack comes looking for the briefcase there. And I don't think you ought to be alone here either, for even a few minutes."

Diane was amused. "Tony Jack again, right?"

"Right."

"And what I want, that doesn't enter in? Even in my own house?"

Kohl ignored that. "I'm gonna stay up," he said. "She can have my room. That ought to keep her out of your way—can you buy that?"

Diane didn't respond. But Bobbi did.

"Boy, I really like this—you two talkin' about me like I'm a dog or somethin'. Like I ain't even here."

"Why don't you go back there now?" Kohl suggested. "You could take a hot bath and relax. I'll check on you later. I'm gonna stay up—I couldn't sleep anyway."

"And *I* could, I suppose?" Bobbi said.

Kohl sat there looking at her and finally she shrugged and got up.

"Oh, why the hell not? I guess I could use a hot bath." She gave Diane a look, a stab at condescension. "Anyway, a body could freeze her tits off in here."

When she was gone, Diane decided to have one last go at Kohl. Looking desperately earnest, she came over and sat down on his chair's ottoman, facing him, and very slowly and reasonably she presented the case for not calling in the police yet—not a legalistic argument about evidence this time but rather her simple fear of involvement, her utter terror at the idea of being charged as an accessory and probably losing her job and her income and her reputation and everything else she had worked so hard to achieve.

"All I ask," she concluded, "is that we don't do anything tonight. That we wait and see. You already checked Tony Jack's house and his strip joint and didn't find anything—no trace of Ken, no sign he'd ever been at either place. So please, Tom, for tonight at least, let's just wait and see. It's what Ken would do—if you were the one missing."

It was an unlikely position for Diane, virtually sitting at a man's feet, her manner earnest, even imploring. And considering the lateness of the hour, she would normally have been wearing one of her handsome robes or elegantly sexy lounging pajamas, not the jeans and Seahawk sweatshirt she had on now. And of course, instead of her hair looking tousled, there wouldn't have been a golden strand out of place. But for Kohl the most strikingly different thing about her was in the cool green of her eyes, in that they were glistening not only with tears but with something very close to desperation.

"Please, Tom—let's not call them tonight," she said again. "By noon tomorrow, if we haven't heard from him—"

"We may *never* hear from him," he cut in.

Tears welled from her eyes, but she didn't abandon her argument. "The same is true now. If those hoodlums got him this afternoon, and if they intended to hurt him—" She didn't finish the thought, but then she didn't have to.

Kohl got up to refill his glass. As he moved past her, he touched her shoulder. "All right," he said. "We'll wait."

At the bar, he dropped some fresh ice cubes into his glass and filled it with scotch. Diane came over and slipped into his arms. He kissed her on the forehead, without enthusiasm.

"Thank you," she said. "I know how it hurts you to wait. And it does me too. It really does." She began to cry then, very softly, and he continued to hold her. She raised her face to him and they kissed, chastely, like friends. Finally she pulled away. "I'm going upstairs and lie down for a while. I don't imagine I'll sleep."

"I'll be right here or out on the deck," he said.

When she was gone, he turned off the outside lights and carried his drink and the .45 out to the deck, where he sat down in the chaise closest to the wall of the house, so no one could come up behind him. He knew that he was acting more than a little paranoid, thinking that Tony Jack might actually come after him or raid the house, looking for the briefcase. But if he was going to err, he decided he would do so on the side of caution.

Beginning with his mother's death, Kohl had long since gotten used to the feeling that he was living someone else's life. The Tom Kohl he thought he was had lived very differently, beginning each day at five in the morning, reluctantly letting go of his young wife's warm and lovely body and dressing in the cold and the darkness, getting ready to do diurnal battle with almost six hundred acres of some of the richest farmland in America. And he'd never really minded the hardship and the long hours, because he innocently thought he was pouring all that labor and concern into something that was his, or at least one day would be his. And he had loved the variety of the work, the freedom to do whatever he wanted, including just shooting the breeze with his father and other farmers at the Blanton café.

That was the life he knew, the life he thought he'd been

cut out for. Nevertheless here he was now, lounging in the dark a couple of thousand miles from home, with a gun at his side and fear his constant new companion, an icy wraith sitting on his lap, snuggling in close. He and Ken and Diane weren't the kind of people who got in trouble with the law—they were the kind who *called* the police when things went wrong. Yet Kohl pointedly wasn't calling in anybody, even though he sat there wondering whether his cousin had been killed that day. And the fact that he knew the reason for his inaction—because most of what Diane said made sense—didn't prevent him from feeling ill with frustration and guilt. He kept remembering the last time he'd seen Ken, on the boat, when his terror had been like an odor filling the cabin. And he'd said to Kohl: "Okay, you win. I'll just sit here and wait for it, like any other asshole on death row."

Kohl's only real hope was that Diane was right, that Ken, running true to form, *had* chickened out at the last moment and was shacked up somewhere or hiding out in a motel. And one other thing she said made sense too: that even if Ken had stumbled into Tony Jack's hands, it was totally unreasonable for the supposed mobster to risk everything over a *traffic accident,* to avenge himself against someone whose only crime was careless driving. If anything, Kohl felt that he himself was a much more likely candidate for retribution, considering that he had threatened Jack in his own office and had waylaid two of his lieutenants.

Maybe there really wasn't anything to worry about, he told himself, sitting there in the dark summer evening, looking out at the lights of Seattle shimmering on the surface of the lake. Sure, he thought, and just maybe the lake was filled with ambrosia instead of water and there weren't any hungry or homeless people lost under all those lovely lights and there weren't any women being beaten or children molested and the desperately lonely weren't lying in their prickly beds listening as the rest of the world made love and laughter.

In the context of all that, cousin Ken was undoubtedly pretty small potatoes, a shallow yuppie who had stumbled, one of life's elect suddenly unelected. But for Kohl, Ken was never *only* that, never only the man he had become. More than anything else he was Kohl's own childhood, the likable little buddy almost always at his side, and sometimes closer, as he was on the nights after a high school football game, when the two grade-schoolers had to cross Kohl's woodland in the dark and Ken's hard little hand would keep reaching for Kohl's until finally, reluctantly, Kohl would give it to him: sanctuary in a dark and threatening world.

When he went back to his room to check on Bobbi, he found her propped up in his bed watching television: Morton Downey, Jr., blowing smoke at one of his guests. Bobbi didn't seem interested.

"Boy, that Diane!" she said, shaking her head. "What a cunt. If I had my car here, I woulda went on home."

"Any news on TV?" Kohl asked.

"I don't know—I didn't look."

He told her that if she wanted anything in the kitchen—any food or drink—she should go and get it. "I don't think Diane would mind," he said.

"Big of her." Looking at him, Bobbi ruefully shook her head. "Boy, how a guy like you could be hot for a girl like that, it just don't figure."

"It's called social climbing."

"Yeah, well, if I was you, I'd rather climb on someone like me."

The way she was lying there, in her customary shorts and T-shirt, Kohl saw her point.

"You take care," he said.

Back in the game room, he turned on the television set there, hoping to find some local late-night news, but it was already past midnight. So he followed the lead of Tony Jack's mother, getting a rock video station but killing the sound, so he could hear her son's approach, if it came to that. And after a short time Diane came down from upstairs, bundled in a terry robe. She sat down next to Kohl on the couch, tucking her bare feet under her and leaning lightly against him. She reached for his hand and pulled it onto her lap, sandwiching it between both of hers.

"There now," she said. "I feel safe."

"Me too."

She looked at him. "There wasn't any news. I watched upstairs."

"I guess you were right," he said. "It doesn't look like we're gonna have any visitors."

She smiled pertly. "Anything you want to know, just ask."

"I'll remember that."

Over the next few minutes they said nothing more as they sat there together watching the videos, the endless sophomoric sagas of apocalypse and heedless sexuality, their absurdity sharpened by silence. Then, on the wall above the television, Kohl saw the light from a car coming up the street, cresting the hill. The light moved slowly at first before zooming across the ceiling as the car turned in and came up the front drive. Gun in hand, Kohl hurried to the window. Immediately he put the gun down.

"It's the police," he said.

Kohl let the bell ring twice before he opened the door. There were two of them, one in uniform and the other in the shapeless brown suit of a detective, though he looked too old for the role, too benign. The one in uniform spoke first.

"Is there a Diane White here?"

Kohl said nothing as she came into the foyer, because it suddenly occurred to him that the elderly man might not be a detective at all, but a *clergyman*. And the thought abruptly took the wind out of him and made his legs go soft.

Diane identified herself and the elderly man asked if he and the officer could come in.

"Of course." Diane gestured for them to enter, and the two men moved just inside the doorway and stopped, like children entering school on the first day. At the same time, Bobbi came hurrying down the hallway from the kitchen. Seeing the two men, she stopped suddenly and her hand went to her mouth, as though to stifle a cry.

"What is it?" Diane asked the men. "What's happened?"

The officer told her that a check run on the license of a Corvette showed that the car had been leased by a Kenneth Ryder. "Of this address," he added.

"I'm his fiancée," she said. "Now tell us—please. What's happened?"

The officer's voice was barely audible. "There's been an automobile accident. A serious one."

Diane stood there staring at the man for a few moments. Then she looked at Kohl, and he could see it hit her, the possibility.

"How bad is he?" she got out.

The officer's eyes skittered toward the elderly man. "This is Reverend Halstrom," he said.

And Bobbi did cry out now. *"No! Oh Jesus Christ, no!"*

Diane opened her mouth as if she wanted to say something too, but no sound came from her. She looked at Kohl again, then at the two men, then back at Kohl, who reached out for her, to hold her, or have her hold him, he wasn't sure which. But she pushed his hands down and started to back away, gesturing for him and the two men to stay where they were. The clergyman cleared his throat and smiled bleakly.

"Perhaps we could pray together," he said.

6 Though Kohl knew he was dreaming, he couldn't pull himself out of it. He felt as if he were floating face-down in water, the water being the dream, a world so compelling he couldn't bring himself to raise his head the few inches necessary to be free of it, to breathe again. What he saw was the mountain road at night, the same identical curve, with Seattle and the Eastside shining in the distance. And though the Bronco was there too, parked at the edge of the drop-off, everything else was different. With Tony Jack looking on, a smiling Ken sat sideways in the passenger seat as the black girl, Heather, performed a kind of table dance in front of him, grinding her nude body against his legs while she groped him with her hands, obviously feeling for a weapon. Kohl desperately wanted to warn Ken, but he was too busy trying to subdue Rusty and the red-haired man, whom he kept punching and kicking with no visible effect, as if his fists and feet were moving through water. And then Tony Jack was up in the driver's seat of the Bronco, gunning the engine and inching the vehicle closer to the drop-off, while Ken sat there with his legs hanging out through the open door and his hands resting on the black girl's head as she began to go down on him. Only it was Kohl who felt her sharp teeth and busy tongue, and as the pleasure mounted in him he longed for the strength to tear himself away, because Ken had begun to realize what was happening and was reaching out toward Kohl just as the Bronco started over the edge, already bursting into flames.

Kohl felt something tighten on his right arm and shake him, and he came rocketing up through the surface of the water like a dolphin at play. Next to him, in the window seat, Diane gave him a look of gentle reproval.

"You were dreaming," she informed him.

His heart was still racing, he had to cover his erection, and under his suit he was drenched. "No kidding," he said.

"People were looking."

"I'm not surprised."

"You ought to have some coffee."

"Probably."

With a considerable sense of relief, Kohl looked around him at the safe, secure world of United first class. No one was being beaten; no one was on fire; alas, no one was being fellated. In addition to all that, Kohl had room for his entire body, which wasn't the case in coach, where his legs and shoulders tended to wander into space paid for by others. He remembered a flight to Seattle to see Ken three years earlier, sitting next to a college student who peevishly asked him to "get out of my space," only to have Kohl inquire if he'd prefer lying stretched out on the aisle floor. Though the kid hadn't uttered a peep after that, Kohl still felt lousy the rest of the trip, knowing that he was in the wrong. So he was glad that Diane had insisted they fly first-class, even though the round-trip ticket to Illinois had eaten up a sizable portion of his capital. After all, a man had to have **room enough for his legs** and shoulders, did he not? It was a thought that stuck in Kohl's brain like an icepick, for it led inexorably to another, similar thought: of Ken's body lying underneath them in the cargo hold, taking up so little of the sumptuous bronze casket Diane had bought for him. But then it really wasn't much of a body anymore, only a pitiful little black thing, fire-consumed, Ken's *remains*, that was all.

When the police came to the house to inform them of the accident, Diane and Kohl were told that no one was needed to ID the body, since the victim's identity could be established only through dental X-rays. The policeman also told them that the rented Corvette was the only vehicle involved in the accident, that a young woman had been with Ken and was also a fatality, and that the car had exploded and burned after rolling down a steep hillside near the suburban town of Woodinville.

Over the next few days, checking out the site and talking with reporters and the police, Kohl learned all he could about the accident, which had occurred near the dead end of a raw new dirt road bulldozed out of heavily timbered ground—a future housing development—in the Cascade foothills about twenty-five miles northeast of Seattle. It was surmised that Ken and the woman, a twenty-three-year-old named Marina Harris, had parked at the end of the road to drink wine cooler and have sex, and that afterward, in turning the car around, Ken inadvertently had backed too close to the edge of the road and the rear wheels had slipped through the soft shoulder. The car had rolled downhill about a hundred feet to the creekbed below, with the gas tank exploding on the way down, causing a fire that consumed not only Ken and the car but a dozen acres of woodland as well. The woman evidently had opened the passenger door and in trying to jump free had fallen under the car as it rolled. Her half-nude body, crushed but unburned, was found just under the collapsed shoulder of the road, near a opened bottle of wine cooler.

Diane had never heard of the woman, nor had Bobbi or Kohl, who was dogged in his quest for information about her, thinking there would be a connection between her and Tony

Jack. But there was none. A native of Montana, she had moved to Seattle three years earlier, had worked as a clerk-typist at Boeing, was unmarried and unattached. She lived in an apartment in the town of Edmonds, just north of Seattle, far from any conceivable route that Ken and the red-haired man might have taken as they carried out the weird business of that weird and fateful day. The girl's presence in the car with Ken strongly supported Diane's theory that Ken had lost his nerve at the last minute, had broken off his tailing of the blue Cadillac in favor of trying to find sanctuary in the arms of a woman, *any* woman.

In his dealings with the police, Kohl had to be very careful, trying to make sure they didn't overlook the possibility of foul play without at the same time revealing his true reasons for suspecting it, since—as Diane continued to point out—any mention of Tony Jack would have led inevitably to the subject of the briefcase, the hit-and-run, and their own involvement. Kohl had told the police that Ken was an incurable womanizer and that there were undoubtedly a number of cuckolded husbands who wouldn't have minded seeing him dead. When the police asked for specific names, he said Ken's affairs had been so numerous that he'd never bothered to keep up. But even as he was telling this to the police, he could see that they were only indulging him, that they thought the circumstances of the accident were obvious. And finally one of the state troopers, a sergeant, patiently articulated this.

"Look, Mr. Kohl, we know you cared for the guy. But as you yourself pointed out, he was something of a cocksman. It ain't hard to believe he'd pick up this chick and park out here. And it ain't hard to see he'd have a problem backing around— you can tell where the road shoulder just crumbled away. And when a car's rollin' downhill with the engine still runnin'— well, they do catch fire now and then. So if I were you, I'd let it go. Your cousin died in an *accident*."

Kohl knew that his quibbles with the sergeant's scenario would sound feeble, but he voiced them anyway: that Ken was a snob and would rather have gone thirsty than drink wine cooler; that he had been burned so badly he could have been beaten to death and the coroner wouldn't have been able to tell; and that the fire trucks had obliterated all other tire tracks, possibly those of a car that had followed Ken—or even brought his body—down the dead-end road.

The sergeant was not swayed. "Well, maybe the girl was the only one drinking. And the other things don't constitute proof of anything. An apparent accident is just that, unless there's proof to the contrary."

Not wanting to come across as a total jerk, Kohl feigned enlightenment. "Yeah, I can see your point," he said. "An accident is an accident—"

"—is an accident," the sergeant concluded, smiling modestly at his erudition.

Diane was only too happy to buy the accident scenario. It not only proved how right her instincts had been on the night the police came, but it also freed her and Kohl from having to come forward about the briefcase and the hit-and-run—and their own involvement. Best of all, it took Tony Jack right out of the picture, and right out of their lives. If he and his cohorts had never made contact with Ken, then they knew nothing about Diane and Kohl. The stranger who waylaid his men in the alley would remain only that, a stranger. As for Bobbi, she was so openly and honestly grief-stricken that there at first didn't seem to be any room in her for curiosity as to *how* Ken died. On the night the police came, it was she, not Diane, who insisted on going with Kohl to view the body, even though the police officer made it clear that no legal identification could be made. Diane said simply that she didn't want to see the body, that she preferred to remember Ken as he was. Though Kohl understood her feelings in this, in fact dreaded what he was about to do, he felt compelled to drive up to the Snohomish County morgue anyway—because he had to *know*, had to see for himself that there actually was a body, and if possible that it was Ken's.

After driving the twenty miles to the small town with the Indian name, Kohl and Bobbi found the funeral home that served as the county morgue. Inside, a man with no hair rolled out the drawer that held Ken's body and Bobbi sagged against Kohl, crying softly. Kohl himself had to bite down hard to stifle a howl of anguish. The body looked like a skeleton covered with road tar. Yet Kohl could see that it *was* Ken. And outside, weeping in the truck, Bobbi agreed.

"I could tell by the side of his eyes," she mourned. "I used to love to just feel his face, you know? His eyebrows was just so perfeck, you know, and right at the end of 'em there was this kinda little round point you could feel. *And it's there, Tom! I could see it!*"

The next day, when Bobbi learned that he and Diane were going to take the body back to Illinois for burial, she hinted not very subtly that she was willing to make it a threesome, saying that though she'd never flown before, she wasn't at all afraid to do so. She also said how lucky the two of them were, being able "to see Kin laid to rest." But instead of inviting her, Diane told Kohl that if he didn't get the girl out of the house she was going to call the police and have her arrested for trespassing.

Once again Kohl packed Bobbi into his truck, this time driving her over to Seattle, to her mother's northside bungalow. He pulled into the driveway to let her out, but the girl didn't move.

"I sure wanta see my babies," she said. "But my ma, now that's a horse of a different color."

Kohl asked her why.

"Oh, she's always on my case about gittin' a job. A *good* job, she says. But all I know is bein' a barmaid. She acts like it's being' a whore or somethin'."

Kohl told her to take care of herself and that he would phone her when he got back from Illinois.

"You promise?"

"Cross my heart."

But Bobbi still didn't get out. "Boy, I hate to come home broke. Kin, he was always givin' me money. It sure helped out, 'specially when you got two little mouths to feed."

Kohl couldn't help grinning. "You know, you ought to get a tin cup and go downtown. You'd be rich in no time."

"Hey, I ain't hittin' on you, Tom," she said. "I was just sayin' what Kin used to do."

Kohl had taken out his wallet. "Would a hundred dollars help?"

"A little," she allowed.

"Good. Then here's a little help."

For Kohl the hundred dollars represented ten hours of hard work, a considerably larger gift than he imagined Ken had ever given her. She thanked him, pocketed the money, and though she had opened the door, she still didn't move. And finally it came—the question Kohl had been hurling at himself ever since the police knocked on Diane's door.

"You think Tony Jack done it?"

"I don't know," he said.

"But what do you *think*?"

He didn't answer immediately, mostly because he still wasn't sure *what* he thought. But when he opened his mouth, there it was. "It's just too big a coincidence—Ken dying on the very day Tony Jack's trying to get his hands on him."

Bobbi looked amazed. "That's just what I was thinkin'! And I just can't buy it."

Now that it was said, Kohl could feel himself already beginning to lose it, like a handful of grain. "At the same time, the thing does look like an accident—the girl being with him and all."

"Maybe that's why she was there."

"You mean, Jack throws the girl in, just to throw us off?"

Bobbi shrugged. "Why not?"

"Because it doesn't make any sense. Even without the girl, there wasn't any solid evidence connecting Jack to the accident."

"So what's gonna happen? You just fly Kin home and bury him? And that's that?"

Kohl already hated his answer, but he couldn't think of another one. "And that's that," he said.

Now, flying six miles above the Great Plains, Kohl continued to be amazed at how easily Diane seemed to accept Ken's death, almost like a widow who had long endured her husband's fatal illness and now felt only release. She even wore the weeds to prove it, a Nehru-type gray suit with black accessories, dark hose, and not a touch of color. At times Kohl halfway expected to look over and find her face hidden behind a veil, though it would have been a totally wasted gesture, since her clear green eyes looked as if they hadn't shed a tear since childhood. As far as Kohl could tell, the main thing Ken's death stimulated in her was a mood of fond remembrance.

"You probably wonder why I'm not more pissed because he had that girl with him at the end," she said, smiling reflectively. "*Practice*, Tom. Practice. You have no idea how women came on to him, especially when he was in advertising and dressed the part—power suits and all the rest. Why, I don't think we ever ate dinner without some waitress or fag sommelier drooling all over him. I could have had on a designer dress—something that would normally stop traffic—and no one gave me a second look, not with Mister Gorgeous across the table from me. So I always made allowances, you know? I mean, the average guy doesn't get hit on when he's with his fiancée, right? But Ken did, all the time. So I figured a dalliance here and there, you really couldn't blame him. Which is probably why I don't care that he had a girl with him at the end." She smiled again, but wryly this time. "Bobbi, yes—that got to me—that his standards had sunk so low."

"Well, it's true she didn't seem like Ken's type," Kohl allowed. And Diane gave him a look.

"More your type, would you say?"

"Could be."

"Men!" Shaking her head in benign exasperation, she began to reminisce about the first two years she and Ken had lived together, in a loft apartment in Seattle's old Pioneer Square district. She lovingly recalled how eagerly Ken had joined her in trying to furnish the place "creatively," how they had scoured both sides of Puget Sound, looking for just the right kind of barber chair and barber pole and the perfect player piano and all the other "funky stuff" that was so "in" at the time.

As she ran on, painting the past in warm sepia tones, Kohl was tempted to inject a note of cold reality into the proceedings, asking her Bobbi's question about Tony Jack; but because he already knew Diane's position on that, he chose a note closer to hers in tone, reflective and almost wistful, yet in essence the same dash of cold water.

"A weird coincidence, wasn't it, him dying on the very day Tony Jack was gunning for him."

"Gunning?" she said.

"Hunting, then."

She looked at him with exasperation again, only this time there was nothing benign in it.

"You're not going to let go of it, are you? Like a dog with a bone. Only in this case the bone is a stick of dynamite. And you're going to keep chewing on it until—"

"What if we had proof Ken was murdered?" Kohl cut in.

"But we *don't.* And the police don't. It was an *accident,* Tom. And if you can't accept that—" She didn't bother to finish the thought.

"I plan to move out anyway," he said. "Soon as we get back."

"And what about the boat?"

"Don't worry, I'll finish it."

She just sat there looking at him like a fond but troubled and disappointed mother. Then she smiled sadly and reached for his hand. "I'm sorry," she said. "But I can't deal with your Tony Jack problem, not now, with Ken's family and all still ahead of us. Without you, I don't know if I could cut it."

"I'm right here," he said.

She squeezed his hand. "Good. And you stay right there, okay? I'm really scared. I've never met them, you know."

Kohl thought of his uncle and aunt and their two daughters, both older than Ken. "They're just people," he said, though there had been times in his life when he wouldn't have accorded them that distinction. "You'll knock 'em dead," he added.

And Diane did. After changing planes in Chicago, she and Kohl arrived in Bloomington in early evening. At first things were predictably stiff and uncomfortable, with old Ralph Ryder trying to bear up under the double burden of grief for his son and irritation at the interruption of his daily fishing routine in northern Wisconsin. Kohl's Aunt Ruth was truly devastated, but the sisters—a divorcée and an old maid—looked as if they had come to the airport chiefly to inspect Diane, the harlot with whom their little brother had been living in sin for so many years. They were no match for Diane, however, who made her considerable living charming all kinds of people. And she did so now, smiling through tears, moving confidently and graciously from one to the other as Kohl introduced her. She wisely only shook hands with the sisters but embraced Aunt Ruth and even old Ralph, who at that moment had the look of Cotton Mather at an orgy, unsure whether to join in or call down the wrath of God.

Diane's beauty and style and warmth obviously disarmed the parents while striking fear and loathing into the hearts of the sisters, both of whom unfortunately resembled their father: tall and gaunt, with the beak and eyes of a famished hawk. Ken's mother, on the other hand, was small and plump, with just a trace left of the cuteness she'd undoubtedly had as a teenager. All of which left Ken something of an oddity in the family, his good looks apparently a fortuitous compromise between the mother's fleeting prettiness and old Ralph's scraggly aquilinity.

Diane's conquest of Uncle Ralph wasn't complete, however, until he saw Ken's casket coming off the plane, dazzling in the late-afternoon sun.

"By God, if that don't look like bronze!" he said.

"That's what it is, all right," Kohl assured him, thinking that he hadn't tried hard enough to talk Diane out of buying the damned thing, though he had pointed out that it would only go into the ground, all five thousand dollars' worth of it. But she was not to be swayed.

"Ken deserves the best," she'd said.

Like a lot of penny-pinchers, Uncle Ralph tended to crow about his purchases, and Kohl had little doubt that in the days to come his uncle would point out to anyone who would listen that his son's solid bronze casket had cost five thousand dollars, without bothering to add that he wasn't the one who had bought it.

Ralph had come to the airport alone in his pickup, so he and Kohl could drive back to Blanton together while the women returned in the family's new Chevy Caprice.

"We got things to talk about," he said to Kohl.

From the beginning, notifying Aunt Ruth and Uncle Ralph of Ken's death had been a complicated affair. Kohl had told the state police that he would take care of the matter, but they explained to him that there also had to be an official notification. After Kohl had phoned his uncle in Wisconsin, telling him what had happened, Ralph and Aunt Ruth were contacted by the police there, who had been notified by the Blanton County sheriff, who in turn had been notified by the police in Washington state. Like Kohl, the various departments had tried to spare Ken's parents some of the details of his death— but not always the *same* details, with the result that Uncle Ralph "smelled a rat," as he put it now.

"Just what is the truth, anyway?" he asked. "Was Ken drunk at the time? And who was this woman he was with? Was he steppin' out on Diane, huh? I want the truth."

"What'd the police tell you?"

"The hell with what the police told me! I wanta hear what you got to say."

Kohl told him that though he didn't know the woman, he figured she was a real estate agent, because she and Ken were driving through land that had just been opened up for development and Ken sometimes sniffed out promising tracts for Diane to invest in.

"She got that much money, huh?"

"She does all right."

"So Ken and this woman was just drivin' out in the woods, huh? And his car just happened to ketch fire and he just happened to stay right there in it until he burned to a crisp, is that it?"

Kohl shook his head. "Uncle Ralph, you know that isn't what I told you. The road was newly bulldozed and the shoulder gave way. The car rolled a good hundred feet down the hill and the gas tank exploded. Ken never had a chance."

Uncle Ralph made do with that, for the time being anyway. He was also interested in Ken's estate, any insurance Ken had or property he might have left. "After all, he was thirty-three years old," the old man said. "He musta 'cumulated somethin' in all that time. And his ma and me, we're his next of kin, remember. He wasn't married."

Kohl told him again—as he had on the phone—that there was no will, that Ken had no life insurance, and that all he'd owned of value was the stolen Bronco.

"What about that boat he was always talkin' about on the phone?"

"It's Diane's."

"Ken never said that."

Kohl shrugged. "Well, you can check on it. You can hire a lawyer and spend money to check on it. But it's still hers. She bought and paid for it."

The old man shook his head in disgust. "Thirty-three years

old—a man—and what did he have to show for it? *Nothin'*."

"Just like his cousin," Kohl said.

Over the next few days Diane put on something of a fashion show for bland old Blanton, changing her outfits two and three times daily, depending on the occasion. There was the "visitation" and the memorial service, the graveside ceremony, and finally a potluck supper at the Ryder home, thrown by the ladies of the Philathea Class of the First Baptist Church. Throughout, Diane performed like a visiting celebrity, doing her star turn to perfection, smiling sadly and graciously in her designer suits and dresses, a congeries of gray and black, including black lace gloves and even a mantilla-like hat. Most of the time old Ralph was at her side, so taken by her that no one dared give her the cold shoulder, since Ralph was still one of the richest men in the area, thanks to the improvidence of Kohl and his parents.

But even when she was alone, Diane managed to maintain her elegance and graciousness, often in the face of real difficulty, such as that presented by gnarled old farm couples who planted themselves in front of her and stared as if she'd just dropped in from outer space. When she reached out to shake the hand of Carl Techsler, a worker at the feed mill, he made a panicked move as though to kiss her gloved hand and then tried to cover his embarrassment by pumping her hand so long and hard that his wife had to dig him in the ribs before he would let go.

Kohl and Diane got through the days of Ken's funeral step by step. Kohl shot the breeze with his old school buddies and farmer friends and even had a short conversation with his ex-wife, Julie, who looked as pretty and childlike as ever. She was engaged to be married again, to the manager of the local Wal-Mart, a job that her parents evidently thought was only one step down from being Sam Walton himself.

Other than his family and Kohl and Diane, Ken's chief mourners were the girls he had dated in high school, a virtual cheerleader squad grown older—some already into dowdy middle age while others looked better than ever—girls Kohl had known well. And it was he they opened up to, crying freely, telling him how close they and Ken had been, even how much in love. And like their mothers and grandmothers, they said, practically in unison: *"He was so handsome!"*

The funeral itself wasn't particularly touching. The pastor, a young Minnesotan new to the area, seemed more interested in saving souls than in the late Kenneth Ryder. The choir was egregiously off-key, and the pallbearers—five farmers and Kohl—experienced some difficulty carrying the heavy casket to the cemetery, which adjoined the church. Once there, however—and once the pastor forsook his own words for those in the Bible—sorrow washed over the crowd like a sudden wind. Through tears, Kohl looked past the casket, down the hill to the area where his parents' graves were, in the shade of a maple tree that had survived a lightning strike. And after the ceremony he walked down to the side-by-side graves and stood alone for a while, an only child still trying to comprehend the loss of the two persons he loved most in all the world. The modest stones he'd bought for them were only about a foot high and wedge-shaped, with room for their names and dates and little else. Anyway, at the time Kohl couldn't think of anything to say about either of them—anything *brief*. It seemed like trying to pour Lake Michigan into a cup.

In time, Diane came down the hill and stood with him. She hesitantly reached out to hold him, then gripped him tightly as he put his arm around him. And they walked that way back to the limo, undoubtedly raising a few eyebrows, especially those of Ken's sisters. Later, after the potluck supper, Diane changed into jeans and a T-shirt and rode with him over to his family's farm, or at least what had once been their farm. Though he normally would have enjoyed her company, he wasn't enthusiastic about her being with him now, since he had a pretty good idea of what lay ahead of him and how he would react to it, and he imagined that she was going to feel like an intruder. But he said nothing, and soon they were driving up the gravel lane in Uncle Ralph's truck to the homely, squarish white house sitting in the shade of a half-dozen oak trees, with a windbreak of pines running along the north and west sides of the farmyard.

The house was more gray than white now, and some of the windows were broken and the side screen door hung askew. The grass was uncut and littered with toys and tires and random oddities, including a Christmas wreath and a baby buggy with missing wheels. Three tiny Mexican children, one of them naked, were playing happily among the clutter. When Kohl and Diane got out of the truck the children's mother came to the side door, chubby and barefoot, looking scared.

Kohl had been told that a "beaner" had rented the house from the company that had taken over the farm, and he could understand the woman's uneasiness, especially if she and her husband were aliens. He told her who he was, that he used to work the farm and that he and his friend just wanted to wander around for a while. She nodded her agreement but didn't say anything, so Kohl smiled and went on, leading Diane out past the barn, which was a charred ruin now, the victim of corporate farmers rashly chocking it full of wet hay. Some of the other outbuildings, singed in the fire, were still standing. But Kohl wasn't interested in the buildings or even in the fields. Rather, it was the oak woods that drew him, just as it had all through his childhood: the cool, dark serenity of the place, like a cathedral to play in, with birdsong instead of choirs and the musk of decayed leaves for incense and the trees as the cathedral's pillars, immense old things, their trunks as thick as cracker barrels.

Diane held his hand as they took the path that led through the woods toward the sulfur pond. "And this is where you two played," she said. "It's beautiful, Tom."

He was silent for a time and then he slowly pulled it out of him, the long, barbed thorn an old friend had casually planted at the visitation. "I hear they're gonna cut it all down," he said. "I guess there's a big market for quality oak. Stouter cocktail tables and the like."

Diane put her arm around him and tried to lay her face against his shoulder, but it was hard to walk that way and she settled for holding his hand again. He helped her through the wire fence where his father had shot himself, but for some reason he didn't bother to tell her what had happened there. They went single-file down the steep hill to the pond itself, and in the moss-rock springhouse there Kohl filled a tin cup with the cold sulfurous water that poured endlessly out of the hillside. Offering the cup to Diane, Kohl kept his silence, not mentioning that he and his father had built the springhouse.

After tasting the water, Diane made a face. "Ugh! People actually drink this stuff?"

"They used to, anyway. All kinds of people used to come down here and fill their jugs and take the water home. Claimed it cured all sorts of ills."

"And did it?"

Kohl thought of his mother. "Not that I know of."

On the way back, he led Diane off the path a short distance to see the creek that cut through the northeast corner of the woods. And while they stood there pitching pebbles into the water, Kohl looked across the narrow stream at the tree in which he and Ken had built a treehouse one summer. A few of its boards were still left, including part of the floor frame, two-by-fours resting securely in the forks of two thick limbs thirty feet above the ground. Once again Kohl almost went on without confiding in Diane. Then he changed his mind.

"See those boards up in the tree over there? It's what's left of a treehouse we built—oh, it must be over twenty years ago now."

"You and Ken?"

"Yeah," he said, knowing that his voice would break if he continued. But he went on anyway. "Yeah, we took a blood oath up there, Ken and me. We vowed that if one of us was ever murdered, the other wouldn't do anything about it. Not one goddam fucking thing."

Lying back in his seat in the dimness, Kohl could feel the thing growing inside him, like a cancer taking root, burrowing in, waxing fat and sleek. What pained him most was the knowledge that it would continue to grow and he wouldn't be able to do a thing about it, or more correctly, would *choose* not to do anything about it. And if he hadn't realized this before, he did now, after a long and at times silly conversation with Diane.

Because of all the summer vacationers, the two of them had to settle for a night flight out of O'Hare, and almost from the moment of takeoff she went to work on him. This time she based her argument not on the practical grounds of evidence and self-incrimination, but on the clichés of pop philosophy: that somewhere along the line a person had to choose between the light and the dark, between life and death, and in his case, between quixotic self-destruction and the mature acceptance of the world as it was. By way of illustration, she ticked off all the reasons for his believing that Tony Jack was guilty of killing Ken, and one by one dissected those reasons, holding them up to the light of feminine logic and common sense, almost indifferently showing him the ragged edges and gaping holes in each of them.

She went on then to tell him what his life would be like if he chose "the light." He was very intelligent, she said. He was physically strong and had "great presence," qualities that would help a man succeed in business the same as in a blue-collar job. His experience in farming and home-building had taught him a lot about finance and machinery and construction, and she pointed out that he already had a couple of years of college. After the boat was finished he should take night-school

THE LION AT THE DOOR

courses in real estate law and financial management, and after he'd completed them she would introduce him to a couple of "developer friends" of hers, men who built industrial parks, condominium developments, and even "whole retirement communities."

"If you got your foot in the door, Tom, you could really score," she said. "In time, you could be rich. You could have everything you want."

"Just like that?"

"Yes, just like that. They'd love to hire you. It's one of the few ways little men can have power over guys like you—by having you work for them."

"Sounds like fun."

"It could be. But only if you wanted it. Only if you decide you want to be a grown-up. Only if you consciously choose the good over the bad, and life over death."

"Only if I forget about Tony Jack."

"Exactly. Because it doesn't go anywhere. It's like quitting during a game. You figure you can't win at life, so you choose—"

"Death."

"Right"

Kohl couldn't help grinning. "You haven't been reading L. Ron Hubbard, have you?"

"I've read him, yes," she said. "And lots more."

"New stuff, uh? Let me guess—*Inspirational Capitalism*?"

"Never heard of it."

"Or then there's *You Too Can Be a Tycoon*."

Smiling sweetly, Diane put her face right into his. *"Fuck you, loser,"* she whispered, turning away from him then and stretching out in her seat, her face just inches away from the jet's tiny window and the starry night outside.

Kohl had settled back after that, thinking he had won the argument, or at least this incarnation of it. But as he sat there in the dimness, smoking and sipping at his drink, glancing occasionally at the hairpin curves of Diane's body and the golden tangle of her hair, he began to go over her argument against involvement. And he was surprised at how incontrovertible it sounded, presented point by point. First, Diane said, there never had been any valid reason to believe that Tony Jack would do anything to Ken once he found out that Ken was the driver of the hit-and-run vehicle. Jack had never made any such a threat. Though he had a criminal record, or at least had been arrested many times, it was for crimes such as loan-sharking and pandering, not for acts of violence.

Second, it made no sense that he would kill in order to try to recover his dead brother's briefcase. All that the items in the briefcase proved was that the brother, Richard—not Tony Jack himself—figured in Ricky Ross's death. Richard could have been carrying on his own loan-sharking operation. And since Richard died in the hit-and-run—and therefore could not be prosecuted—there was no reason for Tony Jack to risk anything in order to acquire the briefcase.

Third, it wasn't Tony Jack who had gone gunning for Ken, but Ken who had tried to neutralize Jack with a preemptive strike. It was Ken's paranoia, not Jack's hypothetical lust for revenge, that led to the contact. In fact, among all the parties, the only *known* intentional violence committed so far was by Kohl himself, in the alley behind the strip joint.

Fourth, if Tony Jack, flying in the face of all reason, had killed Ken—after Ken so conveniently dropped himself on Jack's doorstep—why would he kill the girl too? And in daylight? The mob way would have been a shotgunning or cement overshoes worn somewhere in the Sound. And if Tony Jack had done it out of hubris, to show the world what happened to those who even accidentally harmed a blood brother, why would he kill Ken in such a way that it was judged an accident? He certainly couldn't enhance his reputation as a tough guy that way. No, much better to have Ken shotgunned on Lake Street— while Jack sat among friends and cohorts in a downtown restaurant.

And finally, said Diane, the whole idea was simply absurd. Even if Ken *was* murdered, there was no more reason to suspect Tony Jack of doing it than any number of other people, including Rusty or an unknown boyfriend of Marina Harris, or even a drifter.

Finished, she took Kohl's face in her hands and, having his full attention, softly and slowly summed it all up for him. "It was an accident, Tom. That's all—a stupid, motherfucking accident."

And that was how Diane carried the day, not with her subsequent pop-philosophy disquisition on choosing life over death, success over failure, but with her point-by-point presentation of the case for Tony Jack *not* being responsible for Ken's death. Even then, Kohl wasn't ready to concede, not until later, as she napped and he sat there next to her, sipping scotch and mulling her words. What convinced him finally was the realization that there wasn't one single point she'd made that he hadn't already considered on his own—considered and rejected—because he *wanted* to believe Jack guilty. But hearing the same ideas, the same doubts, from someone as coolly logical as Diane made a difference, in fact made *all* the difference, to the point where he felt he had no real choice except to go along with her.

It was a decision that gave him no pleasure, however, because it meant that he would have to go on living with his doubts, the cancer of suspicion that had taken root in him. But then that was life, nothing more or less. It was but another tough row to hoe. He had done it before; he could do it again.

Having decided this, he signaled to the stewardess and she brought him another scotch, along with a blanket for Diane. When he covered her, she moved slightly, but continued to lie on her side, facing the window. Then a little later, after he'd finished his drink, she rolled over and held her finger to her mouth.

"Sh-h, let me show you something," she said. "Something Ken taught me on a flight back from Hawaii."

While he watched in fascination, she maneuvered the armrest up between their seats and then tripped a lever that allowed her to lift out the plate the armrest had sat on. She then carefully slipped the plate under her seat.

"There," she said, smiling. "Now you can cuddle up and keep me warm."

As she rolled away from him again, Kohl did just as she asked, spreading the blanket over both of them and moving up against her and putting his arm around her, but gingerly, as if he feared being burned. He couldn't help feeling that there was a barrier between the two of them now just as rigid as the armrest had been, only much more permanent. And he believed that Diane felt this too, because she had placed her arm over his, undoubtedly to discourage him from reaching up and holding her breasts. At the same time, because he felt himself growing hard, he edged backward on the seat.

"You sure you want me to hold you?" he whispered.

She took his hand and moved it onto her breast. "I'm sure," she said.

7 Two weeks later Kohl and Bobbi were out on the Williwaw in the middle of the lake, with the engines turned off and Bobbi's radio turned on, playing country music. It was a hot day, over ninety degrees, and when the two of them went swimming off the transom, Bobbi couldn't stop gasping, either at the coldness of the water or at the thought of so much of it—hundreds of feet—between her gooseflesh and the lake bottom. Kohl meanwhile repeatedly dove from the surface, swimming straight down farther than he should have, each time wondering how it would feel to keep on going, past the point of safe return. Afterward Bobbi sunbathed on the foredeck while Kohl sat in the cabin's shade, drinking a beer and glancing over at her now and then, acutely aware of her full figure and how little of it Diane's bikini covered. At the same time, he knew that the girl wasn't coming on to him, that she was still a long way from letting go of Ken, and he liked that in her. He wished Diane felt the same way.

While Kohl was still in Illinois, Bobbi had found a night job as a cocktail waitress in Bellevue, which meant that she had to drive over to the Eastside each day. And, as she began dropping in at the marina most afternoons, Kohl was surprised to discover that he looked forward to seeing her and wasn't even annoyed by her vapid chatter, though there admittedly wasn't as much of it now, with Ken gone.

Kohl had finished working on the boat the previous week and since then had been taking lessons from one of the other marina tenants, a retired ferry-boat captain with a lot of time on his hands and a real need to be out on the water, preferably with someone other than his wife, "someone who don't knit," as he put it. Under his expert guidance, Kohl had learned at least some of the yachtsman's lore, including the fact that nothing in a yacht could be called by its common English name. Stairs were a gangway, the kitchen was a galley, ropes were lines, and so on. In addition, Kohl learned how to take the boat out and in, in rough water and calm, and how to tie it up, how to anchor it properly, even how to pilot the big, lovely thing. Twice he'd taken it across the lake and through Seattle's ship canal and the Ballard locks out into the Sound. The captain taught him how to read depth and tide charts and even gave him an hour's instruction in dead reckoning, though Kohl doubted he would ever need navigation skills, since all he planned to do was demonstrate the boat to prospective buyers.

It was Diane's quite reasonable idea that Kohl learn all this so she could sell the boat on her own, without paying the ten percent commission a marine broker would have charged. Instead she would pay Kohl one-third that amount, a good four or five thousand dollars, depending on the selling price. Kohl willingly had gone along with the idea, even to the point of postponing looking for a new job until after the on-board launch-day party she was busy planning for, and which would include a couple of prospective buyers.

On this particular day, though, Kohl wasn't getting much of anything done. He could have been practicing "clearings" and "landings," as the captain called leaving and returning to the slip. But the air was still and hot and the water much too calm for there to be any challenge in either maneuver. So when Bobbi had suggested they go for a swim, he readily agreed. And a short time later, when she told him she was freezing, he had helped her out of the water and joined her on the deck. Now it was after three o'clock and he knew she had to be at her job by five.

"Time we head in," he said, getting up.

But Bobbi had a problem. "Oh shit, Tom, I'm all sweaty again. I'm just gonna dip in again and come right back out, okay?"

Knowing she wasn't very confident in the water, Kohl followed her down the ladder to the transom. Also, by being there he was able to give her a hand again coming back aboard, which wasn't an easy task on the Williwaw, since the ladder didn't extend down into the water. Back inside the cabin, Kohl restarted the engines while Bobbi went below to change. When she came back up, she gestured with the bikini.

"What do I do with this? If Diane finds out I wore it, she'll burn it, right?"

"At least."

Bobbi smiled. "Maybe I should just take it with me."

"Or maybe you should just hang it out in the sun—how about that?"

"Killjoy," she said.

After hanging up the bikini, she came back in and stood close to Kohl, with a hand on his shoulder to steady herself, since even in calm water there was a degree of motion when the boat was underway. They were still about two miles out, heading southeast toward Yarrow Bay. The water was deep-blue and sun-spangled, and the engines purred like fat cats as the boat moved along at a modest ten knots.

Bobbi shook her head admiringly. "Boy, I bet this is just what Kin had in mind—sittin' right where you are, headin' across the water, everything just perfeck, you know?"

"Yeah, I imagine so," Kohl said.

"Only he woulda had on one of them little billed caps like the captain wears."

Kohl grinned. "That's a fact."

"And a blue blazer."

"With brass buttons."

Bobbi's eyes brimmed. "And he woulda been just beautiful," she said.

When Kohl got home, Diane was finishing up with the caterer, a woman who looked eerily like Diane herself, only brunette and a decade older. In spite of this, the two of them appeared to get along beautifully. They had spread a catalog out on the dining-room table, and while Diane paged through it the woman was making out a list of some kind. Diane interrupted their labors only long enough to introduce Kohl as "my captain, Thomas Kohl," and Kohl had all he could do to keep from saluting smartly. Though he left the room as they got back to work, he was still able to hear their deliberations.

"Smoked salmon, but only as an hors d'oeuvre."

"And Sauvignon Blanc, you say?"

"Oh yes, definitely. And almost any of the state labels will do. They're really fine."

"I'm still uneasy about having only one steward, though. Some of the men will want hard liquor, you just know the bastards will. So the boy will be busy with that."

"But it's a question of room, my dear. You can't have that many people on that size boat and still have a full staff."

"Just *two*," Diane pleaded.

And the woman laughed. "All right, then—*two*. And I know just the couple for you. Filipinos. A tiny little couple, and *so* efficient you won't believe it. You won't even know they're there."

"Excellent."

Later, after the caterer was gone and after Kohl had show-ered and changed, Diane came back to his room, sipping at a glass of champagne.

"You weren't exactly Mister Warmth, were you?" she said.

"Is that required of your captain?"

"I thought it was of everyone. At least in a civilized soci-ety."

"So that's what this is."

Having just showered herself, she was wearing a terry robe and had her hair turbaned in a towel. She smelled delicious and looked even better, especially as she gave him a smile, ironically pouting.

"Let's not fight," she said. "I have a client dinner later, and right now I'm in dire need of one of your famous massages."

It had become their private joke, a code word, starting soon after their return from Illinois. Diane had come home late from work so tired she didn't even want to eat, and Kohl had wound up giving her a massage, in her room, on her bed. And in time they made love, not as passionately as they had on that first night, but then neither was it so maddeningly perfunctory and unsatisfying as their second time together. He still had to use a condom, but along the way Diane did much more than just lie back and *take*. In fact, there were moments when she was almost ardent, and Kohl as a result got so carried away with desire for her that he didn't give a moment's thought to Ken. And it had been much the same since then, with her suggesting a massage or smiling in a certain way, always the initiator, always in control. For if it was Kohl who made the first move, nothing happened—she would have a headache or some pressing engagement or simply wouldn't feel like it.

Kohl also found it frustrating that in between their cou-plings they didn't behave at all as lovers, didn't kiss hello or goodbye, didn't cuddle in front of the fire or indulge in horse-play or even sleep together—because that was the way Diane wanted it. But he was so filled with the woman—so driven by love or lust—that for a while anyway he had no trouble overlooking such shortcomings. Her cool green eyes and perfect smile and softly authoritative voice so mesmerized him that he sometimes wondered if there was anything she could say or do that he would not accept. Naked, she was truly something to behold: small-boned and slender, yet so well-knit he could see the line of muscle running from her breasts to her pubis. And when she lay on her side her hip seemed virtually boneless, a swell of flesh so maddeningly perfect that he practically growled as he nipped at her and kissed her, often running his mouth down the whole lovely roller-coaster of her, from golden hair to vermilion toenails. And once, as he was going down on her, she burst into laughter because of his hairy back, saying that now she knew how Little Red Riding Hood had felt. Although the laughter hadn't lasted, the sex was good, the feelings were good.

Unfortunately those feelings didn't exist outside her bedroom. Once out of there, it was back to business as usual, with Captain Tom still sleeping in the servant's room and Princess Diane going on about her affairs. And Kohl was getting angrier by the day at the situation. He tried as dispassionately as he could to analyze that anger and decided finally that it was threefold: because she was treating him like a stud horse; because he wanted her so much he accepted such treatment; and because of guilt over Ken. And the fact that Diane didn't seem to share this feeling of guilt only served to strengthen it in Kohl.

So he was not in the best of moods as he followed her up to her room for yet another "massage." And he was not overly gentle as he kneaded her back and shoulders with what she continued to refer to as his "big mitts." But she didn't complain at all, and later, when he made love to her the same way, in a cold rage of lust, she seemed to enjoy herself more than ever. Afterward, rather than stay for the few minutes of tenderness she normally allowed them, he got out of bed and slipped into his robe.

"What's the big hurry?" she asked.

"I'm going to shower again."

"Why? Am I that unclean?"

"Of course not."

"Well, what is it, then? Is it Ken?"

Kohl looked at her. "Ken who?" he said.

As he headed in his truck out across the Evergreen Point bridge, Kohl had the odd feeling that he wasn't consciously choosing to do what he was doing but rather was acting out of a compulsion so deeply set in him that he had no business questioning it or even trying to analyze the thing. All he wanted was to *act,* to roll up his sleeves and climb right down into the corral with the beast and learn where the breaking point was— in him or in it. And the only way to do that, he knew, was through pressure, by taking hold of its tail and twisting until the beast twitched, until it bellowed and kicked and finally lowered its thick, ugly head and charged into the chute—and helplessness. Either that or the exact opposite, for there had been times when Kohl, working with bulls, had seen the damnable creatures tear down most of a corral out of nothing but irritability.

He drove on past the university and around Lake Union and up the steep hill to the Queen Anne district, turning finally onto the short street that came to a dead end at Tony Jack's house, with the familiar spaceship hovering over the backyard hedge. The structures nearest the house were a condo apartment building on the downhill side of the street and a wooden Victorian mansion on the other side. Kohl parked just past the mansion, facing Jack's house, so he could observe it with ease—and be seen doing just that. Knowing it might be hours before anyone in the house saw him and even longer before they tried anything, Kohl had brought a thermos of coffee with him, along with the .45 automatic. As before, he didn't believe there would be any need for the weapon, but he felt a good deal safer with it lying next to him on the seat inside a brown paper bag.

If Diane had known what he was doing and had asked him what he hoped to accomplish by it—staking out the man's house—he would have been hard pressed to come up with a reasonable answer. For one thing, the likelihood was that Tony Jack would be at his place of business all evening and that someone else—his wife or mother, or the oriental maid—would see Kohl first and instead of phoning Jack would simply call the police to come and check out the suspicious-looking man parked in front. If that turned out to be the case, Kohl accepted it that he would have some tall explaining to do, especially if the police discovered what was in the brown paper bag.

On the other hand, if Jack was at home or if he returned during the course of the evening, he might be the one to phone the police. And that, Kohl decided, was his best reason for being there—to find out if Jack *would* turn to the police. An innocent man almost certainly would. But Kohl was betting that Jack would do just what he had done after Kohl's visit to the strip club and the alley behind it: *nothing*. There hadn't even been a news report about the incident, and since Kohl knew that a number of onlookers had seen him and Bobbi drive off, with his Illinois license plate in plain view, and since the police had never contacted him, he surmised that Tony Jack had dissuaded his brother and the redhead from pressing charges. *But why?* That was what Kohl wanted to know. Could it be, as he suspected, that Tony Jack simply didn't want the police even to *think* about a possible connection between him and the late Kenneth Ryder?

Kohl continued to sit there in his pickup truck, smoking cigarettes and having an occasional cup of coffee while he watched and waited. He had arrived at about eight in the evening; and because it was August now, that meant he had almost two hours before nightfall. And even after ten o'clock he knew he would be plainly visible, since his truck was the only

THE LION AT THE DOOR

vehicle parked in the street—the condos having their own parking facilities, just as the mansions had their three- and four-car garages. In addition, the street was well lit, as the streets of the urban rich tended to be.

In the hour between nine and ten, Kohl saw someone looking out at him from a front room in the house, a hand bending the blinds down for a better view. Then, at around ten, Tony Jack himself drove slowly past in a white Mercedes 450 SL, glancing over at Kohl in the truck but continuing on into his driveway and pulling around to the back, where the garage was. By then Kohl had his hand inside the paper bag, ready to bring the gun out at any moment. Unfortunately, within a few minutes of Jack's arrival, an elderly man in a silk bathrobe came out onto the Victorian mansion's huge wraparound porch and stood there looking at Kohl, shielding his eyes against the streetlights so he could see better. When he went back inside, Kohl didn't doubt that the police would be arriving soon.

A few minutes later he saw the headlights of a car coming very fast down the short street. Just as it was passing him, the car braked suddenly, tires screeching, and he saw that it was the redhead's old blue Cadillac as it slid into the curb in front of him. At the same time, the Mercedes came shooting out of Tony Jack's driveway and angled in behind Kohl's truck, braking sharply. Kohl had a bad couple of seconds, with shock or fear momentarily sucking the blood out of his head and extremities. Then the feeling passed and he quickly started the truck's engine, just to have it running, and stepped outside. Using the open door as a shield, he motioned with his gun to the redhead, who had come bounding out of the blue car, waving a tire iron.

"*Both of you—on the sidewalk!*" Kohl shouted, turning in the direction of Tony Jack, who was empty-handed, apparently unarmed.

Jack threw up his hands in a gesture of good-hearted consternation. "Okay, okay," he said, moving toward the sidewalk. "But what the fuck's with you, man? Why the fuckin' gun? I just came out here to talk with ya, ya know? Find out who the fuck you are and what's eatin' ya. You invade my house, you beat the shit outa my employees, and now you turn a gun on me. *And I don't even know who the fuck you are!*"

He was smiling and shaking his head and still holding up his hands, the incarnation of amiable puzzlement. Next to him on the sidewalk the redhead looked as if he were about to explode, his eyes were that round, his splotchy face that puffed up. Among the splotches were a couple of fresh scars, still red and ugly.

Kohl lowered the gun slightly. "I already told you. This cousin of mine who got in touch with you—who left certain items at Leschi and the Art Museum, which Red here picked up—"

Tony Jack was still grinning. "So?"

"So I warned you not to hurt him. Yet he died that same day." Kohl's eyes at that moment were locked on Tony Jack's face, searching it in the light of the streetlamp for the slightest tic of panic or fear.

But the elderly man had come out onto his porch again, waving a cane now and yelling something. Behind him, a white-haired lady stood in the mansion's doorway, looking out.

"Oh, for Christ sake," Jack muttered. "Not that old fart again."

The woman turned on the porchlight as the old man came down the stairs, still shouting. "That you, Giacalone? What in God's name are you up to now? What sort of neighborhood do you think this is, anyway? This time you've gone too far! This time you're going to have to answer to the police, Giacalone! They're on the way here right now!"

At that moment Kohl did see something new in Tony Jack's face, almost a canine snarl of rage and hatred as he turned toward his neighbor.

"You get back inside, you old fucker, and call off the police!" he yelled. "You hear me, you deaf old cocksucker? You call them back—and I mean *now!*"

"Like hell I will!" the old man bawled.

None of this was going the way Kohl had thought it would. He wasn't learning anything, wasn't getting any closer to the truth. All he knew for certain was that the longer he remained there, the more he had to fear, if not from Tony Jack then from the police. So while Jack was distracted by the old man, Kohl hurriedly slipped back into the truck and threw it into gear just as the redhead struck, smashing the tire iron into the windshield and pulling back to strike again, only to have Kohl peel out, burning rubber as the truck shot forward and slammed into the right rear corner of the Cadillac, tearing up the trunk and fender and—judging by the sudden odor of gasoline in the air—puncturing the gas tank. There was no explosion, however, not yet anyway. Kohl rammed the gearshift into reverse and went roaring backward toward Tony Jack's car. He heard the mobster yell *"Hey! No!"* just as the Chevy's massive bumper caved in the side of the Mercedes sports car, unhinging the door and smashing the driver's seat over to the passenger side. And it was evidently the door clattering to the pavement and striking a spark that set off the gasoline, creating a bright ribbon of fire that tore under Kohl's truck straight over to the blue Cadillac, which suddenly looked like a tin can trying to contain the sun, with doors and other debris flying in every direction as the car itself, a blackened silhouette now, bucked up into the air and slammed back down, burning brilliantly in the darkness.

Kohl managed to avoid the fireball as he swerved across the street and up onto the grassy parkway, U-turning back onto the pavement, headed in the other direction. Incredibly, Tony Jack had come running out into the street, waving his arms in front of the truck like a reasonable man, a traffic cop trying to establish some semblance of order. Kohl slowed down but kept moving, forcing him out of the way.

"Look, I just wanta talk with ya!" the mobster bawled. "Christ, what can you lose? I'll drive! You can hold your fuckin' gun on me!"

187

This too was something Kohl had never expected, yet he found himself braking now and throwing the door open. As he slid over to the passenger side, Tony Jack clambered in, bringing with him a pall of cologne so sweet-smelling that Kohl almost gagged.

"Stick shift!" Jack exclaimed. "Christ, I ain't drove one of these forever."

But he remembered how and very quickly they were at the top of his street and turning onto another, with Kohl looking back in amazement at the blazing car and the redhead in silhouette, standing there like a workman tending a fire. Soon Kohl and Jack were on a thoroughfare, heading steeply downhill toward the bay and the lights of downtown Seattle beyond. As they descended, a police car and a fire truck came roaring past them, heading uphill, sirens blaring.

"I guess you want to get out of the area, uh?" Jack said. "That old motherfucker next door to me, he'll have the National Guard out lookin' for us."

"This side of Lake Union," Kohl said. "The parking lot. We can talk there."

Lake Union was a working lake. Located almost in the center of Seattle, its shoreline was crowded with restaurants and condos and boatyards and other marine businesses. On its western shore, behind a virtually solid phalanx of buildings, a narrow parking lot ran almost the entire length of the mile-long lake. It was there that Kohl had Tony Jack park the pickup, on the outer lane, facing the street, so they could watch for police cars. And Kohl was struck by how peaceful it all seemed, the sounds of the city counterpointed by those of the waterfront: boat horns and whistles, the chugging of a diesel, the cry of an occasional insomniac gull.

The first thing Tony Jack did was get out his cigarettes and offer one to Kohl, who declined it. Settling back, Jack lit up with a monogrammed gold lighter.

"You musta thought I was wacko, huh?" he said. "Gittin' in here with you. But I figured if you was gonna shoot me, you'd already done it back there, right? I said to myself, hey, this guy's got a real beef with me, so why not git to it, uh? Why not talk it over and find out what the fuck's buggin' him?"

Though Kohl still had the gun in his hand, he had it pointed at the floor now. "Yeah, why not?" he said.

"Okay. So out with it, uh? What's all this about your cousin?"

Driving down to the the parking lot, Kohl had decided that to get anywhere with Jack, he would have to tell him the truth, about Ken anyway. As for his own involvement and Diane's, he saw no reason to mention that.

"Your brother Richard was killed by a hit-and-run driver on the Eastside, right? Well, that driver was my cousin Ken. He said your brother stepped right out in front of him. But Ken had had a couple of drinks that night and he already had one DWI conviction, so he just took off. Anyway, other people were there, he said. People who could have helped your brother—if he could have been helped. At any rate, Ken took off and got rid of his pickup—where, I don't know. He never said."

Kohl was watching Jack very carefully and he could see that the man was not surprised by any of this, that Ken undoubtedly had told him much the same story on the phone.

"What about you?" Jack asked. "Didn't you think he oughta turn himself in?"

"I didn't even know what had happened, not for a couple of days. But when he finally told me about it, yes, I advised him to go to the police. He wouldn't listen, though. Anyway, as he probably told you on the phone, when he hit your brother, your brother's briefcase came right through the windshield, and he wound up with all this stuff—evidence that your brother was a loan shark and that just before the accident he paid a visit to a client named Ricky Ross, whose body was found a couple days later. According to the coroner, Ross died of a heart attack brought on by a beating."

As Kohl said this last, Jack's eyes registered nothing at all.

They looked like slots in a gun turret. Kohl might as well have been telling him about the weather in Illinois. Finally, though, the man shook his head in denial.

"That's bullshit," he said.

"I don't think so," Kohl countered. "I've seen the stuff in the case. And so have you—at least the two samples Ken planted for you, to establish that he had the rest. Anyway, his big fear was that if the police ever nailed him for the hit-and-run, you'd come after him, have him hit on the street or in jail. I guess he figured if your little brother carried around a bloody baseball bat, you'd be a lot worse. So he was terrified. Which is why he tried that stupid little treasure hunt with you—to scare you off, warn you that if you ever hit him, the briefcase would go to the police."

This, finally, had an effect on Jack. He was smiling wryly and shaking his head, a man teetering between amusement and disbelief. "So that's what he wanted, uh? Man, I just couldn't figure what he was after. I mean, he said something on the phone about buying insurance, you know? That this stuff of Richie's was gonna be his insurance—but insurance against what, he never said! And I never knew till this minute! I never coulda guessed! I mean—*how could I?*" At that point Kohl could see the man sliding into anger, the eyes narrowing even more and the beefy face reddening in the light of the streetlamps. "Just cuz I'm Italian, is that it? Is that what your pretty-boy cousin figured? Cuz I'm Italian I automatically gotta shoot some poor asshole who runs over my brother—*by accident?* I mean, what kinda weird logic is that, anyway? I ain't Al Capone, you know!"

Like a cracked phonograph disk, Kohl's mind had stuck on the one phrase. *"Pretty boy,"* he said. "How would you know that? I thought you'd never seen him."

"I didn't! I guess it was just the way he sounded on the phone. Like one of them pansies, you know?"

No, Kohl didn't know. But for the moment he decided to let it pass. "Go on," he said.

"Well, like I was sayin', my business is girls and parking

lots and tow trucks—good honest businesses. I don't loan-shark no more. If I'd found out about your cousin, I'da called the police myself, that's what I woulda done. Like any other citizen. So you're barkin' up the wrong tree, my friend."

Kohl lit his own cigarette. "Maybe," he said. "And maybe not. After all, you did send your people out to find the stuff Ken stashed for you, right?"

"So what? I figured the man was looney tunes, but you never know. And anyway, I wanted to find out what the fuck was goin' on. I was *interested*, ya know?"

Kohl knew that they were there now. If Tony Jack was ever going to betray himself, reveal any fear or panic, it would be now. So Kohl proceeded very deliberately, watching his man as if he had him under a microscope.

"You sent Red and the black girl out to find the items. And Ken followed them. Then he disappeared and wasn't found until late that night. That is, his *body* was found."

Jack's only reaction was to toss his first cigarette out the window and to light another. "So how'd he die?" he asked.·

"You don't know?"

"Indulge me."

"He burned to death in a car, out past Woodinville. Supposedly he was parked with some girl and when they started back, the car rolled down a hill and exploded."

"Kinda like Red's car, uh?"

"You could say that."

"The girl die too?"

"Yes."

Tony Jack shook his head again. "Jesus, you got a real high opinion of me, don'tcha? I knock off some girl too, just cuz she happens to be there?"

"It's done."

"Not by me it ain't. And that goes for your flaky cousin too. I don't kill nobody. I hire sexy girls to shake their little pussies at hard-up guys. I used to have an escort service. And I even ran a numbers game before the state got into the business bigger and better than I ever dreamed. But I ain't no killer, my friend. And especially I don't kill nobody over no fuckin' *accident*—you got that?"

"Maybe you had someone else do it for you."

Tony Jack laughed coldly. "Jesus, you must think I'm the CIA or something. Your cousin calls me and I send Red out to get the stuff and someone else to watch your cousin watchin' Red? What am I, a fuckin' genius or somethin'? And anyway, why hit the man in the first place? That way, all I do is guarantee that Richie's briefcase goes straight to the police. Which you gotta admit ain't too bright."

"Maybe you had a simpler motive."

"Like what?"

"Like revenge."

"Yeah, and maybe you're fulla shit too—you ever thoughta that? Like tonight. Just for that little scene, you could do time—you realize that? Of course, they'd have to know who you was, which they don't. And which I don't know either, for that matter—not Thomas Orwell and his cousin George anymore, I take it. And I say let's keep it that way. I got car insurance, Red's got car insurance, all God's chillun got car insurance. So I say why not let bygones be bygones—okay?"

"Why so generous?"

Jack threw up his hands. "Who knows? Maybe it's cuz I like a man who cares about family. Or maybe I like a man with balls." He laughed coldly then. "Frankly, I don't want to cross you, friend—you got *too much* balls for your own good. I figure why not you go your way, and I go mine. Fair enough?"

By then Kohl suspected that the only fear or panic he would see this night was by looking in a mirror, for he was beginning to feel like an utter fool, a wild-eyed fanatic who at that moment was not headed for jail or a cemetery plot largely because of the patience and good sense of the "evil" Tony Jack. Not that Kohl was totally convinced the man was innocent—there was simply no way of knowing that. But he had to admit that Jack's behavior on this particular night certainly pointed in that direction. So he decided it was high time he pulled back a little, time he tried to make his way to safer ground.

"Could be I owe you an apology," he said.

Tony Jack looked at him and smiled broadly, scoring his beefy face with a hundred lines. "Could be," he allowed. "Listen, man, we all make mistakes."

"It was just such a coincidence," Kohl said. "Ken contacting you and then winding up dead that same day."

"Yeah, I can see that. Only it's like I said—I'm in the pussy business. Murder? Christ, I don't even own a gun."

Kohl tried to smile too, not very successfully. "Well, I guess it's like you said, then. You go your way, and I'll go mine."

"Fair enough."

Tony Jack suggested that Kohl drop him off downtown near his strip club rather than run the risk of returning to Queen Anne Hill, since the police might still be on the scene there. "They'll probably be lookin' for you," he said. "But don't worry about it—I'll make up some story, tell them I don't know you from Adam. Which happens to be the case, right?"

Kohl nodded. "I hope so."

The two men changed places in the truck then, and on the way downtown Jack said that he was worried about his sister-in-law and her kids, that they would suffer added grief if the police or media got hold of his late brother's briefcase, "with all that Ricky Ross junk in it."

"If you don't wanta give it to me," he went on, "I'd be willing to buy it. Say, a thousand bucks. How's that sound?"

"There's no need for that," Kohl said. "We've got a boat, and soon as I can, I'll get the briefcase out of the bank and deep-six it, along with everything inside. No one will ever see it again."

Tony Jack smiled again, but not very warmly this time. "Whatsa matter?" he asked. "You don't like the color of my money?"

Kohl didn't answer.

***

When he got back to the house, things seemed at first like a faithful re-creation of the night of the hit-and-run. Diane was in the game room again and she was wearing the same robe she had had on when he came in after ditching the Bronco. She was on her feet and smoking a cigarette, doing a pretty fair impression of Bette Davis in a snit. And to complete the picture, Johnny Carson was again holding forth on the television, albeit a much younger Carson, a ghost out of the past.

As Kohl went over to the bar, Diane tried to scorch him with her gaze.

"Too bad you missed the late news," she said. "Some asshole with a truck just like yours was over on Queen Anne Hill tonight. Destroyed a couple of cars and kidnapped Tony Jack, of all people. You wouldn't know anything about that, would you?"

Kohl was trying unsuccessfully to find a bottle of scotch. "You know, it's weird," he said. "I think Ken bequeathed me his taste for scotch. I used to kid him about it. Now it's my drink."

"Fascinating."

Kohl got out a bottle of vodka and dropped a handful of ice cubes into a tumbler. "Guess I'll have to settle for a Russian vodka-tonic," he said, pouring the liquor over the ice. "Look, Ma, no tonic."

"Being cute is not your forte," she told him, pronouncing it *fortay.*

"*Fort,*" he corrected. "The *e* is not accented."

She regarded him coldly. "Enough, all right? You kidnapped the man? You *actually* kidnapped him?"

Kohl dropped heavily into one of the leather easy chairs. "Not at all. I was just trying to get out of there. He waved me down and jumped in, said he wanted to talk."

"You can't be serious."

"Afraid so. And are you ready for this? The man sold me. I hate to admit it, but I seriously suspect he didn't have anything to do with Ken's death."

Diane looked at him in disbelief. "You mean the two of you really *talked*? You're trying to tell me that you and Tony Jack sat together and *talked*? Like a couple of civilized human beings?"

"Something like that."

She seemed almost disappointed. "Well, that's something anyway."

"I thought so."

But she still had a lot of anger to use up. "Not that it solves anything, not by a long shot. The police are after you, do you realize that? Did you think you could just waltz over there and wreak havoc and get away with it?

"Wreak havoc?" he said.

"Oh, fuck you, Tom! Just fuck you, that's all!"

Kohl didn't know what to say. He realized he was being insufferable, but Diane seemed to have that effect on him. "I'm sorry," he said finally. "I knew it was stupid and reckless, but there were some things I just had to find out."

She wasn't listening. "And what really pisses me is that you'd pull a stunt like this on the night before the launch party! You know how important it is for me, and how hard I've worked on it! Yet you blithely go ahead and muck up everything!"

"I said I was sorry."

"Sorry, my ass. The truth is you could care less what I want. The hell with Diane, right? Who gives a fuck about her?"

"Look, it's not as bad as you think. I doubt if the police are even looking for me."

She tossed her cigarette into the fireplace. "Oh, you doubt it, do you? I wonder what all that was on TV, then? They even had a chopper over the scene, for God's sake! It looked like a war zone—cars burning, lights flashing all over the place. And this neighbor of Tony Jack's—a real elegant old guy—he described you to a T. 'A big fella with curly dark hair,' he says, 'and a forty-five automatic, and driving an old Chevy pickup with big tires and big bumpers and an Illinois license plate.' You know anybody like that?"

195

Kohl drained his glass. Going over to the bar again, he patiently explained to Diane that Tony Jack wasn't going to sign a complaint against him and in fact was going to tell the police that he didn't even know the miscreant's name or anything about him.

"The man's willing to forgive and forget," he said.

Diane was not so inclined. "The police don't give a damn what he says. They know what *you* did—the felonies *you* blithely committed—and they'll keep after you, whether he signs a complaint or not."

Fresh drink in hand, Kohl went back and sat down again. He told Diane that even if the police had his license-plate number—which he didn't believe they did—and even if they were able to find him, all he'd face would be reckless driving and a weapons charge, and even those charges would be debatable, since he'd had good reason to believe that Tony Jack and the redhead meant him harm, the way they had sandwiched him in. A lawyer could reasonably plead him innocent because he acted in self-defense.

"Who cares? I'm not going to worry about it," she said. "It's your neck, not mine. And if you can't pilot the boat tomorrow night, I'll get that old guy who gave you lessons. Probably should have hired him in the first place."

"That's the attitude."

"I'm going to bed," she announced. "If they come for you, I don't even want to know about it."

Kohl told her that he had put the truck in the garage. "And I probably ought to leave it there for a while," he added. "You think you could get me a deal on a rental car?"

"Oh, sure thing. Just what I need—to become an accessory to *your* crimes now." She went into the foyer, heading for the stairs.

"Goodnight, Diane."

Halfway up, she stopped and looked back at him. "Remember what I told you on the plane? About choosing life over death, success over failure?"

"How could I forget?"

"Well, I guess you've chosen, haven't you?"

"I guess so."

She shook her head in solemn regret. "Too bad. You know, you didn't have to be a loser, Tom."

He didn't respond until she was almost all the way up the stairs. "Sure I did," he said.

Sitting out on the deck in the dark, Kohl tried to pretend for a time that the alcohol was doing its job, making him slow and sleepy and carefree. He looked out at the lake and the lights of Seattle and tried to forget that he himself had added real fire to those same lights a few hours before. He tried to forget, but couldn't. Relentless as the tide, his problems kept moving in upon him, each wave seemingly higher than the last.

Oddly, he seemed to hate Tony Jack now more than he had before, probably because the man had so infinitely complicated everything. Before their conversation, Kohl had been virtually convinced of Jack's guilt, at least emotionally, in his gut. Now he wasn't sure of anything. On the one hand, it was patently absurd to believe that on the day Ken contacted the mobster and threatened him and tailed his people—that on that very day he would burn to death in an improbable accident on a remote country road in the company of a girl he apparently never even knew. Yet it was just as absurd to believe that Tony Jack in the span of that half day could have set up and executed so perfect a murder.

Kohl's head ached with the effort of trying to find his way through this thicket of contradiction. It was an effort he had to make, however, because of the ache in his heart, because he was only now beginning to understand what Ken's death meant for him, that he had lost not only his cousin and boyhood chum but also a good part of his own life, in that there was no one left now who really *knew* him. He had taken his other losses pretty much in stride—his wife, his mother and father, his home—had taken them because there wasn't much else a man could do, except hurt and grieve, and he had done his share of that. But after his trip home, burying Ken and standing at his parents' graves, he had begun to realize just how totally alone he was, how bereft of his own life, his own past, because there was no one left who had shared it except in bits and pieces, a friend here, a lover there. And he suddenly understood the old men who sat in bars talking *at* each other, never listening, pathetically trying to unburden themselves of histories known only to them, tales they would have to take to their graves.

Kohl knew that this was not exactly a rare occurrence in modern America, where the happy, extended family was one of its most cherished myths. In reality, even country families scattered before the slightest of winds, heading for sunshine and sand and other chimeras. And when death and divorce were factored in, Kohl knew his situation was even less unusual. Still, with the vodka's help, he managed to feel thoroughly sorry for himself, if not quite thoroughly drunk.

When he finally got up and went inside, he made his way carefully up the stairs and into Diane's room. Later he wouldn't remember if he woke her or if she was awake when he came in and pulled a chair over to her bed. He would also have trouble remembering what he said to her as against what he only *thought*, downstairs, out on the deck. He remembered her complaining bitterly to him about needing sleep and how quiet she became when he told her to shut up. And he was fairly sure that he explained to her how Ken, in dying, took a large part of their lives with him to the grave.

He hoped he didn't go on about the goddam country and how it was just a lot of scattered families and broken dreams, lonely footloose bastards drinking vodka in the dark and thinking unwholesome thoughts about death and revenge. But he did remember sitting there next to her bed in the dimness—the only light coming from downstairs, through the open door—and looking at the way her body sculpted the bedsheet and how her hair radiated across the pillow. And he knew that if he'd been less drunk he would have tried to get in bed with her. Rebuffed, he would have begged, would have *paid*.

"You're so beautiful," he said, slurring his words as he reached out to touch her. "Like your hip right here, the way it curves down to your waist and then starts up again. It's so damned beautiful, Diane. So perfect. Like the rest of you. Too perfect, I guess. For me anyway."

As he remembered it, she had just lain there watching him, saying nothing, as he ran on.

"Sometimes I think what I need is a cross between you and Bobbi. Someone smart and beautiful like you, but softer, you know? Sweeter. Someone I wouldn't feel like saluting. Just someone to really care about. Someone to care about me. You wouldn't think that'd be so much to ask, would you?"

And he seemed to remember her eyes filling with tears. He seemed to remember her reaching out and lightly taking hold of his hand.

"No, you wouldn't," he thought she said. "You wouldn't think it'd be so much to ask."

8 The police didn't come for Kohl that night, and the minuscule news stories in the Seattle papers the next day indicated that they wouldn't be coming anytime soon either, since all they had was a description of the culprit and his vehicle, a pickup truck with Illinois plates whose number no one evidently had caught. And Tony Jack, true to his word, had reported that the man responsible for all the mayhem was essentially unknown to him, the anonymous ex-husband of one of his ex-dancers, a young woman he had known only as Peggy Sue.

So the next evening Kohl was able to pilot the Williwaw for Diane's launch party. The weather was perfect, clear and warm, with enough of a breeze to disperse the city's summer smog and bring out the mountains that ringed the area, especially Mount Rainier sixty miles to the south. With its base shrouded in moist air, the mountain seemed to float above the horizon like a dream of perfection, a paradigm before which grubby little human beings might be expected only to gape and won-

THE LION AT THE DOOR

der and hold their peace. But Diane's friends seemed not even to notice the mountain. Instead they ate and drank and danced and argued and finally two of them got into a fight and one of them vomited—in the lap of his business partner's wife.

For the first few hours, though, the party went along smoothly enough. The guests were mostly in their thirties and early forties, successful entrepreneurs and professionals used to the best of everything, well traveled and well fed. Dress was casual, with everyone in deck shoes and either slacks or shorts, with a lot of T-shirts advertising where they had been and what they were wearing: Kitzbühel, the Seoul Olympics, Nike, Lauren. Some went in for humor, like the fat man whose paunch displayed a head-on view of a very large hog, above the caption FEED ME.

While the Filipino couple hustled quietly behind the bar, the women lounged out on the shaded deck and a number of the men gathered around the helm, with Kohl. Some expressed their admiration for the boat, comparing it favorably to their own yachts, modern fiberglass "vulgarities," as one man termed them, before adding, "Of course, mine sleeps more people and will go about twice as fast as these old wooden tubs can—and on half the fuel."

For the most part, though, Kohl found the guests to be pleasant and attractive people. A number of them spoke to him about Ken, saying how much they had liked him and how unfair it was, someone that young and vital dying in a stupid accident. Just as in Illinois, the women eventually got around to his good looks, one of them even going so far as to say that without Ken the Northwest wasn't all that beautiful anymore. On those occasions when the conversation was about Ken, Kohl waited in vain for Diane to join in, say even a word or two about her longtime lover. Instead she would turn away and hurry over to some other group, playing the hostess-in-demand. Above all, Kohl wanted to hear her remind the guests that the Williwaw had been Ken's idea and dream, and maybe even that she wished he could have been there with them, as their host and captain. But she did not. And the times Kohl mentioned it himself, he felt uncomfortable doing so, because he sensed in many of the guests an almost prurient interest in him, as the cousin who had so swiftly replaced Ken in Diane's house and bed and now at the helm of her yacht.

They left Yarrow Bay at about eight o'clock, after everybody had had a couple of drinks as well as all the smoked salmon and other delicacies they cared to eat. As Diane directed, Kohl took them across the lake and through the ship canal to Lake Union, where they circled slowly, enjoying the view of the city's downtown skyline and also the city's view of them in the handsome, classic old yacht, with its lovely straight lines and warm hues of mahogany and polished brass.

They returned to Lake Washington and cruised south to Mercer Island, where it was rumored that during an economic recession the locals often fed their dogs dogfood. Many of the guests lived on the island, and Diane managed one way or another to point out the waterfront homes she had sold there, causing some of the women to wink at each other or roll their eyes, for their hostess was obviously much more popular with their husbands than with them.

Halfway along the island's western shore, Kohl turned the boat around and headed back north, since it was already dark and some of the guests were beginning to complain that they were cold. Diane playfully advised them to dance some more and even turned up the music, but only a few bothered to comply. For the most part, they gossipped and talked about business and their possessions—their new cars and boats and airplanes—and above all, where they had traveled and the new restaurants they had tried, the dishes that met with their approval and those that did not.

Among the guests was the real estate developer Diane hoped to sell the boat to, not to mention Kohl as well, as a future employee. His name was Robert Twigg, and though he was about Kohl's age, he was only half his size, which didn't seem to bother him in the least. He had the habit of tipping back his head so he could more easily look down his nose at one while he explained how things worked. Having heard that Kohl was an ex-farmer, a victim of the farm depression, Twigg thought it might be helpful to instruct him in what was wrong with the farm economy, pointing out that as long as Washington kept buying the farm vote with "farm welfare," the industry would never become profitable. Kohl asked him what he would do in his own business if he knew that money was going to be very tight for the next couple of years. Would he retrench?

"Of course."

"Cut staff and inventory?"

"Whatever it took."

"The farmer can't do that," Kohl said. "He can't cut staff because he usually doesn't have any staff except his wife and kids. And he can't cut inventory because he doesn't have that either. So he does just about the only thing he can, which is plant every square inch of ground he's got and pray for good weather. Otherwise, he starves—not to mention the rest of us."

Twigg smiled indulgently. "I'm afraid it's not all that simple, Kohl. The trouble with the Midwest farmer is that he's kept hanging on to the feed-grain concept long after it's become obsolete. Corn-fed beef is a drug on the market. What people want today is fruits and vegetables and the lighter meats—fish and fowl. In today's world, you either change or you perish. It's that simple."

By then the two of them had a small audience, including Diane. And Kohl knew that he probably should have discussed the matter further, politely pointing out to Twigg that the demand for feed grains grew year by year, that the Midwest didn't have either the growing season or enough field workers for vegetable farming, and that a man already mortgaged up to his eyeballs didn't have a whole lot of flexibility. Kohl knew that he should have said those things, but he didn't.

"Gosh, Twigg, I wish I'd known all that before I went belly-up."

That was what he said, and most of their audience laughed. Not Twigg, though. And not Diane either. Stepping between the two of them, she put a hand on each man's shoulder and asked Twigg if he'd like to take the wheel for a while.

"Tom says she handles beautifully," she added.

Twigg was still smiling indulgently. "Diane, these old wooden yachts are for show," he said. "Like antiques. But they handle like barges—didn't Kohl tell you that?"

Then he and the others drifted away, leaving Diane to take out her disappointment on Kohl. "Well done," she said. "You're just a born salesperson, aren't you?"

"No—more a labor person, I'd say."

At that, she dug him in the ribs and whispered "fuck you" before moving on.

Behind the bar, the Filipino couple kept dishing out the food and pouring drinks. In time the man in the FEED ME T-shirt became drunk and got into a shouting match with a lady lawyer, who claimed he had copped a feel. Her husband then took the side of the FEED ME man and openly copped a feel himself, only to get his face slapped. After that two other men got into an argument about capital punishment, one predictably claiming that it was institutionalized murder while the other held that it was a vital public ritual, an affirmation of the sacredness of life.

By the time they reached Yarrow Bay and Kohl had maneuvered the boat into its slip, everyone was ready to leave, either for home or to continue the party elsewhere. Diane had advised Kohl earlier in the day that the Twiggs might invite her and Kohl to join them at their waterfront home after the cruise and that of course they would go. Kohl could forget about cleaning up the boat or anything else that had to be done—he could save all that for the next day, she said, which was a Saturday. But the Twiggs didn't invite them along and the only group that did included the lawyer's husband and the hog-shirted man, and Diane regretfully declined, saying that she had an "absolutely hellish weekend of showings" ahead of her and needed as much sleep as she could get.

After the Filipinos had packed up and left, Kohl got a beer from the refrigerator and went out onto the stern deck, where he sat back in a canvas chaise and lit a cigarette, figuring that he had earned a few minutes of peace and quiet. But Diane was in a lather of disappointment and resentment, and she knew just what to do with it.

"Well, at least you handled the boat all right," she said.

"That I did."

"And the fact that Twigg might have bought it—and even could have been your ticket to a decent career—none of that stacks up alongside the old Kohl ego, does it?"

"I guess not."

"The man's your age and he's worth probably twenty million bucks. Does that say anything to you?"

Kohl blew a lungful of smoke over the railing. "That he's a great man. A superior human being."

"You bet your ass he is."

"He'd be pretty easy to bend, though."

Diane shook her head sadly. "I might have known it. How do we bring a giant down to our level? With a *pun,* and a bad one at that."

Kohl was grinning happily. "I know, I know, I'll probably hate myself in the morning."

"Well, that'll make two of us."

Kohl looked up at her. "Diane, do you ever listen to yourself? Where did you ever get the notion that you could talk to people the way you do? Because Ken put up with it? Well, lady, I ain't Ken."

That seemed to confuse her, and for a few moments she had nothing to say. She leaned back against the railing and sighed. "I guess I just had such high hopes for tonight."

"That's no excuse. Christ, sometimes I listen to you and I think that without ever going through the rites of love and marriage, we're in the middle of a divorce."

She shook her head in bafflement. "I don't know—you bring

it out in me. Your fucking aplomb maybe. Or your goddam size. Maybe you make me feel insecure—"

"Insecure!" he interrupted. "I seem to remember a night not too long ago, right out there in the rowboat, you telling me how *safe* I made you feel."

"That was then—"

"And this is now—right."

He had wanted to say something to her about Ken, about her curious inability even to mention his name during the party, but in the end he decided to let it go. He doubted that he would have gotten a straight answer anyway.

"I'm going on home," she said. "I suppose there are things here you still have to do."

"A few, yes." As she turned to leave, he reached out and took her hand in his. "It was a fine party, Diane. Everything was perfect—except for some of the people. Like me."

She started to reply, then thought better of it and smiled, even squeezed his hand before moving to the gangway. "I'll see you," she said.

"Right."

Kohl stayed on the boat that night, trying to sleep out on the deck, on one of a half-dozen air mattresses Diane had bought, evidently for emergency pajama parties. The night air was cool, the sky was bright with stars, and the sounds of the marina—the lapping water and creaking boats—could have lulled a speed freak to sleep. Yet Kohl lay there for hours wide awake, unable to turn off his mind. When he closed his eyes, he saw a kind of light show, an aurora borealis of mental agitation. Occasionally he would smoke a cigarette or get up and drink a glass of water. But it made no difference—he went right on thinking about his conversation with Tony Jack, specifically the mobster referring to Ken as "pretty boy," and later offering to buy the briefcase.

206

Even at the time, Kohl was not convinced by Jack's explanation of the "pretty-boy cousin" remark: that Ken had sounded like a "pansy" on the phone, and that as far as Jack was concerned, all pansies were pretty boys. But Ken's voice wasn't in any way weak or effeminate, and he didn't have any "pansy" mannerisms either, not in the way he moved any more than in the way he spoke. At the time, however, Kohl had given Tony Jack the benefit of the doubt, figuring that Ken was undoubtedly terrified when he made the phone call to Jack and probably hadn't sounded anything like himself. Yet it took a real stretch for Kohl to believe that Ken would ever have come across as effeminate. At the most, he might have sounded nervous and quavering, which in Kohl's mind was a long way from being pansylike. And even if Ken *had* sounded weak and effeminate, a reasonable person would not likely leap from that perception to the conclusion that he was therefore a pretty boy. All of which gave new life to Kohl's old suspicion that Tony Jack might have seen Ken after all, which meant that he might also have killed him. At least, Kohl couldn't totally rule it out, not yet anyway.

As for the briefcase and "all that Ricky Ross junk," as Tony Jack referred to it, Kohl had no problem understanding why the mobster had offered only a thousand dollars for it. He obviously wanted Kohl to believe it was of no real importance to him, nothing more than an embarrassment to his late brother's wife and kids. He would pay a few bucks for it to save her from added grief, that was all. One would have thought that he or his brothers were linked to murder on a daily basis, for that of course was what the briefcase items did: pointed to the fact that Richard Giacalone had been at Ricky Ross's and had probably robbed and beaten him, contributing to his fatal heart attack. And that was first-degree murder in any state in the Union.

On the other hand, maybe Tony Jack was as sophisticated as Diane about the "chain of evidence" and other legalisms. As a card-carrying wiseguy, maybe he knew that the briefcase and its contents were tainted as evidence and couldn't be used against him or anyone else in a court of law. It was possible that Tony Jack knew this, but Kohl didn't believe it for a second. Rather, he believed—felt it in his bones—that the mobster wanted the briefcase so badly he hadn't dared put a more realistic price on it, lest Kohl discover what a valuable piece of property he had. Also, Jack might have only wanted to find out where the case was, so he could pick it up much more reasonably later, by force.

As the night wore on, Kohl's mind gradually wore down, until he finally fell asleep just before dawn.

Late the next morning, Kohl tried to find the briefcase on the boat. The story he'd told Tony Jack—that the case was in the bank—had only been a ruse to keep the mobster from coming for it until after Kohl had decided whether to deep-six the thing or actually put it in a safe-deposit box. But after a half hour's search that turned up nothing, he phoned Bobbi in Seattle and asked if she knew where Ken had stashed the briefcase.

"I sure do," she said. "It's in the trunk of my car."

"You free for the next couple hours?" he asked.

"Free, white, and twenty-one."

"Good. I'll drive over and pick you up."

"Wow, how neat," she said. "Is this gonna be like a date?"

"Not exactly."

A half hour later he was parked in front of Bobbi's house, sitting with the briefcase on his lap, opened, while he carefully checked its contents again, hoping he might find something he'd missed before, not a new item so much as the significance of one he'd already seen, one that might yield an answer to the questions that had kept him awake most of the night. But he found nothing new.

Almost indifferently then, he took the briefcase and slipped it under the seat.

"What now?" Bobbi asked. She was standing outside the pickup, leaning back against its opened door.

"How about we go for a drive downtown? Only in *your* car."

She smiled impishly. "Why? You think someone might be lookin' for an old pickup with big bumpers and a Illinois license plate? How was it they described the driver on TV? 'A big guy with curly dark hair'—something like that."

"Yeah, I know, I know," Kohl said. "I heard it all before—from Diane."

Bobbi pretended chagrin. "In that case, mum's the word."

"Good girl." After lighting a cigarette, Kohl told her much of what had happened the night before last, with Tony Jack. "And it's turned me into a real Doubting Thomas," he went on, not proud of the pun. "Now I don't know what to believe. I don't know which way to turn. I think I need another opinion."

"Whose?"

"Remember the black girl at Leschi?"

"Sure."

"I thought I'd have a little talk with her."

"Well, I guess you already 'talked' with the redhead and the brother, right?"

"You could say that."

Frowning, Bobby looked down at her feet. "You know, Tom, I ain't into all this as much as you might think. I mean, I don't wanna git killed, you know? My babies kinda need me."

"No problem," Kohl said. "I can handle it alone. All I need is your car. The less I drive my truck, the better."

"I can believe it."

"I'll have the Buick back by the time you go to work."

Bobbi shook her head. "No. I want to go along."

"You sure?"

"I'm sure."

"Suit yourself. There's really nothing to be worried about anyway. I just want to talk to the girl."

"Let's go, then."

Within the hour the two of them were driving slowly

through the downtown traffic, past Tony Jack's strip joint. A short time later Bobbi found a parking place up the hill from the Pike Place Market, which was one of the city's main tourist attractions, a sprawling semi-open-air market in which dozens of mom-and-pop vendors sold everything from artichokes to fresh salmon to expensive jewelry. Since this was the height of the tourist season, the sidewalks and streets as well as the market itself were approaching gridlock.

Taking Bobbi firmly by the hand, Kohl towed her through the throng until they located a phone booth—fortunately the old-fashioned enclosed type—near a small health-food restaurant. After looking up the number, Kohl phoned Tony Jack's and asked for Heather. In the minute or two that passed before she came on, he readied himself, trying to squeeze his 230 pounds of blue-collar ex-farmer into the svelte three-piece-suit persona of a young investment banker with the voice to match, Southern patrician, polished in the Ivy League.

"Heathuh, this is Randall Holmes," he said. "You don't know me—ah'm in the bankin' business—and ah caught your act a few weeks ago, at the tail end of a somewhat drunken bacheluh party, ah'm afraid, and—"

"Just what the fuck to you want?" he heard.

As Randall Holmes, Kohl went on then and told Heather that he would consider it a great favor if she would be his date for the Symphony Ball, the purpose being to drive his ex-wife— "the gold-digguh from hell"—crazy with jealousy. He would pay Heather five hundred dollars for the night and also buy her a dress for the occasion.

"And no strings attached," he said. "No sexual favuhs expected."

"You serious, man?"

"Puhfectly."

"Then why don't you come by and we talk about it."

Holmes laughed daintily. "Cuz ah already got a table ovuh heah at Cuttuh's. You know the place? Only a couple blocks from you."

"Yeah, I know it."

"Well, come on ovuh, then. We'll have a champagne lunch and ah'll give ya two-fifty down. Later we go pick out a dress for ya. How's that sound?"

Bobbi had opened the door a crack to listen in, and for most of the conversation she was either laughing silently or shaking her head in disbelief. After he'd hung up, she gave him a look.

"Boy, remind me never to trust a word you say—*Randall*."

"We're in luck," Kohl said. "She's off for the next hour— said she'll be at Cutter's in fifteen minutes. You might as well go back to the car and wait for us."

"Whatever you say."

As Bobbi hurried off, Kohl stopped at a fruit stand and bought a small bunch of bananas. Leaving the market and crossing the street, he gave all but one of the bananas to a wino beggar, who looked as if he'd just been handed an assortment of dead rats. Walking on, Kohl worked the brown bag down around the lone banana, trying to make it look and feel like a handgun. Near the corner of First Avenue, he stopped in front of a shoemaker's tiny shop. From there he could see Tony Jack's place on the next corner south. Whichever of the two possible routes Heather took, he would have it covered.

He lit a cigarette and stood there smoking while he waited. Within a couple of minutes he saw her come out onto the sidewalk and immediately possess it, long-legged, gaudy, insouciant, a queen out for a stroll. As she came to the corner, Kohl moved closer to the door of the shop, deeper into the shadows, to watch her unobserved. She crossed the side street against the light and followed the crowd across First Avenue, heading straight toward him in her skimpy bright-orange dress and brassy jewelry. She had her hair pulled back into a bun of curls, in the manner of Scarlet O'Hara, and she turned a number of heads, literally, though Kohl's was not among them. Waiting for her to pass, he gazed absently into the dark little shop and found himself staring into the frightened eyes of a tiny old oriental man standing behind a counter. Kohl smiled,

211

but the shoemaker didn't change his expression, didn't show his large yellow teeth until Kohl started to turn away.

Following Heather, Kohl moved down the street. At the corner in front of the market, she turned right, heading for Cutter's, and Kohl let her proceed, staying about ten feet behind until they were approaching the next street, the one on which Bobbi had parked the car. Then he moved in close, taking the girl by the arm and shoving the bagged banana into her slim, hard waist.

"I just want to talk," he said, trying to reassure her, wipe the sudden look of terror from her eyes. As she started to pull away, he squeezed her arm and shook her. "Don't be an ass. If I don't shoot you, I'll stomp your foot and you'll limp the rest of your life. Honest, I just want to talk."

Whether or not she believed him, she did as she was told, going with him up the steep street to Bobbi's car. Kohl pushed her into the backseat and climbed in next to her, not bothering anymore to hold the bagged banana against her ribs.

"Who's she?" Heather asked.

"My chauffeur," Kohl said. "She's gonna drive, and we're gonna talk."

"Where the fuck you takin' me?"

"Nowhere. We're just gonna drive. And after you've told me what I want to know, we'll drop you back at Tony Jack's."

"S'pose I don't *know* what you want to know?"

Kohl lit another cigarette but didn't offer her one, for fear she might stub it out on his face. "I think you will. I don't need a whole lot. I'm just trying to fill in the blanks."

"Where we goin'?" she asked again.

And Bobbi echoed her. "Yeah—where?"

"Go east on Yesler," Kohl said. "Straight back to Leschi— maybe it'll help her remember a few things."

"Like what?" Heather asked.

"Like what happened to my cousin."

"I don't even know your fuckin' cousin."

Kohl had decided that he didn't want to smoke after all,

that this was no time for it. And just as he leaned forward to drop the cigarette out the passenger window, Heather suddenly struck at him, much as Rusty had done, swiveling in the seat corner and drawing up her dancer's legs and kicking out at him, driving her spiked heels into his side with such force he felt as if he'd been stabbed. In a rage of pain he lunged against her, ramming her upper body back into the corner with one arm while he drove her legs down with the other, finally pounding the nearest leg twice, using his fist like a sledgehammer. When he pulled back, she crumpled against the armrest and window, squealing and crying, hugging her leg.

"Motherfucker, you broke it!" she wailed. *"Jesus, it hurts! Jesus!"*

"My gut doesn't feel so hot either," he said. "What the hell's wrong with you? Why'd you do that?"

"Why you think? I want outa here!"

Kohl had felt inside his shirt and was surprised when his hand didn't come back bloodied. "Now you know the score, anyway," he said. "You tell me what I want to know and I'll leave your other leg just like it is."

"Motherfucker! I woulda told you anyway!"

"Sure you would."

Yesler Avenue passed through the Central District, Seattle's version of a slum. There were more black faces here than there were downtown, but the shops all seemed to be thriving, there were few abandoned buildings, the houses were painted, and the lawns were mowed. But according to the media, it was also the place where crack was king, where the ubiquitous L.A. gangs carried on their violent drug wars. As such, it definitely was not the sort of place where Kohl cared to be seen abusing a black woman. So, as Bobbi drove on through the area, stopping for an occasional traffic light, Kohl put his arm around Heather and even kissed her on the cheek a couple of times, trying to make it appear that they were a pair of lovers enjoying themselves in the backseat of a car.

"After my cousin phoned Tony Jack," he said, "you and

the redhead went to Leschi Park and the art museum, right? To pick up the stuff my cousin planted."

"I went along, that's all," Heather said. "Tony don't tell girls his business, you know. He talked with Red."

"And you just went along?"

"That's what I said, din't I?"

"And was there a second car—say, Tony Jack and his little brother watching the whole thing—seeing if anyone was watching you?"

"Lemme tell you again—Tony don't tell me nothin'. Cuz I'm a woman, see? And far as he's concerned all women 'cept his mama is whores. Sometimes we good whores and sometimes we bad whores, but we always whores, you unnerstand? The good whores, we suck his fuckin' cock *whenever* he says. That's the main difference."

"So you don't know if there were two cars?"

She shook her head. "Far as I know, just us and the handsome dude followin' us from Leschi."

Kohl said nothing for a few moments. He felt as if he'd just been slapped awake. "Handsome?" he said finally. "How could you tell?"

"Well, I couldn't tell then, you know. I mean, Red just seen this car in the mirror, stickin' to us like glue. But I didn't really see him till the doughnut."

By the time they reached the lakeside park at Leschi, Kohl judged that he had learned about all Heather could give him, at least without the stimulus of added pain. And he had no stomach for that, already felt lousy enough about hitting the girl as hard as he had. Going on, she had told him that after Red spied Ken's car following them, he went ahead to the Art Museum and pretended not to be able to find the second item near the doughnut. Gesturing failure to Heather, he returned to his car and the two of them drove off. Ken, who had parked some distance away, then hurried over to the doughnut himself to see what had happened to his second "sample." Red meanwhile made a U-turn and came creeping back in the old

Cadillac, following Ken as he walked from the doughnut back to where he'd parked the Corvette. And there Red "just took him over," jumping out and slamming a gun into his ribs and pushing him on into the Corvette, forcing him to drive them to the garage of the Aabco Towing Company, which was owned by Tony Jack and managed by the little brother. Heather followed in Red's car and saw Ken being taken into a back room there. After that, the little brother drove Heather back to the strip club and dropped her off, telling her what to say to Tony.

"And what was that?" Kohl asked.

"That they had him—the fella on the phone. That they was gonna ask him some questions. And that they'd come by later and fill Tony in."

They were parked at Leschi by then, looking out over the narrow strip of lawn and trees at the lake, and across it, the Eastside, with its cluster of skyscrapers that Ken had never owned.

"Can you walk?" Kohl asked.

"If I can, it's no fuckin' thanks to you."

"I'll hold your hand."

She laughed coldly. "What a sweet li'l mother you are."

Bobbi started to get out of the car too, but Kohl asked her to stay where she was. "Might be better," he said, "if there are things you don't hear."

She frowned at that. "Come again?"

"Think about it," Kohl said. "Your babies, remember?"

Shrugging, Bobbi pulled the door shut and waved them on. And Kohl did take Heather by the arm, walking her to the shore and helping her sit down on one of the breakwater boulders.

"I feel lousy about hurting you," he said.

The black girl gave a sharp laugh. "I ain't zackly enjoyin' it either, you know."

"I guess you know what I'm gonna ask," he said. "And look, I realize you've got no reason to trust me, but I promise anyway—I swear Tony Jack will never find out who told me."

"Told you what?"

"What happened to my cousin. Exactly how he got from the tow company—alive—to where they found him that night—dead."

Heather shrugged. "How should I know? What you think I am, anyway—Tony's right-hand man or somethin' like that?"

"He sent you along with Red to pick up the samples."

"Sure—and you know why? Cuz some white dude customer was hasslin' me. Thought he was in love or somethin', and he was parkin' outside my apartment, which is near the Art Museum, you dig? Well, the super calls me and says this dude is there again, and I tell Tony, and Tony says go along with Red, so Red can throw a scare into the guy later if he's still there. And that's the only reason I went along. What d'ya think, I'm some kinda gangster or somethin'?"

"Don't forget, I saw you in the office with your boss. You ain't just one of his dancers."

"I never said I was. I'm his *top* dancer."

Kohl was becoming impatient. "When Red and the brother came back, what did they say to Tony?"

Heather laughed in Kohl's face. "You puttin' me on, man? What you think they say? They say some big mother just kicked the shit out of 'em, that's what they say."

"I mean after that."

"You mean after they stop Red bleedin' like a stuck pig?"

"Yeah, after that."

"Man, his face looked like hamburger, you know that?"

Kohl stood there waiting, trying to be as patient as he could. And Heather coolly met his gaze. Finally she shrugged again.

"I got no idea," she said. "I was back in uniform by then, shakin' my cooze in some asshole's face."

At the end of his rope, Kohl found himself reaching down and placing his fist on Heather's good leg, tapping it lightly, not hurting her at all, in fact knowing he *couldn't* do it, not again. Nevertheless tears welled up in her eyes and she began to tremble.

"My cousin," he said. "Who killed him?"
"I don't know, man! Honest to Jesus—*I just don't know!*"

That night Kohl again slept on the Williwaw, but not alone this time. After he and Bobbi drove back downtown and dropped Heather off near Tony Jack's, Bobbi revealed that she had lost her job the night before, her boss having labored under the misapprehension that his position permitted him to pinch and pat his barmaids at will. To set him straight, Bobbi hammered his offending hand with a beer mug, breaking his knuckle and index finger and losing her job all with one stroke. So, after they returned to her mother's to pick up Kohl's truck, along with the gun and briefcase, she talked Kohl into spending the rest of the day out on the water. For all the good it did her, she might as well have stayed on shore. She wanted to swim, but Kohl did not. She wanted him to open up the throttles and fly over the water, but Kohl set the engines at slightly above idle and was content to cruise slowly up to the north end of the lake and back, standing at the helm, thinking and worrying, trying to decide what to do.

Giving up on him finally, Bobbi settled for sunning herself on the foredeck, right under his lugubrious gaze. Twice Kohl phoned home, in case Diane was trying to reach him, but each time all he got was the recorder and her brightly businesslike voice: "Please leave your message at the tone and I'll get back to you as soon as I can. Have a nice day." Earlier he had bought food and drink—again, scotch instead of beer—so when they got back to the marina there wasn't much left to do except eat and settle back with a drink and watch the day fade, the blue sky and blue water turn gun-metal gray and black. And Bobbi did her best to lift Kohl's spirits. Once she came up behind his chair and tried to massage his neck and shoulders, but her fingernails were too long and he gently pulled her off him, saying that she'd make a better surgeon than a masseuse.

"Why don't they call them massagers?" she asked.

Kohl had never thought about it. "It's a French word," he said. "And the French are crazy."

"Crazy for sex, right?"

"No, just crazy. Everything in their world is either a he or a she, did you know that? Like this chair, it's a she. If I asked you where the chair is, you'd say, 'She's right over there.' Stupid, uh?"

"How come you know all that?"

"I had one year of it in college."

"Can you speak it?"

"Sure. *Je parle le français* real good."

"What did you say?"

"That I lie a lot."

"I don't believe that."

"See?"

All she had on was a sweatshirt over her bikini, and she was sitting with her feet resting on his chair, sometimes on his lap. The way she kept smiling at him, he could see that things between them had undergone a certain change that day, at least on her part. And he did nothing to put her off, in fact began to look forward to bed, unable to imagine a better way to give his mind a rest.

"There's still something I wonder about," she said.

"What's that?"

"Whether you ever believed me."

"About what?"

"That the blackmail thing wasn't my idea. It wasn't, you know. It was Rusty's all the way. I blabbed like usual, but I never would've blackmailed anybody." Her eyes had grown moist, and she looked grave and vulnerable. "And it bothers me a real lot that you think I did."

Kohl looked at her. "I don't anymore," he said.

"Honest to God?"

"Honest to God."

She smiled like a kid with a new puppy. And Kohl smiled too, but not convincingly enough.

"I guess you're still wonderin' what to do," she said.

"You could say that."

"Heather didn't help much, I take it."

"She did and she didn't. I know I'm on the right track now, but I also know I'm in over my head—to mix a couple of metaphors."

"Whatever that is."

"Right."

"Well, if you know you're in too deep, maybe it's time to call the police."

She was right, Kohl knew, but he also knew that he was not there yet, not ready to make the call and accept its consequences. "Not yet," he said.

"So what happens? You gonna take them on yourself?"

"As what—a *vigilante*? I hit them and go to prison for it— I can't see that does Ken any good. Or me either."

"That's for sure."

"Anyway, I'm no Rambo. I've never even been in the army. I've hunted ducks and rabbits. And a couple times Ken and I went deer hunting with my dad. But the only time I had a buck in the cross hairs, I didn't shoot. Don't ask me why."

"So what happens?" Bobbi said again.

Kohl looked at her. "You tell me."

She shrugged and smiled. "Oh, we could forget about it all. For a while anyway."

And that was exactly what they did. Afterward, lying together in the bow-cabin bunk, Kohl found himself wishing once again that he could somehow take Bobbi and Diane and blend them into one, into a woman who would interest and challenge him as much as Diane did, yet would be as comfortable as Bobbi. At the moment, though, that sense of comfort was already fading, even as the two of them lay there in the dark, with Bobbi snuggled against him, her head on his shoulder and her leg draped across his body while her fingers played with his chest hair, twining it into curls. In his mind he was already back across the lake by then, in the alley behind Tony Jack's, dealing with the brother and the redhead, though realizing now that they had just finished with Ken, had already killed him, or at least had beaten him, making sure of the information they were about to give Tony Jack. And knowing Ken, Kohl could only assume that his cousin had told them everything, right off, not held anything back, in the understandable hope of avoiding pain and disfigurement. Yet they wouldn't have been satisfied with that, not the redhead anyway. He would have wanted to find out if Ken would hold to his story or would change it under duress—would have enjoyed finding out.

That left Kohl with the big question still unanswered: whether or not Ken was still alive at that time, and if he was, whether Tony Jack then led his brother and the redhead back to the Aabco Towing Company garage, to take Ken or his body and the rented Corvette out to the remote foothill road northeast of Woodinville. As for the girl, Marina Harris, Kohl couldn't figure that one at all: how she got into the act or why she was killed. But at least he knew now what he'd wanted most to know—that Ken had not died in an accident, that he had been killed by Tony Jack or the men who worked for him, which amounted to the same thing. What he didn't know was what he could do about it.

Even as he was thinking this, he felt a slight tremor pass through the boat, a starboard roll of no more than a quarter inch, virtually imperceptible had it not been for the fact that the lake was calm as ice. And he knew that a forty-foot yacht in still water wouldn't move even that much unless it had suddenly taken on a considerable amount of weight, two hundred pounds or more. Because he had the hatch open as well as the portholes, and hadn't heard anyone moving along the dock, he sensed immediately where the weight—the *man*— had set foot: on the transom, the narrow platform running across the back of the boat, a foot above the waterline. It was not only the platform they swam from, but also the place where one stood to load fuel, slip the gas-hose nozzle into the gas pipe.

"Don't talk!" he whispered to Bobbi. "Hurry, we gotta get

out of here!" He was already pulling on his jeans.

Swinging a small hinged ladder down from the ceiling, he climbed up it and moved silently through the hatch onto the foredeck, where he crouched, peering through the windshield and lightless cabin at the stern deck. But he saw no one. Then, as Bobbi joined him, still naked, an aura of light, a flickering glow, appeared above the stern railing. Down below, out of sight, something was burning. *A fire had been lit.*

Immediately Kohl hooked Bobbi with his right arm, much as if he were tackling her, and dove over the railing, carrying her with him down into the water, where she immediately began to fight against him, desperate to surface. But he held her for five or six seconds longer, stroking with his free arm, moving under the dock and between two sailboats on the other side, both of which looked like whales from underneath, great long black shapes giving definition to the dark gray of the lake's surface. Then abruptly it was daylight up above them, brilliant high noon, and a shock wave rolled through the water, throwing them against the hull of one of the sailboats, which itself pitched violently in the water. Fearing that Bobbi had been knocked out, Kohl clamped his hand over her nose and mouth and towed her under the sailboat's bow and up to the surface, where she gulped the air as ravenously as he, even though the night was drizzling fire, flaming bits and pieces of the Williwaw still falling about them, into the water and onto the dock and other boats as well.

Bobbi had the dull, wide-eyed look of someone in shock, and as she tried frantically to hold on to him, even climb on him, he maneuvered behind her and took her by the hair, close to the scalp, so he could hold her head up out of the water as he swam. Towing her that way, he moved past the stern of the sailboat and out across the narrow waterway to the next row of slips—the last row—where the captain kept his twenty-four-foot fishing boat. Kohl figured that they would be farther from the fire there, as well as from any other explosions that might occur as the yachts closest to the Williwaw went up in flames. Also, he knew where the captain kept an extra key to his boat's cabin.

He wasted no time in getting up onto the transom and pulling Bobbi after him. As he got the key—from inside a light fixture—sirens began to wail in the distance: fire trucks in Kirkland and Bellevue already on the way. His idea was to find a sweatshirt or fishing jacket, something for Bobbi to wear as the two of them tried to make their way to shore through the gathering throng of firefighters, police, and onlookers.

As he was opening the door, he glanced out over the low-set cabin's roof at the lake, and *there they were*, about 150 feet out: two men in a rowboat, the smaller one frantically paddling with a single oar, first on one side of the boat and then the other, making no headway at all, while the husky one, in the stern, kept pulling in vain at the starter cord of a small outboard motor. In the light of the fires Kohl had no trouble making them out: the burly body and red flattop, the miniature version of Tony Jack. And Kohl's brain, like the outboard motor, seemed to stick: *They tried to kill you,* he told himself. *They just tried to kill you.*

"You go inside," he said to Bobbi. "I'll be back."

"Where you going?" she cried.

But he had already swung his legs over the side of the boat and now he slipped down into the water, barely going under before he began to swim toward the rowboat and the two frantic men inside it. Knowing that they would quickly spot him if he continued to swim on the surface, he dove under as soon a he cleared the marina, still stroking as hard as he could, in the hope of reaching them before the outboard motor caught. Hatred and rage had pulled him down into the water, and he knew that those same feelings were fueling his arms and legs now, yet he somehow felt cool and calm in his mind, as if it were wholly separate from the rest of him. Oddly, it occurred to him that the scene was not without an element of comedy: the two murderous clowns frantically wanting to flee their fiery handiwork, but stranded there in the tiny boat, virtually be-

222

calmed, one of them trying to paddle with an oar while the other pulled viciously at the motor's starter cord, undoubtedly cursing it, sweating like a hog at market.

Kohl breathed twice on the way to the rowboat, letting his head come slowly up out of the water before pulling it back down, trying not to roil the surface any more than he had to. The second time, when he was still about forty feet from the boat, they saw him. Afraid they would shoot him or try to hit him with the oar as he drew close, he dove deeply and didn't begin to come up until he saw the rowboat's black shape directly above. Passing underneath it, he came up on the side away from the fires, gripping the boat's gunwale and pulling it sharply down, causing water to pour into it at the same time the redhead went pitching out of it, toppling into the lake right over Kohl's head and screaming as he fell.

"No-o-o!"

Kohl didn't see or care what happened to the brother. The redhead was his quarry, and he was on him immediately, hitting him in the face before plunging with him down into the freezing blackness, frantically trying to pull the man's powerful hands from around his neck. And until that moment Kohl hadn't known for sure what he was about, had thought he would probably subdue the man and tow him to shore for the police to deal with. But that illusion vanished as he realized he was fighting for his life, tumbling into the void with this bull of a man, this raging underwater beast. So Kohl raged too, gouging and kicking and struggling, until he managed to work himself onto the redhead's back, able to reach under his thick arms and lock his hands at the back of the man's beefy, hairless neck. They tumbled that way into the weeds, the trefoil, at the lake's bottom, forty or fifty feet deep at that point. Kohl's lungs were bursting, his body was screaming for air, but he held on, using all his strength and thinking that the man's neck was about to give, snap like a dead oak branch. When it didn't, Kohl loosened his aching fingers for a fraction of a second, trying to get a firmer grip. And in that moment the flattop head came snapping back up and Kohl felt the red-head's thick torso abruptly expand as he took a deep and greedy breath—*of water*. The man shuddered then, apparently in shock, and the writhing, powerful body of a moment before went suddenly limp, became nothing but weight, flotsam. Kohl let go of it and felt it drift away as he pushed off from the bottom.

When he finally broke the surface, he gulped the air, sucked it down, savored it, the sweetest draft in all his life. His heart was banging in his neck and his ears were ringing, *but he was alive,* and for the moment that was all he cared about. Toward shore, the fires were still burning in the marina and the sirens were wailing louder than before. In the other direction the little rowboat was moving slowly out across the lake, its motor chattering softly while a tiny figure huddled over it, making good his escape. But Kohl couldn't have cared less. All that mattered now was putting one immensely heavy hand in front of the other. All that mattered was reaching the captain's boat.

9 By the time Kohl reached the captain's boat, fire trucks and police cars were already arriving on the scene, some with their sirens still wailing while others had scaled down to a haunting growl. Even though the Williwaw's dock was now a wall of flame and smoke, engulfing a half-dozen yachts, beyond it Kohl could see the flashing lights of the vehicles as they came down the hill from Lake Street and disappeared behind the great long sheds that sheltered about a third of the boats in the marina. Bobbi gave him a hand as he climbed into the captain's boat. Then she fell into his arms.

"You were down so long!" she cried. "I thought—"

"I know, I know." He was so short of breath he could barely speak.

She was still naked, evidently having stood there watching the whole time he was gone. "Who was it?" she asked. "Flat-top?"

Kohl nodded. "And the brother—he got away. Come on, we have to get some clothes."

Inside, he found a couple of yellow rain slickers, one of which he hurriedly helped Bobbi put on.

"We can't use the dock," he said. "Even if we could get through the fire, the firemen or cops would stop us. There'd be questions."

"How, then?"

"Underneath." He handed her the other slicker. "Here, you carry this for now. And wait here a second. I'll be right back."

Slipping into the water again, he swam over to a dinghy tethered in front of the nearest sailboat. He untied its line, then took hold of the stern and swam the tiny craft back to the captain's boat, so Bobbi could step down into it. Steering it with his arms and propelling it by kicking his feet, he proceeded under the dock, turning when they reached the main part, which ran perpendicular to the shore. And as they moved slowly along between the pilings, Kohl could see and hear the firefighters up above, running and connecting hoses, shouting back and forth. Closer in, some of them had gone out to the slips and were yelling for anybody aboard the boats to abandon them and get ashore.

Kohl knew that he and Bobbi eventually would have to come up on top—soaking wet and wearing the slickers—and face the scrutiny of at least some of the police and firefighters. Though he seriously doubted the two of them could make it through them all, reach his truck unchallenged, he gave it a try anyway, abandoning the dinghy at the innermost row of slips, which was sheltered under one of the sheds. There he and Bobbi made their way along the shed wall to the nearest boat and climbed into it. He put on the other slicker, and in a utility compartment next to the engine he found some old rags, which he and Bobbi used to dry their faces and hair. Finally he whispered to her.

"We're lovers," he said. "We hold hands. We're shocked by all this. And we're not in any hurry."

Bobbi smiled wanly. "No shit."

Kohl climbed out of the boat onto the dock and Bobbi followed, taking his hand. As they neared the marina's chain-link gate, Kohl kept looking back at the fire and shaking his head, feigning shock and amazement. In the distance, a fireboat came roaring into the bay, its sirens adding to the din. Kohl pulled Bobbi close to him, still glancing back at the fire as they made their way over the hoses and past the firefighters and police at the gate. When he saw one of the cops looking them over too closely, he smiled and shook his head again.

"Jesus, what a mess," he said. "We didn't even have time to get dressed."

The cop did everything but wink as they passed on, heading for Kohl's truck in the parking lot. When they got there, he discovered that his jeans were so wet and tight that he couldn't get the keys out of his pocket—Bobbi had to do it for him. In the truck finally, he drove very slowly, not wanting to draw the slightest attention. As they went across Lake Street and started up the hill, Bobbi exhaled as if she'd been holding her breath for a week.

"Jesus, Tom," she said, "you sure know how to entertain a lady."

The street they were on was the same one Ken had turned onto after the hit-and-run. When they reached the top of the hill, Kohl pulled off the blacktop onto the gravel shoulder, at approximately the same spot where he had forced them off the road on that night back in June, when the nightmare began.

"What's up?" Bobbi asked.

He didn't answer. Feeling dizzy and nauseated, and for some reason thinking he saw the redhead's body, he opened the door and got out, halfway expecting to vomit in the roadway. But he didn't. Instead he stood there trembling and sweating, looking down the hill at the almost postcard-pretty holocaust the redhead had created. On any night the bay was a thing of beauty, situated as it was at the bottom of the bluff and ringed by the lights of the city. But on this night the fires added to the spectacle, flickering under the floodlit, arching geysers of water the fireboat and land-based firefighters were pouring onto them. Everywhere emergency lights glittered and flashed, bathing the scene in red and yellow and blue, the primary colors, the colors of disaster. But it was the water that Kohl kept looking at, water still coal-black and calm as ice, reflecting nothing because of the steep angle he was looking down from. He didn't quite know what was going on in his head, why he'd felt dizzy, or what it was he'd seen, or *thought* he'd seen—the figure floating facedown in water, with only the back of its head and its shoulders and arms protruding through the surface. And he had to see, he had to look.

But there was nothing, at least not out there where they had fought, about two hundred feet from where the fireboat treaded water, its cannons shooting water onto the dying fires and gutted boats. No, there was nothing, no body floating in the blackness. The terrible secret was still his, his and Bobbi's.

She was leaning out the truck window. "Hey, you okay?"

"Yeah, I think so," he said, getting back in.

"You don't look so hot."

He lowered his head against the cool plastic of the steering wheel. "Listen, what happened between me and the red-head—that's our secret, okay?"

"Sure—if that's what you want," she said. "But he tried to *kill* us, Tom. You were only—"

"I know. But for now, it's just between us, okay? I'll tell Diane later."

"You got it."

He put the truck into gear and they moved slowly back onto the roadway, heading for home. He still felt weak and drained, and he wondered how he could possibly do what remained to be done, that very night.

After they entered the house, Kohl called upstairs to Diane, figuring that because of the hour—almost two in the morning—she might think that burglars had broken in.

"It's me, Diane!" he said. "You'd better come down. We've got problems."

She evidently had already gotten out of bed, for almost immediately she was coming down the stairs, tying on her robe. She looked half asleep—until she saw Bobbi. "What the devil's *she* doing here?"

"That's what I wanted to tell you," Kohl said. "We're all in danger. Tony Jack had the redhead blow up the Williwaw. We were in it. We got out at the last second."

Diane stopped on the bottom stair and stood there looking at him. "Are you serious?"

"Very."

"They blew it up? My boat!"

"Sky-high. Didn't you hear the sirens? The fire took a half-dozen other boats too."

"My God."

"The police will probably be here soon. And I don't think you ought to tell them anything—I mean, that we were there, on the boat. It would just confuse the issue and probably get me arrested. They might think *I* blew it, so you could collect on the insurance."

Diane shook her head. "Beautiful. Just beautiful."

"I think you two could be in danger, the same as me. It might be a good idea if you went to a hotel and stayed there till I—" He faltered at that point, not at all sure what lay ahead of him.

"Till you *what?*"

"Defuse the situation."

"And what the devil does that mean?"

"I'm going to find out."

"You're just going to wing it, uh? Like the night on Queen Anne?"

"Something like that."

"Well, that certainly gives me a lot of confidence."

By then Kohl was wondering why he didn't just forget about

her, let her stay right where she was. With her brass-plated arrogance, she probably stood a better chance against Tony Jack than he did anyway. Nevertheless—wearily, patiently—he forced the words out.

"Let me repeat—I think we're all in danger. I've got to hit them first. It's that simple."

Diane shook her head, in disbelief or denial. "My God, has it really come to this? I listen to you, and I can't believe this is my life, actually *my life*."

"I know the feeling," Kohl said.

"Do you really?" She went on into the game room and got a cigarette, lit it. "Look," she continued, "I can see why Tony Jack might be after your ass—but why mine? I haven't beaten up his employees. I haven't wrecked his car. I—"

"I've been living here with you, remember? And Ken before me. Jack's gotta be wondering what you know."

At that, fear touched the cool green of her eyes. "You think so?" she said.

"I think it's possible, yes. I could be dead wrong, of course. But why take any chances? Why don't you just pack up a few things, give Bobbi some stuff to wear—"

Diane laughed. "What do you expect us to do—*room together*?"

"Why not?"

Bobbi looked at Kohl. "I can tell you why not—cuz I ain't goin' nowhere with her. I got babies to look after. And anyway, I feel a whole lot safer with you."

"Well, that solves *that* problem," Diane said. "But I'm afraid there are a few others, Tom. You see, unlike some people, I don't live in a cowboys-and-Indians world. Where I live there are these messy little things like boat insurance to take care of and lawyers to confer with and clients to deal with."

"You can do all that from the hotel. Just call the police and tell 'em where you are. Say you saw a cockroach in the house and you've got a phobia. Something like that."

Diane made a face. "A *cockroach*? In *my* house?"

Kohl started up the stairs. "I'm gonna find Bobbi some clothes."

Diane ran after him. "Oh no you won't! I'll take care of that."

"Do it, then." He came back down, passing her on the stairs. "I'll get my stuff together. And if the police come before we can get out, we're not here, understand?"

Though Diane didn't respond, Kohl knew that she had heard him. He went back to his room and put on some dry clothes, got out the .410 shotgun, and strapped on a hunting knife. He had only the vaguest idea of what lay ahead of him, but he figured it couldn't hurt anything to have a little extra muscle of his own.

When he was ready, he went out to the foyer to watch for the police and wait for Bobbi, but she was already there, wearing deck shoes and a flowered wraparound dress that fell below her knees.

Seeing Kohl's reaction, she smiled wryly. "Diane claimed this is all that'd fit me. I feel like my goddam grandma."

"Then you got a very sexy grandma."

"What a bullshitter." She was following him out to the garage, where he'd parked the truck.

After they reached it and got inside, Kohl told her that he was letting her come along only as a lookout and backup.

"You're not going in with me," he said.

"In *where?*"

"Wherever they are."

"You're gonna take them on all by yourself, huh?"

They had turned out of the driveway and were heading down the narrow blacktop street. "Something like that," he admitted. "And if I don't come out, you go to the police. Tell them everything."

"Don't talk like that," she said.

He repeated the message. *"Tell them everything."*

"Everything?" Bobbi shook her head in dismay. "I could never get it all straight. They'd think I was a retard."

"Not if you had a body to show them."

"What body?"

"The redhead's. Who else's?"

She was looking at him with tears in her eyes. "And don't you forget it," she said.

Like most things in Seattle, the Aabco Towing Company was situated in relation to a hill, in this case at the bottom of one, about a mile southeast of downtown. By parking on a side street that climbed the hill, Kohl had a bird's-eye view of the whole operation: a grimy corrugated steel building with a connecting fenced-in lot that held over twenty cars, probably impounded. Lights were burning in the corner office and two huge tow trucks were parked in front, next to four other cars, one of them a gray Mercedes 450 SL. Around the back, near an assemblage of garbage cans, a rowboat with an outboard motor sat on a small two-wheel trailer. Under it a pool of water glistened.

"What happens now?" Bobbi asked.

"We wait."

"Forever, I hope."

On the way to Seattle, as they drove across the bridge, Bobbi had reminded Kohl of what he'd said before the fire—that he wasn't a vigilante or Rambo, that he was a hunter of rabbits, not men. And he had asked her if she still wanted him to call the police in.

Her answer was another question. "Don't you think you should?"

"Probably," he said. "Only I keep seeing myself sitting in the police station—answering questions for days—while you and Diane are out here alone with Tony Jack."

"He's not after us."

"The girl who died with Ken—I wonder if she thought the same thing."

Bobbi was sitting with her head bowed and her hands pressed between her knees, like a child waiting outside the school principal's office. "What will you do?" she'd asked.

"Stop him somehow."

"Like you did the redhead?"

"I didn't kill him, Bobbi—he drowned."

"Oh."

They drove in silence the rest of the way. And they weren't doing a lot of talking now, angle-parked on the steep side street, looking down at the towing company. Kohl was surprised to see that the office was still open, the business apparently operating through the night. He surmised this not so much because the office lights were burning—that could have been the case if only Tony Jack and his brother were there—but because of the four cars in front, which indicated that there were at least two other persons inside the building, probably a dispatcher and driver. Judging by the large number of cars locked inside the chain-link fence, Kohl assumed that the company's main function was the towing and impounding of illegally parked cars—a business performed around the clock.

He realized that Tony Jack might not even be there. The Mercedes could have been the little brother's, though Kohl was inclined to doubt it, reasoning that a man as vain and cocky as Tony Jack wouldn't look kindly on an underling—even an underling *brother*—driving a car as expensive as his own. Judging by the disparity in their clothing—the brother's taste for red double-knits and white shoes—Kohl wouldn't have been surprised if one of the cars out in front had been a pink Eldorado. So he figured that the Mercedes was Tony's, either a car he'd already traded for or one that he'd rented while his own was being repaired. In any case, Kohl knew that he couldn't do much of anything here, not with other employees of the Giacalones on the scene. About the most he could hope for was that the man himself would leave the building on his own, come to Kohl, rather than the other way around.

"What're you going to do?" Bobbi asked.

233

"I'm not sure." As he opened the truck's door and started to get out, she reached over and grasped him by the arm.

"Don't, Tom," she said. *"Please."*

He put his hand over hers and gave it a reassuring squeeze. "Don't worry—I'm not gonna try to bust in on them. I'm just gonna wait outside and see what develops. If I drive off with someone—someone in *my* control—you just follow. Don't go to the police unless—"

"Unless it's too late," she broke in.

Her eyes had filled, but that only strengthened his resolve to keep pressing, make sure in any way he could that Tony Jack would never harm her or Diane. He leaned back into the cab and kissed her.

"I'll be all right," he said.

Carrying the shotgun, he made his way down the steep brambly hillside to the outer chain-link fence that enclosed the entire operation. He climbed the fence and moved across the open ground, keeping the two parked tow trucks between him and the building's lighted front windows. The second truck was his goal, and when he reached it, that was where he stayed, in the lee of it, in the deep shadows on the side away from the building's entrance and the front windows. He felt lucky that it *was* a tow truck, since its very structure—the winch and boom and other apparatus—allowed him to remain in the shadows and yet see through to the front of the building. On the other side of the truck was the gray Mercedes sports car, toylike in comparison.

While he waited, he hungered for a cigarette, but didn't want to take the risk of lighting it in the darkness. He also had to urinate, and this he allowed himself, even though it meant he might have to go into action with his cock hanging out. Occasionally, peering from behind the tow truck, he saw someone moving about in the office: once an elderly black man; another time a fat young man with blond hair. But Kohl didn't see either the brother or Tony Jack until a good twenty minutes had passed, when the front door swung open and out

234

came the little brother, looking scared and harried. He went straight over to the Mercedes and was starting to get in when Kohl came around the back of the truck, shotgun at the level. Giacalone spun around, fish-eyed, his hands going out in front of him just as his brother's had before the hit-and-run.

"Jesus, I thought you was dead!" he gasped.

"Take the position," Kohl told him. "Pretend I'm a cop."

"Sure, man! You got it!" Giacalone quickly leaned against the car and spread his legs. "Listen, none of this was my idea. I—"

"Shut up."

"Right. You got it."

"Your brother inside?"

"No. Honest to Christ—he ain't here."

"Where, then?"

"I ain't sure. The club maybe."

Giacalone was shaking badly as Kohl patted him down, running his hands over clothing still wet from the lake. Not until he got to his shoes—a pair of short dress boots—did Kohl find anything, a compact .22 caliber automatic tucked into an ankle holster. After pocketing the gun, Kohl abruptly punched the man in the kidneys, hard enough to drop him onto the ground.

"That's for my boat," he said, surprised at his choice of words, that he had grown that proprietary toward the craft.

Holding the shotgun in one hand and Giacalone in the other, by the nape of his neck, Kohl got into the cramped sports car and scooted over to the passenger seat, dragging the brother after him, forcing him behind the wheel. All the while the man kept whimpering.

"My God, my back! Oh Jesus, Jesus, it hurts! I can't drive, man! I can't, I really can't!"

Kohl stuck the muzzle of the shotgun into the man's soft middle. "Start the car," he said.

And Giacalone did so, continuing to complain as they crossed the gravel lot to the front gate. Up on the hill the pickup's headlights came on and Kohl opened the car window and signaled thumbs-up to Bobbi, though he doubted that she caught it.

"Drive to the strip club," he said.

"You got it, man. But Tony, he probly ain't there still—it's almost three, ya know."

"Go there anyway."

"Right. But listen—ya wanna know somethin'? Tony didn't have nothin' to do with all this any more than me. It was Red all the way. Honest to Christ. Red's a crazy man, a real head case. He really is—or *was*, I guess I oughta say now, huh?"

"Shut up and drive," Kohl said.

"What're you gonna do to me?"

Kohl didn't answer. They were on a two-way, four-lane avenue, heading downtown, and considering the hour, there was a fair amount of traffic. Nevertheless Kohl was able to keep track of Bobbi in the pickup, holding at a half block behind them.

"Look, there's no reason to do me or Tony," the brother argued. "You already got the guilty party. Red's the one who whacked your cousin and the other two. Honest to Christ."

Other *two*. The word hit Kohl slowly, like a dental probe nearing the nerve in a deadened tooth.

"*Two?*" he said—just as Giacalone swerved to the left and braked, skidding the Mercedes into the path of an oncoming car, so Kohl would take the collision broadside. But the other car turned sharply to *its* left, smashing into the rear of the Mercedes and sending it pinwheeling across the pavement, directly into the path of a following truck, which did hit it broadside, but on Giacalone's side, throwing Kohl violently against him, using the little man as a kind of cushion, a human shock absorber. Somehow, in the midst of the crash, Kohl was aware that the sports car had wedged under the truck's bumper and that the two vehicles—like a snowplow and its blade—were skidding down the street, throwing up a rooster tail of sparks. By the time they came to a stop the Mercedes was a pile of junk and Kohl was bleeding from the head and face, feeling the first faint stirring of pain in his left leg and in his ribs, below his heart, pain that he knew would soon have him by the throat. But he saw that Giacalone was in much worse shape, unconscious, bleeding heavily, his body woven into the wreckage. The key was still in the ignition, and though Kohl doubted that the motor was still running, he pulled the key out anyway and pocketed the set. Overhead, he saw that the car's roof was curled open like the lid of a can, and he struggled upward, pushing himself out over the top of the passenger door, much as if he were climbing a fence. Toppling to the pavement, he was amazed to discover that he still had the shotgun in his hand. Instinctively, he held it close, trying to conceal it.

The truckdriver had come down out of his cab by then, and his only concern seemed to be his driving record.

"It wasn't my fault!" he yelled. "Jesus Christ, you came spinnin' right at me! What could I do, huh? You came right at me! It wasn't my fault!"

As he got to his feet, Kohl saw that the other car had come to a stop in the middle of the street, a half block farther down. The driver had gotten out and was standing there, looking back at the wreck. Others, though, were beginning to gather—pedestrians, a motorcyclist, drivers from other cars—and Kohl saw now that one of them was Bobbi, running toward him, her face a cry of anguish. She started to hug him, then pulled back as he reacted in pain. He put his arm around her neck, bracing himself. Then he turned back to the truck driver.

"I'm going to the hospital," he said. "With her. But the driver, he needs an ambulance. Make sure someone calls it in."

The man didn't seem to hear. "It wasn't my fault," he insisted. "You came right at me."

Bobbi was pulling Kohl toward the pickup. As he went along with her, he was relieved that whatever was causing the pain in his leg didn't prevent him from walking.

"You okay?" Bobbi asked. "You gonna be all right?"

"Sure," he said. "Just shaken up."

She started to come around the truck, to help him in, but he waved her back to the driver's side. Once inside, she found a rag and blotted the blood on his head and face. Forcing a smile, he took the rag from her.

"Let's go, okay?" he said.

"Right. Sure." She started the motor and they drove off. "Where to? Harborview Hospital's probably the closest."

"Not there," he said.

Kohl could see that Bobbi thought he'd gone over the edge, and for all he knew, she might have been right. But his own instincts told him that he was doing the right thing, the sensible thing. The cuts on his head and face were still bleeding, but not very heavily, and though he imagined that he had some broken or cracked ribs, he was able to breathe and he wasn't spitting up any blood. The pain was there, of course, just as in his leg, which he figured had suffered nothing more than a severe contusion above the left knee. But he was able to walk, and he believed he could handle the pain, for a while longer anyway. So it made sense to him to get on with what he was doing, finish the heavy business of this long and heavy night. For certain, he didn't want to be laid up in the hospital when Tony Jack came looking for him. Or for Bobbi. Or Diane.

Bobbi had pulled over to the side of the alley and parked. And though she had switched off the headlights, Kohl could see her clearly in the city lights, her childlike face temporarily aged with dread and fear. He had told her to drop him off and park at the other end of the alley, where she could have kept an eye on things—the strip joint's back door if nothing else—and not have been in danger. But she wouldn't hear of it.

"The same thing still goes," he said now. "If I'm not out in twenty minutes, you go to the police. Don't hesitate. And don't do anything stupid, okay?"

238

"You mean, like you?"

"Exactly." He took Giacalone's little gun out of his pocket and gave it to her. "Here. You hold on to this. And use it if you have to."

"On what?"

"On rats. Two-legged rats."

She was looking at him as if she hated him. Her lower lip was trembling, and Kohl for some reason felt closer to her than he ever had before. He leaned down and kissed her, hugged her despite the pain it caused him.

"I'll be all right," he said.

And she nodded, in desperate agreement.

He got out and went over to the alley door, trying one after another of Giacalone's keys until the lock finally turned. Going inside, he found himself at the back end of the narrow hallway that ran from behind the bar past Tony Jack's office. And even though it was after three in the morning, long past closing time, rock music was still pounding in the showroom, and Kohl could see through the open door at the end of the corridor that the light show was running too, the luminous roaches still crawling endlessly across the walls and ceiling of the room. He closed the door behind him, leaving it unlocked so he could exit more quickly if the need arose. Then he made his way slowly along the darkened hallway, in between all the cases of soft drinks. And when he came to Tony Jack's office, he saw that though a light was burning inside, no one was there.

Continuing toward the showroom, he was surprised at how calm he felt, almost as if he'd come for a late-night job interview, something not particularly pleasant but not all that daunting either. Having already been firebombed and half drowned and injured in a head-on collision, he figured he could face the prospect of a showdown with Tony Jack without too much trouble. The problem was he didn't even know if the man was there—not until he came to the doorway behind the bar and peered into the showroom, which was dark and smoky, glittery with lights that seemed only to add to the gloom. The mobster was sitting across the room in a corner booth, with his back to the wall and a gun lying on the table in front of him, near a bottle of Christian Brothers brandy, a glass, and a plastic tub of ice. Next to him sat Heather, wedged into the corner of the booth and wearing only a tiny show bra as far as Kohl could see. He also saw that she was in pain, crying softly as she fingered her left eye, which was discolored and swollen almost shut.

In between them and Kohl was the only other person in the room, a girl dancing nude on the stage—the same one who had served him when he first entered the place, on the day Ken was killed, a young woman with maroon hair and skin of such whiteness it appeared almost phosphorescent under the spotlights. She was swaying as though in a dream state, so listlessly it could hardly be called dancing. And Tony Jack did not approve.

"I told you to move your fuckin' ass!" he bawled suddenly. "I wanna *feel* somethin', you understand? Somethin' *good* for a change! So move it, baby! *Move it now!*"

At that, she took hold of one of the stage posts and began to make love to it, simulating feverish copulation. Considering her sudden animation and how incandescent she appeared under the spots, almost like a pillar of fire between him and Jack, Kohl did not even bother to crouch as he crossed the room toward the mobster, holding his shotgun on him every step of the way. And when Jack finally saw him, he jumped like a frightened cat, practically knocking over the table in his sudden terror. His gun clattered to the floor.

"*Aw, no!*" he cried. "*No, come on! Oh Jesus, oh Christ!* I thought you bought it, man! Arnie just told me on the phone—you and Red both! Oh Jesus, oh Christ!" Disconsolate, he put his face in his hands and then reached out to Kohl, as if to ward him off, the final brother to do so. "Listen, man, you can't just whack me now. Not like this. It ain't right. *Cuz you already got the right guy.* Red was your man—wasn't he, Heather? Go on, tell him! Tell him, goddammit!"

Heather was busy righting the bottle of brandy and picking up scattered ice cubes. When she said nothing, Tony Jack turned on her in a rage.

"You tell him the fuckin' truth, you hear me!"

She managed a shrug. "Oh yeah, oh sure—whatever you say, Tony."

He immediately backhanded her across the mouth. "She knows the truth!" he bawled. "But she's got it in for me! Bitch wants to get me killed, that's what!" He looked at Kohl with a conspiratorial grin, as if the two of them were old friends, buddies in league against an absurd world. "And you know why, don'tcha? Cuz she was Red's girl. Cuz she loved the ugly fucker, can you imagine that? And she figures I got him wasted—which is a laugh, it really is. Christ, I tried to talk him outa doin' you. And I woulda warned you—honest—only I didn't have no idea how to get in touch."

Kohl shook his head, even smiled a little. "You're a prince, you are." Still standing about a dozen feet away from Jack's table, he was reluctant to move any closer, since that would have put the dancer at his back. As he signaled for her to come down from the stage, he heard movement behind him and quickly whirled with the shotgun, only a twitch away from blowing a very large hole in Bobbi, who had followed him in and now stood there looking scared and embarrassed.

"Let me help," she said.

She had her hands behind her back, probably holding Arnie's gun. Kohl wanted to show anger, yell at her and send her running back to the truck for her own good. But he couldn't bring it off.

"You sure you want to be here?" he asked.

"You're here."

He smiled in spite of himself. "You're too much, you know that?"

Turning back to the others, he asked if there was a storeroom or some other place where he could put the dancer. "A place that locks from outside," he said.

Heather nodded. "Sure. The lady's can."

"Where's the key?"

She pointed. "On the wall over there, behind the bar."

Kohl asked Bobbi to get the key, which she did. The nude dancer picked up her discarded garments and went into the ladies' rest room. Bobbi locked her in and came back toward Kohl, who was already closing on the corner booth by then. He picked up Jack's gun, a snubnose .38, and pocketed it. Shifting the shotgun to his left hand, he then backhanded Jack across the face, just as the mobster had done to Heather, only a good deal harder. Blood began to run from Jack's nose and mouth, but he didn't cringe or whimper, as his brother had done. Instead, the blow seemed to fortify him.

"He do that to your eye?" Kohl asked Heather.

Again she shrugged. "I can't remember."

Kohl prodded Jack with the shotgun. "You know, you're one stupid bastard. Yesterday this girl lied like hell to protect you, and this is how you repay her."

Jack looked at him with cold hatred, evidently having decided that tears and contrition weren't going to buy him much of anything. "Like I told ya—*I didn't do nothin'*," he said. "So I don't need no protectin'. A fair hearing—that's all I need."

"And you're gonna get it," Kohl said. "Right now."

Seizing him by his pompadour, Kohl dragged him out of the booth and walked him over to the stage. He placed a chair under one of the spotlights and prodded Jack up into it with the shotgun.

"There—the perfect place for a performance," he said. "Only I don't want a *performance*. I want the truth." He looked over at Bobbi and told her to take Heather to the control booth and turn off the music.

"Look behind the bar too," he added. "There should be a bamboo stick there—a kind of club. Bring it to me."

While they waited, Tony Jack sat on the stage with the air of a noble, long-suffering victim, much as if he were a political prisoner, a lifetime guest of the gulag. When the pounding rock music suddenly ended, the silence hit Kohl like the icy water of the lake, something one could drown in.

Bobbi gave him the bamboo club, which was about a yard long and over two inches in diameter, so hard and light that Kohl had no trouble understanding the bouncer's attachment to it. One could take a man out with a single shot and not run much risk of killing him in the process.

"Heather, you sit over there," Kohl said, directing her to a table on his right. "And Bobbi, keep an eye on her, okay? I have no idea whose side she's on, except her own."

"Well, you got that right anyway," the black girl said.

"You okay?" Bobbi asked Kohl. "You know what you're doin'?"

He tried to smile. "Probably not." He placed the shotgun on the nearest table and moved closer to the stage.

"All right, Mister Tony Giacalone," he said, tapping the bamboo lightly against the floor. "It's time you answered a few questions. And every time you lie, I break a bone. One of *yours.* Fair enough?"

Tony Jack looked down at him, probably barely seeing him in the glare of the spotlights.

"How will you know if it's a lie?" he asked.

"I'll know."

"Sure you will."

"First—did anyone try to sell you information on the hit-and-run?"

The mobster sneered. "You must mean that hippy asshole, that Dogpatch cokehead who comes in here one day and tells me he knows who ran over Richie and he'll cough up the guy's name for five large—five thousand, to you."

Bobbi broke in, her voice soft, awed. *"Rusty?"* she said, looking at Kohl. "He really did sell out Kin?"

"What happened to him?" Kohl asked. "The cokehead?"

"Asshole was just like you," Jack said. "He figures I'm some kind of vigilante hoodlum, not a respected businessman with a payroll to meet and family responsibilities and all the rest.

Figures I'm gonna pay him off and whack some jerk because he had a car accident—real smart, huh? And when I tell him no deal, to take his little story to the police—well, he storms outa here like I hurt his feelings. So I send Red and Arnie out to the boonies to ask him a few more questions, you know? And Christ, they coulda been Jehovah's Witnesses, for all he knew. Yet he comes flying outa his trailer with a shotgun— you believe that?"

"So they killed him," Kohl said.

"Who knows?"

"What'd they do with the body?"

Tony Jack shrugged. "How the fuck would I know? Red's got his secrets. I don't ask."

"Sure you don't," Kohl said. "But getting back—my cousin."

"Yeah—your cousin."

"This how you did it with him? You sit him down in a chair, or tie him to a post, or what?"

"I don't know—I wasn't there."

The bamboo club seemed to vibrate in Kohl's hand, almost as if it had a life of its own. "Then who was there? Who killed him?"

"You want to know who really killed him?"

"That's the general idea."

Tony Jack didn't answer immediately. He took a deep breath and sighed as he let it out. "*You did,* my friend," he said finally. "You killed all of them."

"Is that a fact?"

"Yes, it is."

Kohl's hand was sweating on the bamboo. "You're running out of time," he said.

"Maybe so, but its' still the truth. All I told Red to do was hold him there, at the garage, and I was gonna question him later. And if his story held up—I mean, if it turned out he was who he said he was—the guy who ran over Richie—then I was gonna turn him over to the police, so help me God. It never hurts to make points with the police. But no—*you* gotta stick

your nose in. *You* gotta beat the shit outa Red in the alley—
sweet old Red Einhorn, who scares the livin' piss outa me, mister, even though he works for me! Anyway, from that moment
on, all Red cares about is findin' out who the fuck you are, so
he can kill your ass. He's lookin' like dog meat. His face is a
bloody mess. But I can't stop him. He goes back to the garage
and leans hard on your pretty-boy cousin, to find out who the
fuck you are and where he can get his hands on you."

Kohl was beginning to feel weak, ill. The bamboo club almost slipped out of his hand, and he wondered if his voice
would quaver, as the brother's had, earlier. "Go on," he said.

As the mobster did so, he began to stammer. "Like I said,
by the time I-I-I got there—Red, he tells me your cousin must've
had a heart attack or something like that. Honest to Christ, by
the time I got there he was already gone. So I had no choice—
I had to go along with Red. He's a crazy man. Ask Heather,
she'll tell ya. You wanta live, you don't cross Red Einhorn,
lemme tell ya that."

"So you took my cousin out in the country—took his *body*,
that is."

"Yeah—Red lives out that way. He owns some lots on that
road. That's how he knew about it. He set it up, the whole
thing, tried to make it look like—"

"The girl," Kohl interrupted. "Tell me about the girl. How
was I responsible for *her*?"

Tony Jack's cockiness was gone now. He had sunk down in
the chair. His head was hanging. He had clasped his hands
and raised them to his mouth, as though in prayer. And he
had begun to cry. "She just drove in on us, the poor stupid
bitch," he wept. "Maybe just to park and get drunk—I don't
know. But Red, he didn't want no witnesses—"

"Red strikes again," Kohl said.

Tony Jack held up his hand. "As God is my witness! It was
him—Red—the whole way! I couldn't stop him! I swear to God!"

Kohl looked at the man as a child might regard a dead dog
lying on the highway. His hand tightened on the bamboo club,

but he couldn't bring himself to use it, not on a man slumped in a chair, weeping. Suddenly Heather spoke up.

"He said just ask Heather. So why don't you?"

"All right," Kohl said. "I'm asking."

She laughed softly, in contempt. "Well, he's lyin' in his ugly teeth, of course. Red Einhorn ever touch me, I'd take a bath in Lysol. That crybaby up there—" At that point she spat in the direction of the stage. "That fuckin' crybaby, he's the one gives all the orders. He's the one we all gotta be suckin' off all the time."

Kohl had reached the point where he didn't want to hear any more, not from either of them. His head felt as if it were bursting, as if vermin were spilling from every orifice. Wearily, he lifted the club, preparing to toss it away—a movement that Tony Jack evidently misconstrued as the signal that his time was up, for he came bounding like a big cat out of the chair and dove from the stage onto Kohl, yelling as he struck, knocking Kohl down and sending the bamboo club spinning across the floor. Squealing and cursing, the mobster fought with everything he had, clubbing Kohl with his own head and digging at Kohl's eyes and throat with his malletlike hands while his legs churned in an attempt to get a knee into Kohl's groin or stomach. Yet it wasn't pain or fear Kohl felt but something very like joy, because he knew that finally he could unload it all, purge himself however briefly of the frustration and hatred that had been building in him ever since Ken's death.

As the man kept butting him and kicking at him, Kohl caught him twice in the stomach with hard right hands, then dropped him with a forearm to the face. Holding him down from behind, he jammed the mobster's arm up his back, at the same time taking a handful of his hair and yanking his head up.

"I got a warning for you," he said. "That girl over there is Bobbi. Then there's the girl my cousin lived with in Kirkland. Her name is Diane. You listening to me?"

Jack tried to nod.

"They're both important to me—you understand that? I'll be leaving town soon, but I'm gonna keep checking with them. And if either of 'em so much as gets a toothache, I'm gonna come back here and take you out in the woods and beat you to death. You understand that?"

Again Tony Jack tried to nod.

"Another thing—I'll have the briefcase with me. They won't have it. You're just gonna have to forget all this, Giacalone. You're gonna have to live and let live. *Capische?*"

Kohl didn't wait for a nod this time. Scrambling to his feet, he pulled the mobster up with him and dragged him over to the wall, where he began to slam him into it, over and over. Finally, surprising even himself, he held Jack up with one hand braced against the back of his neck while he punched him in the kidneys as hard as he could, three times, silently tolling them off: the first one for Ken, the second for the girl, the third for himself. When he let go, Tony Jack slid down the wall like a splattered egg.

"Couldn't happen to a nicer guy," Heather said.

Tears streaming down her face, Bobbi came over to Kohl and tried to embrace him or fall into his arms, but he was too wound up for either, was breathing too hard. Instead he patted her, almost in commiseration, as if to apologize for what he'd put her through, what he'd made her witness.

"Let's go home," she said. "Please?"

Kohl looked at Heather. "What are you gonna do?" he asked.

It was a matter she apparently had given some thought. "Well, I'd say things are kinda over for me here, wouldn't you? So after you take off, I figured I'd let Taffy out of the girls' can and call the ambulance. And then I'm outa here. Let the cops try to figure out what happened."

"Looks like we'll just have to trust you," Kohl said, picking up his shotgun and the bamboo club.

Heather laughed at that. "Sheeit, man, I still don't know who the fuck you are. And if you think I'm gonna get on your bad side—tell the police about you—you must think I'm a whole lot dumber than I am."

"Fair enough," Kohl said.

He followed Bobbi across the showroom and down the hallway to the back door, a journey that seemed to take forever. Outside, the sea-salted air felt cool and fresh, but it was not enough to invigorate him. More than exhausted, he felt close to collapse. He leaned on Bobbi as they walked to the truck. He let her help him into the passenger side, and after they drove away he propped his head against the window and felt sleep coming at him like a long dark tunnel.

"What about his gun and that bamboo thing?" she asked. "How come you brought them along?"

"I don't know—fingerprints maybe. I'll toss them later."

"Did you mean that about leaving town?"

He was almost in the tunnel by then. "Yeah, I guess so."

"I'll miss you," she said.

"I'll miss you too." He wasn't sure whether he actually said the words or only wanted to, tried to, before he went roaring into the darkness.

10 Kohl was barely aware that Bobbi had taken
him to her mother's house that morning. He
remembered hearing children crying and beds
being moved around before he drifted off
again, reliving in dreams the worst moments of the previous
night—the explosion and fire, the fighting and drowning, the
disintegrating Mercedes—as if the real thing hadn't been bad
enough. He also remembered waking occasionally, shivering
under blankets in a bright, summery room; and then it was
nighttime again and Diane was there, helping Bobbi dress him
and get him out of bed and onto his feet. And he remembered
how comical it seemed, leaving the house and going out to
Diane's car, with one woman under each arm, like a pair of
crutches.

Diane took him to the offices of a Kirkland physician she
somehow had convinced to come in after hours. With the help
of his wife, an ex-nurse, the doctor removed the scabs from
many of Kohl's cuts, then cleansed and stitched them. He X-

rayed Kohl and bound up his ribs, two of which were cracked. And finally he shot him full of antibiotics and painkillers before returning him to Diane with a handful of prescriptions and his considered opinion that "the man belongs in a hospital, phobia or no."

Even though he was running a four-degree fever, Kohl insisted on going home, where there would be no one to ask questions about his injuries, no busybodies making unwelcome connections between him and a certain accident with a missing victim. And anyway he felt that he could get by on his own now, all sewn up and with a goodly supply of medicine. So he settled into his bed at Diane's like a bear into its winter cave, confident that sleep and time would mend him.

By the next evening he was able to get up and hobble around the house, testing his leg. Diane had left a note beside his bed, saying that she was at a party and wouldn't be home till late. Nevertheless he called upstairs for her, in case she had changed her mind. Getting no answer, he limped back to the kitchen and had some scrambled eggs, washed down with orange juice and coffee.

The doctor had explained to him that he had two deep bruises on his thigh which would be slow to heal, that only warmth and rest and time would do the job. With this prescription in mind, he fired up the whirlpool spa on the game-room deck and spent the rest of the evening stewing in the 115-degree water. He found two current issues of the Eastside newspaper and looked for any stories covering the events of that night, but the only item of interest was the Yarrow Bay fire, which according to the paper was still thought to be the work of arsonists or vandals, though the spokesman for the fire department emphasized that this was still just a theory, since the fire had consumed all the evidence, as well as six yachts. There was no mention of any bodies being recovered, no mention of a Red Einhorn.

Kohl brought a portable television out onto the deck so he could watch the eleven-o'clock news while he soaked. For a time he thought that the electronic contingent wasn't going to give him anything on Tony Jack either. Then a good-looking young woman came on, reporting on the funeral of Arnold Giacalone. She said that Arnold had been killed in an automobile accident early Monday morning on Rainier Avenue—just a few hours before Tony Jack himself was found severely beaten in his downtown nightclub. The anchorman asked the reporter if the police were any closer to solving the "mystery of the Tony Jack affair."

"Well, if they are," said the reporter, "they're just not saying. As you know, Aaron, the whole thing started with the hit-and-run death of the youngest brother, Richard Giacalone, last June. So far there have been no arrests in that case. Then there was the fracas last week outside Tony Jack's house on Queen Anne Hill. And now, in the course of a single night, the middle brother is killed in an auto accident and Tony Jack is attacked and severely beaten in his own nightclub, and in fact is still in intensive care. And then the most intriguing element, Aaron—the disappearance of Tony Jack's right-hand man, Ernest Einhorn. Einhorn matches the description of the mystery man reported to have been in the car with Arnold Giacalone at the time of the fatal accident. Supposedly, he left the accident scene and went straight to a hospital—but no one's seen him since."

The anchorman came on again, shaking his head in mild consternation. "More questions than answers, that's for sure," he said, turning to his cherubic weatherman. "Well, Harry, I sure hope that isn't the case with you." And it wasn't. From that point on, the newscast was all smiles and sunshine.

The next morning Kohl found the last two issues of the *Seattle Times* in a wastebasket in Diane's room. The second, delivered the previous afternoon, had two fairly extensive stories on the Giacalones, one about the accident and the beating and the other an overview piece detailing the family's long history of criminal involvement and speculating on the possibility that the Monday-night violence was the beginning of a power struggle—a civil war—between various underworld "families."

But it was the other article that gave Kohl the detailed information he wanted, such as the fact that Arnold Giacalone had died of massive head injuries incurred in the auto accident. As for Tony Jack himself, he reported that he had been attacked by two young black males as he was locking up and leaving his strip club Monday morning. However, he was found *inside* the club by police after they received an anonymous phone tip, presumably from a woman. Jack suffered a concussion, a lacerated eye, loss of teeth, and a crushed jaw as well a severe internal injuries, including the loss of a kidney in an emergency operation performed at Harborview Hospital. Police were reported to have serious doubts about his account of the attack, since he wasn't robbed, nor was anything reported missing from his club.

Returning to the subject of Arnold's death, the article speculated on the disappearance of Red Einhorn, expanding on the television report about Red supposedly having been a passenger in Arnold's car at the time of the crash. Immediately afterward, bleeding heavily himself—*and carrying a shotgun*—he reportedly had hitched a ride to the hospital. And that was the last anyone had seen of him.

Kohl's most pressing need was simply to find out where he stood, to learn what if anything the police knew about him. Since Arnold Giacalone had never regained consciousness, it all came down to Tony Jack, and he apparently was doing his level best to keep Kohl's name out of the investigation, undoubtedly because that was the only way to ensure that the deaths of Ken and Marina Harris wouldn't become part of the case also. In addition, there was the warning that Kohl had hurled into the mobster's ear. He liked to think that played at least some part in the man's fanciful storytelling.

Despite all this, Kohl still didn't feel very secure. He knew that in the end stone walls crumbled, often where one least expected them to. Red Einhorn's body could come popping up at any time; Heather might get high and say the wrong thing to the wrong person; Arnold Giacalone might have confided in his wife before he died; Bobbi's mother might say too much over the back fence; and Tony Jack himself might simply change his mind, turn gutsy and try to pin everything on Kohl. So Kohl was not in doubt about the necessity of leaving town; the only question was when.

As for feeling any guilt or remorse over what had happened, he felt not one drop of either. Out in the lake with Red Einhorn, tumbling into the freezing blackness, he'd had a simple choice of kill or be killed. And it was Arnold Giacalone, not Kohl, who had swerved the 450 SL across the divider line and into the path of the oncoming vehicles. As for beating Tony Jack, Kohl only wished he'd had the stamina to work on the man a half hour longer, maybe break his kneecaps and a vertebra or two while he was at it—because out of all that happened, the one thing branded forever into Kohl's mind was a scene he had never even witnessed, that of Ken being beaten to death. And while Ken's death easily justified for Kohl all that he had done, it now had a downside as well: the mobster's unsettling accusation that Kohl himself was responsible for what had happened to Ken, that if he hadn't charged into the picture and beaten up Red Einhorn, *then none of it would have happened.* Ken wouldn't have been beaten to death. Marina Harris wouldn't have been killed in the cover-up. And, unfortunately, Red Einhorn and Arnold Giacalone would still be alive.

Intellectually, Kohl knew that it was a ludicrous argument, the moral equivalent of an airline hijacker complaining that if only his victims had behaved properly, he wouldn't have had to shoot them. Nevertheless, Tony Jack's words kept eating at Kohl, whether he was lying awake at night or watching daytime television or soaking his leg in the whirlpool out on the deck. Each time he would consider the accusation and then reject it as absurd, yet never with a feeling of relief or finality, as if he'd finally worked his way through to the truth. Instead, he would be left with a feeling of uneasiness and doubt, and he would wonder what might have been, if only he hadn't followed Red Einhorn and the brother down that fateful alley.

Bobbi had found another job, this time as a waitress in the bar of a Seattle restaurant. So she was able to come over and see Kohl only in the afternoon, and not very often at that, since her mother threatened to kick her out of the house if she had anything more to do with "that big hoodlum" who had bled all over her sheets and pillowcases. The few times Kohl saw her, Bobbi seemed like a different person, thoughtful and subdued, almost wistful. She kept asking him to tell her stories about him and Ken growing up, especially any that involved Ken's drop-dead looks and the devastating effect he had on the hearts of schoolgirls.

As for the present, anything about Tony Jack or his cohorts or the police investigation, she was totally uninterested. Instead, she would ask him about his plans: when he was going to leave, and how Diane felt about his going. And on her last visit, she even asked him if he and Diane were in love. They were out on the deck at the time, Kohl soaking in the whirlpool while Bobbi sat across from him, dangling her feet into the steaming water.

"What makes you ask?" he said.

"Well, you're still living here with her."

"Only for a few more days. Soon as the leg's normal, I'm on my way."

"But that don't mean you're not in love with her."

"No, I guess it doesn't. But as it happens, I'm not. Diane and I simply aren't right for each other. For one thing, she's way too smart for me."

"Could be you're too nice for her."

"Not very likely."

Bobbi smiled shyly. "Is that the way it is with us? I mean, not being right for each other."

Kohl didn't know what to say. "I don't know—you tell me."

"Well, you're too smart for me—I know that."

"Then you know more than I do."

"Or maybe you're too nice for me."

He laughed at that. "Oh hell—probably both."

"Now you're making fun of me," she said.

He was at a loss. Normally Bobbi didn't talk about love and relationships; normally she just took off her clothes and got down to business. But that didn't seem to be the case anymore, and he wasn't sure how to act with her or what to say. In time, feeling thoroughly stupid, he went the way of habit.

"Why don't you peel down a bit and join me in here?"

She shook her head. "That's my problem. I'm always so easy, guys don't take me serious."

"We could just sit here in the water and talk," he said. "I could put my arm around you and give you a hug—no more than that."

Her smile turned her into a child. "Really? You mean it?"

He started to make a face, a caricature of woeful exasperation. But her smile forced him to smile. "Of course I mean it," he said.

Lying awake one night, Kohl pondered which woman—Bobbi or Diane—would have made the better pioneer wife, the one he would have wanted at his side had he been unlucky enough to cross the continent in a covered wagon. And he decided that while they were both tough and fearless—though in different ways—he would have had to give the nod to Diane not only because she was more intelligent but because she would have scared the hell out of the Indians. He was still amazed at her coolness throughout the Tony Jack mess. Just hours after her yacht was blown to smithereens and Kohl set out after Tony Jack, the woman *went to work*—and probably sold a couple of houses, for all Kohl knew. And the following night, when Bobbi called her, she could have taken the easy way out and phoned for an ambulance, had him carted off to a hospital, covering herself in the bargain, or at least not continuing as an active participant in the cover-up. Admittedly her plucki- ness in this regard wasn't on a par with Bobbi's—actually going along with Kohl, even following him into Tony Jack's—but Bobbi had spent most of her life knocking around in a much tougher, poorer neighborhood and was no stranger to vio- lence and lawlessness. Diane, on the other hand, was a quin- tessential yuppie, a college graduate whose previous experience of criminality was probably confined to jaywalking. Yet ever since the hit-and-run—and Ken's fateful decision not to turn himself in—she had coolly gone along with the cover-up. Granted that, later on, her own vulnerability as an accessory undoubtedly contributed to her continuing silence, but Kohl still believed that a vast majority of women in the same fix would have tearfully informed on him and Ken—while saving their own necks in the process.

And Kohl respected this in her, her coolness and loyalty. At the same time, he was often dumbfounded at her ability to carry on business as usual no matter what was happening in her personal life. The day after she brought him home from Bobbi's she had held a six-hour open house and by ten that night had a closing on a lakeside condo. And the very next day, with her lawyer in tow, she had put sufficient heat under the insurance company that it settled on the Williwaw, agree- ing to pay her the full $140,000 face value of her policy even though fire marshals were still poking around in the ashes at the marina.

Kohl had told her that he would be leaving as soon as the swelling went down in his leg, probably within a week, and though she pretended to be disappointed at the news, he could see that she was anything but. So he was surprised when she came home early one day with some stylish new clothes for him, including a sport coat and a pair of handsome pleated slacks that easily accommodated his swollen leg. She showered and put on a cocktail dress and took him out to dinner, at

Toby's Lakeside. As was her custom, she got exactly what she wanted, an umbrella table on the deck, in the row closest to the water. Though it was September now, the weather was still clear, if a touch cooler. The sun was setting flamboyantly behind Seattle, turning every north-facing window, every reflective bit of glass, into gold leaf.

Diane as usual looked stunning and confident, a winner among winners. And after a couple of drinks and a number of interruptions, saying hello to her many friends, she got down to business. It seemed that she and two of her fellow agents, both men, were forming a corporation to buy up bargain houses and apartment buildings—"dogs," as she called them—properties that they would rent out for the present, then remodel during the next recession for sale later on, when the market grew hot again. What she and her partners needed, she said, was a manager who could also serve as a handyman and rent collector, the kind of fellow deadbeats wouldn't argue with.

Kohl couldn't help smiling. "For this you brought me *here?*"

She looked hurt. "It's a job offer, isn't it?"

"Diane, you seem to forget—I'm leaving town."

"I know you're leaving my house—but why *town?*" She lowered her voice. "Hell, you're not in any danger anymore. You canceled all their tickets except for Tony Jack, right? And from what I read, he'll be parking with the handicapped from now on."

Kohl sipped at his scotch, thinking that, yes, the Indians would have fled in mortal terror. "Would you have liked to be a pioneer woman?" he asked.

"What is this—twenty questions?"

"No, just one."

"In that case, the answer's no. I like it here and now."

"I guess I knew that."

"Then why ask?"

"Brain damage?"

"Apparently."

Neither of them said anything for a while. Looking out

over the water, Kohl fixed his gaze on some sailboats running with the wind. He was afraid that if he let his attention wander, he would end up scanning every square foot of the lake. When he looked back at Diane, she was smiling at him.

"You wonder when he's coming up, don't you?"

"You could say that."

She nodded thoughtfully. "Yes, I suppose I'd want to leave too, if every time I looked out at the lake—"

"I know, Diane," he said. *"I know."*

The next night she came home late from an office party and went straight up to her room. Kohl was already in bed, lying in his jockey shorts in the dark, wondering if he'd ever again fall asleep the second his head hit the pillow, as he usually had on the farm. He heard her bathing upstairs and a little later he heard her in the kitchen, banging cabinet doors and humming tunelessly. Finally she appeared in his doorway, wearing a short oriental robe and carrying a glass of champagne. The only light, coming from the kitchen, made her hair appear halolike, an illusion she obviously didn't care to foster.

"There he lies," she said. "The Lion of Illinois."

"You found me out."

"Early to bed, early to rise—that's the ticket, uh?"

"The ticket to hard work and poverty, yes."

Smiling reflectively, she sipped at her champagne. "Foolish me. I keep expecting you to come knocking at my door some night. But it never happens. I guess you don't like me anymore, is that it?"

"I like you fine."

"You just don't desire me, then."

"Wrong again."

She came on into the room and sat down on the edge of his bed. "Then what is it?" she asked. "And mind you, I'm not trying to seduce you. I'm just curious as to what it is I've lost and where I might have lost it. If I find out, perhaps I can get it back."

Kohl lay there looking at her, wondering whether to play along with her. "Diane," he said, "if you'll remember, I was in a pretty serious accident last week."

"But you seem perfectly normal. Everybody at Toby's yesterday, I bet they thought you were in the pink."

"But I'm not."

"No, obviously not."

He did want her, of course, especially if she could have forced herself to be the slightest bit affectionate in the bargain. But something in him held him back, something new and unsettling, and he didn't like her pressing him on the subject. So he dissembled.

"If you wait a couple of days, I imagine I could service you as required. Morning, noon, and night, if necessary."

"Wouldn't that be something of a stretch?"

"I would hope so."

She shook her head admiringly. "*Quel* virility. And to think, it's not there now, but in a couple of days—*zowie!*"

"It *is* kind of awesome, isn't it?"

"Definitely. Why, it's almost unbelievable."

He placed his hand over hers, like a cleric, benign, fatherly. "There's just no explaining it," he said. "Why, it's almost like I left a part of me down there in the lake. Or like every time I hit Tony Jack, it was me I crippled." He had meant for it to sound ironic and mocking, but it was not. It was his guts, spilled, lying there between them, foul and shining in the darkness.

"Oh, that's such a lot of bullshit," she said.

Kohl spoke not out of conviction so much as to hear what he would say, learn what was in his heart. "Maybe a guy only has one choice. Maybe he can be a lover. Or a killer. But not both."

"More bullshit."

"Or how about his? Maybe when a guy gets his cousin killed—his best friend—maybe he's not a lion anymore. Maybe he's a pussycat."

She lifted Kohl's hand off hers and dropped it as if it were a crab. Getting up, she tossed off the rest of her champagne and moved toward the door. Haloed again, she looked back at him, sadly shaking her head.

"Next time I want a few laughs," she said, "I'll know where *not* to look."

Then she was gone.

Fortunately, they didn't part on that note. In other ways, Diane did everything she could to help him. When he was still recovering, she and a fellow agent drove to Bobbi's house and picked up Kohl's truck. She had a new windshield put in it and even threw in a new set of tires. And finally, going above and beyond any possible call of duty, she generously insisted on paying him a $4,500 "commission" on the insurance settlement on the boat. And that was big money for an unemployed ex-farmer. So he figured that he was in pretty good shape, financially at least, when he left town.

The night before he set out, Diane stayed home and they sat together on the deck till after midnight, drinking and talking, even reminiscing about Ken. Later, at the foot of the stairs, he took her in his arms and kissed her goodbye, much more passionately than he had expected to, and she laughed uneasily, as if his ardor embarrassed her. He saw, though, that her eyes had filled with tears.

She was at work when he packed up and left the next day. On his way out of town, he drove over to Bobbi's to say goodbye. She came outside to see him off, and she too was tearful, even before he gave her her goodbye present, an envelope containing twenty one-hundred-dollar bills. At first she insisted that she couldn't accept the money.

"We're *friends*," she said. "You don't owe me anything."

260

"It's only a gift," he told her. "And actually, I owe you much more than money."

Her mother kept watching them from the front window, probably itching to call the police, but Kohl took his time anyway. He told Bobbi that she was special in his life and that he would stay in touch with her.

"You don't have to do that," she said.

"But I want to."

She looked away from him. "Will you be staying in touch with anyone else?"

"Probably."

"I was afraid of that," she said.

When he took her in his arms and kissed her goodbye, she held on to him much longer and more tightly than he'd expected her to. But it made him feel good, made him feel almost happy. And he wondered if that was how Diane had felt the night before.

Soon he was on his way again, heading toward the freeway a mile or so ahead. He knew that when he reached it, he could take the first ramp and head south for California or he could drive under the freeway and take the cloverleaf, go north to Alaska. There he could hole up along the coast somewhere, build a cabin miles from anyone else and try to scrape by, alone, in the wild. It was a prospect that had a certain appeal for him, the idea of solitude and the forest and the sea. But for that very reason he distrusted it, sensing that he wouldn't be able to lose himself there as easily as he could in California, in a rented room in downtown L.A. It turned his gut, just the thought of it, the noise and the crowds and the endless, smoggy sun. At the same time, he suspected that he wouldn't be terribly out of place there, would probably fit right in with all the others who had washed up on its gaudy shores over the years: the rootless and the maimed and the dispossessed as well as those like him, those with blood on their hands and doubt in their souls.

When he came to the freeway, he turned onto the first ramp and accelerated slowly. He wasn't in any hurry.

261